C000274589

THE PICK-UP ARTIST

CHRIS HILL

This is a First Edition of the paperback

The Pick Up Artist:

a lad lit rom com about dating in the digital age

Copyright © February 2015 Chris Hill

ISBN: 978-1-910094-16-7

eBook ISBN: 978-1-910094-17-4

Published February 2015

By Magic Oxygen

www.MagicOxygen.co.uk

editor@MagicOxygen.co.uk

Edited by Tracey West

A catalogue record for this book is available from the British Library.

Printed by Lightning Source UK Ltd; committed to improving environmental performance by driving down emissions and reducing, reusing and recycling waste.

View their eco-policy at www.LightningSource.com

Set in 11.5pt Times New Roman

Titles set in Luckiest Guy

ALSO BY CHRIS HILL

Song of the Sea God
Published by Skylight Press

ABOUT HIS WRITING

"Funny and tender and ironic and crafted, bursting with great images and wonderful turns of phrase."
Kate Atkinson, author of Behind the Scenes at the Museum

"Chris Hill has delivered a masterly first novel, one that is crafted and measured yet shining through with the intensity and passion that comes from deep inspiration."
P.E Wildoak, author

"Song of the Sea God is a remarkably original work, one of the boldest and most striking novels I've read in recent years."
Novelist Garry C Powell

"With a voice that is as raw, unpredictable, and beautiful as the sea, Chris Hill delivers a hauntingly singular, rich debut novel in Song of the Sea God."
Novelist Jesse Giles Christiansen

DEDICATION

For:

Claire

Joseph

and Matthew

CHAPTER 1

"So why *did* you throw a spider at her?"

"I don't know, it seemed like a good idea at the time." Rob Johnson was remorseful and dehydrated, he slurped full sugar Coke and inexpertly stifled a burp.

"Mind you, they'll probably put that on my gravestone."

His mate Sam nodded sympathetically: "After you kill yourself in your bachelor flat full of old newspapers and rotting takeaways."

"Cheers, that's cheered me right up."

"You'll have wanked yourself to death most probably, cried and masturbated yourself into a little desiccated lump."

Rob spat a suspect bit of his bacon sandwich onto the paper plate.

"And you're my best mate."

"Tough love son. So, tell me the rest of it, how did it go?"

"Oh, I dunno, when you left the bar there was just me and her and she was too beautiful, that was the problem and she was Spanish."

"From that language college, next to the Tailors pub?"

"Yeah, that's right. We had about a half hour of nothing conversation about that, plus me trying to explain the difference between a boil and a wart."

"What?"

"You know, I had that boil removed."

"Yeah, but why tell her about that? I mean, why? An available Spanish sex goddess, you and her, having a drink, why with the boils?"

"Well, I was saying, a boil is to a wart, as a mountain is to a hill, but she didn't really get what I was on about and, you know, I didn't know the Spanish for boil."

"Pity she spoke any English at all. So, what happened then?" Sam went up to the café counter to pay, returned to the tiny Formica table to hear the rest of Rob's tale of failure.

"Well then, spider. I dunno why. I panicked. She was too attractive and it was going nowhere. She spotted this spider scuttling across the table, started squealing and backing off. I thought it might be amusing if I picked it up and threw it at her. So I did."

"And?"

"Well, there was a big reaction. You know, a tsunami of Spanish swearing."

"How did you know, you don't speak Spanish?"

"You can tell, believe me. She was dancing around, brushing herself down. Anyway, turned out she was allergic."

"What did she say?" Sam was laughing, but in a despairing, head shaking way."

"She said, 'If it bite me, I die!'"

"That's priceless. 'If it bite me, I *die*', fuck me, that's bad."

Rob was heading out of the door. "Come on, we'll be late for work."

"You're supposed to chat them up, not give them anaphylactic shock."

They were ten minutes from the office and five minutes late already.

Rob was six foot one which didn't make him big among his peers but meant he looked down on most of the people from the previous generation who were his superiors at work. Sam had the sort of red hair that makes you enemies at school and at five foot eight was short enough to make a giraffe of Rob.

Rob seemed apologetic about his height, stooped a little when he spoke to people and hid behind his fashionable fringe. He was living in a limp bed-sit in a hopeless part of town and working in the advertising department of the local rag.

It was the sort of job where you didn't need paper qualifications, just bottle and chutzpah, neither of which he had. But he thought he did, which goes a long way with that stuff. Other stuff too.

I mean, Rob Johnson wasn't that bad looking, that's my opinion. Maybe his nose was a little big, but so what? Perhaps his ears stuck out more than he would have liked but luckily the young were wearing their hair shoulder length this year. The problem was that what he saw in the mirror varied dramatically depending on the day. Sometimes he saw a well-made, earnest young man, clean-shaven, no worse looking than most. Other days a grinning, leering Caliban confronted him in the glass.

8

When he tried to speak to a girl he liked he couldn't get his words out. He felt scared he would not manage to express the essence of himself, that he would seem just like all the others. But Rob knew that once found a girlfriend he would be constant and kind. That was the plan at any rate, to repay the faith she showed in him by proving he was deeper than she believed men could be. Mostly Rob felt high-minded about women, sure that he was searching for a soul mate. Other times he would catch sight of a girl whose challenging eyes or cheeky smile stirred him so nothing else mattered.

The newspaper office was several old buildings bashed together into one. The frontage was cod Regency and glowed with white paint. Inside, the original character had been stripped away so efficiently that you would guess the place was less than ten years old. What did it look like? It looked like all offices.

If you wandered in there you'd amble absently over to your desk and wonder who put gonks on it and pictures of somebody else's kids.

In the tearoom, Sam emptied the kettle into a stained flotsam of mugs.

"So not a huge success then, overall?"

Rob danced from foot to foot a little.

"Yeah, your wedding invite's in the post. I thought it would be a laddish thing to do with the spider, you know, coquettish."

Sammy stuck the teas on an old bar tray.

"Maybe it's my hair they don't like," said Rob, "I could go for a new look."

"Nah, mine's ginger and I do okay, for a ginner. That's what they said at school anyhow," said Sam.

Rob had a long critical look at Sam's head. "It's not *that* red," he said diplomatically. "It's kind of dark red, I'd say auburn, but that sounds a bit girly. It's not like it glows, you know. You're not pasty and all splattered with freckles."

Sam shrugged non-committally. Rob didn't want to make a big deal of the whole red hair issue anyway, it struck him it was one of the few things it was still acceptable to bully people for, that and being Welsh, and having a moustache. Was Sam Welsh? Some people were and you couldn't tell.

"On a serious note though," Sam said, "it has to be a high-risk, low-return sort of strategy doesn't it?"

"What?" Rob seemed genuinely perplexed.

Sam shrugged. "Approaching women you don't know, where they are feeling vulnerable anyway as they're on their own and among strangers. Are they not simply liable to think you are a pervert and see you as threatening, rather than feeling whatever emotion you were after, let's say, lust?"

Some things just sound like sense and you have to let them percolate for a while, so Rob said nothing and simply stirred sugar into his instant coffee.

After a pause Sam tried again.

"What's wrong with the girls in this place? It's an advertising department. It specialises in pretty young girls, many of the men are gay. It should be like falling into a bucket of tits surely?"

"And I'm worried I'll come up sucking my thumb."

They sniggered like you do at old jokes, recognition of something shared. Sam added milk to some of the mugs, then tried again.

"What's wrong with Alice? She's magnolia."

Alice was dark, plump and gobby, pretty, late twenties. On the base of her spine she had a gaudy floral tattoo.

"I am worried that I'll come on to some girl. Make our relationship sexual rather than just friendship and she'll give me the usual big fuck off. Then I'll have to get in the lift with her every day for the rest of my life for socially uncomfortable trips to the second floor."

Sam grabbed brews in both hands.

"Eventually you would retire."

"Yeah, no. I think the thing is, you can leave your failures behind you in a bar. It's anonymous. Like speed dating with added drunks."

He thought about it for a moment though. Alice scared him, she was too full-on for a first attempt.

"What about Pamela the librarian, she's quite hot," he suggested. Indeed she was, in a cool, rock chick kind of way.

"Nah, she sups from the furry cup," Sam seemed certain.

"How would you know?"

"Know people who know."

Sam moved off to distribute the largesse.

"Oh er, what's magnolia?" Rob called after.

"Goes with anything."

Rob handed out the brews in geographical order round his section of the office. He had about half a dozen on the tray counting his own. He saw Alice glancing towards him as he approached her terminal, black hair tied up, white teeth with a fake ruby set in one of the front ones. He swerved off and gave Daphne Morris her tea; fifties, smelt of lavender. When he turned round from pleasantries with her, Alice was deep in conversation with one of the telesales girls and he left her coffee on her desk, moving on without catching her eye.

As he walked back to his desk she shouted after him.

"No sugar in it this time is there darling?"

Looked back at her shaking his head, "You keep telling me you're sweet enough."

"I am lover, maybe you ought to have a taste."

She cackled with telesales girl. The pair of them bent towards each other in loud mirth as Rob quickened his step, despite himself.

"Where you going hon? You in a hurry all of a sudden?" she called after him and they laughed again, this time with Daphne joining in from across the aisle.

"Leave him alone, he's sweet. Don't you upset him, he's my baybee, aren't you Robbie?"

Jesus Christ. Luckily, he was far enough away now just to keep going as though he hadn't heard. Rob was glad to reach his desk and tuck his legs in under it, pulling its familiarity around him like a duvet.

He picked up a worry ball in the shape of a light bulb, a leave behind from a local PR company. It looked like a dog had chewed it. He worked it thoughtfully in his left palm, glancing over the other personal items arrayed in front of the VDU. There was a small pot model of an old style manual typewriter, a photo in a cardboard frame of his nephews with their gran, his mum. There was a peach granite pebble too, from the beach near where he was born and, Blu-tacked to the edge of the computer screen, a quotation on yellowing newsprint.

I have spent half my life trying to get away from journalism, but I am still mired to it, a low trade and a habit worse than heroin, a strange seedy world full of misfits and drunkards and failures. A group photo of the top ten journalists in America on any given day would be a monument to human ugliness: Hunter S Thompson.

He put down the light bulb and picked up the pebble. Cool and smooth and dense. Eventually he tired of staring at the black screen and turned on the computer. Almost as soon as Outlook had booted itself up, there was the ping of a new email in his box.

"You're too scared, it's a confidence issue, you need coaching. Try TPUA.co.uk"

He sent back. "If she's been with everyone, does that include you?"

Then, when there was no reply, turned scornfully to his diary to see who he was down to pester for ad revenue that morning.

Shite. Crazy Al from Crazy Al's doors and windows. Perhaps he could get away with just ringing the crazy fucker up but he knew the formidable Susan, in charge of his department, would scare it out of him that he'd not been down there and then he'd be in the stocks come the next team meeting; he picked up the phone and rang Crazy's to sort out a visit.

Bored sounding woman picked up at the other end.

"Crazy Als. Crazy guy, crazy prices. How can we help you?"

"I'd like to make an appointment to see Mr Crazy please. It's Rob from the Post."

"The what?"

"You know, the local paper. I manage Crazy Al's advertising account. I'd like to meet him to see if there's anything we can do to maximize his sales potential."

She snorted down the phone at him, "Yeah, well he said to say he's in a meeting if any of you lot call."

Rob assumed an air of calm indifference.

"Oh yeah, he'll mean those other idiots who call up pestering from internet and the radio and them little magazine people. He doesn't mean us, we have an official account with you. I'd better let you book me in quick for today so's he won't miss out on our current promotions."

She seemed unsure of her position now, thrown by his self-assurance.

"Well, okay, if you think that's what he'd want."

"I'm certain of it, he more or less invited me back down there last time we chatted."

"Say three?" she said, relenting.

"Say now," he came back. "He won't want to miss these offers, promise, I can be down there in half an hour."

Best get it out of the way, plus it would mean he could skip the team brief, the painful shambles of a morning meeting where Sue Crag, his line manager, gave them all a wild-eyed pep talk-come-bollocking.

He was just heading out of the door when Sue came in.

She was shivering a bit in her taupe trench coat and holding a takeaway cup of Starbucks.

"Where you going?"

He half paused in the doorway.

"Got to see a client, have to leave early 'cos the pool car's knackered again and, as we've discussed, I don't have a car."

Only his face left behind now, the rest of his body heading for the exit.

"It'll keep you fit. You can go right after team brief."

Bollocks.

It was as grim as usual.

Sue was earnest and keen to succeed. She was reed thin with bleached hair and sometimes looked fit if she was made up and had a little black dress on for a Friday night leaving do. But the rest of the time she just looked malnourished and a little desperate. Like she'd been starved as punishment for not meeting her monthly ad revenue targets and she was determined not to miss out on lunch again this fiscal period.

Most team leaders passed the brief out to read, or joked through it, but she read it out ponderously in a flat drone while wearing an earnest, worried expression which forced Rob and the others to take it seriously.

The others were the three wise monkeys, Jude, Alan and Colin. All older - forty something/fifty something - Rob didn't know. They had been around the office since the dawn of time, so remained jovial and unflustered by Sue's daily prophesies of economic catastrophe.

"So in summary, it's going really badly," she finished. "Now, questions?"

There had to be questions - she'd have them sitting around here all morning otherwise, as she jiggled up and down in front of them like a small bird warning of nearby cats.

"Perhaps they should improve the bonus structure," grumbled Colin, last man in Britain to keep faith in the comb-over as a fashion statement.

"It would incentivise us more," chimed in flowery Jude.

"It's good to be incentivised" said rotund Alan.

Sue bent over to write 'incentivise' on her pad.

As she did so, Rob could see right down her blouse where her small breasts nestled snugly in a black bra.

"Rob?"

"Sorry?"

"Your input?"

He thought for a while. Of breasts mainly.

"I think it would be good to be further incentivised too," he concluded.

"They could incentivise me with a company car for example. Then I wouldn't have to walk every sodding where."

Sue peered at her pad again.

"I shall report back to the senior management team viz the general feeling of the group re: restructuring of current incentivisation structures," she piped robotically."

"That's a good girl," murmured Jude contentedly.

"Won't make any bloody difference though," grumbled Alan.

"No bloody difference at all," said Colin.

"Who's turn is it to make tea?" Sue asked brightly. "Rob?"

"I've got to see this client," he told her, grabbing his bag.

Sue's lip curled as she saw him hoist it over his shoulder.

They didn't like the man-bag, he knew this already.

Maybe one day they would let it pass, but not today.

"Bless 'im with his man-bag," said Sue, sticking a bony arm around him

"What have you got in there darling? Your sandwiches?"

He adopted a mock dignified tone.

"I have my sandwiches in there until lunchtime and afterwards, only the sandwich box."

"Weird that you even bring *in* sandwiches," Jude said. "You young ones think that's what McDonalds is there for, don't you."

"Don't change the subject," Sue instructed. "We are talking about the man-bag."

It was brown leather with a canvas strap. He'd had it as a Christmas present from his aunt, mum's younger sister, who still considered herself a bit 'with it.'

Sue and Jude looked like they might be about to pull it off him and turn it out on the office carpet.

"Why not a ruck-sack?" demanded Sue.

"A ruck-sack would be more manly," said Jude.

"I come in on the bus," Rob explained.

Sue and Jude gave him a bored look to show that an inquiring one would be beneath them. Both did that right away. It was as though all human behaviour, even jokes, were pre-programmed.

He did his best to clear the matter up.

"If a bloke gets on the bus wearing a ruck-sack, he inevitably looks like Forrest Gump. You think, 'What have you got in there love?' Your comfort blanket and your medication? The overgrown schoolboy look is never a good one. You can get away with a ruck-sack if you're riding a bike."

Sue shrugged as though she maybe got it.

"Think website," she trilled after him, as he made once again for the exit.

She wasn't a bad sort, Sue, he was thinking to himself, as he let himself out of the front door and down the steps to the street.

She was eager to do well, competent at her job. She wouldn't deliberately stab you in the back and only gave you a ticking off if she felt you genuinely deserved it. Plus, he did genuinely fancy her, though only in random bursts. Perhaps he *ought* to give more thought to Sam's idea of bringing his never-ending quest to find a girlfriend, closer to home.

As he pondered this some more, heading down lower High Street on the way out to Crazy Al's ring-road barn, he realised that, although he had a clear idea what he thought of Sue Crag, he hadn't the vaguest notion what she might think of him. Her thought processes on the subject were opaque, he got nothing, it was like staring into a smoke-filled room.

Of course, he knew what she thought of him as an employee. Her jargon-filled annual appraisal, just a few weeks previously, had clued him in on his usefulness to team morale, his eagerness to learn and his regrettable tendency to give humorous back-chat to more senior members of the team.

But as far as a more personal appraisal went, nothing.

It was a general problem, he realised. It was not that Sue Crag was an unknown country to him so much as that *all* women were an undiscovered continent, shrouded in baffling mists.

Crazy Al's place was a small shed up past the drive-in McDonalds. It was oblong, functional and aluminium; it looked a little unloved. You've have thought there was some kind of engineering firm in there rather than something public facing.

There was a big garish sign on the side of the unit with a photo of a chubby balding man in middle years. He was wearing a brown suit and a strange intense smile. He held a cowboy hat which he was lifting away from his head in a 'Howdy!' gesture. There was a speech bubble coming from his mouth, "Welcome to Crazy Al's!" it read. The scarlet letters were tilted this way and that, to demonstrate the true level of their craziness.

There was a large glass porch on the front of the aluminium shed with brochures on stands inside, it was basically a factory unit with a conservatory. The idea, Rob supposed, was to display Crazy Al's craftsmanship right from the get go.

Through the porch there was a white plastic door and beyond that the showroom. Spacious, with a tiled floor and pale walls, every effort made to decorate the place until just above head height. Everything beyond that had been left as the construction firm intended; concrete lintels, steel joists and bare strip lights with the wires exposed. The room was filled with strange oases of domesticity. Front doors leading to nowhere, porches, conservatories and hot-tub rooms perched incongruously on the tiles. They looked like zoo cages, Rob thought, where homo sapiens could be exhibited in their natural habitat.

A callow salesman approached in oversized grey suit.

"Welcome to Crazy Al's. Crazy guy, crazy prices. Can I help you with anything sir?"

Robert Johnson from the Post. I'm here to see Al."

The sales guy pulled a face. He was maybe nineteen, probably a college student with a part-time job. He was on commission and clearly brassed off at dealing with anything which didn't earn him any.

"You've come in the wrong door. Office entrance is round the side."

Rob remained standing where he was, next to a display of triple glazed windows with brown laminate frames.

"Okay well, if you go through that door at the far end of the showroom, you'll come out at the rear of the office - please remember for next time," and he stalked off to paw pointlessly at a computer terminal.

The office was much like the showroom except there had been no effort to decorate below the eyeline as well as above. There was a desk in the corner and a girl with long bleached blonde hair sitting behind it. She had pale brown lipstick and a sunbed tan. Californian she looked, and wholesome. Rob liked this type of girl, but then again, he liked many types.

"Hi, I'm Rob. I rang earlier."

She looked up and started slightly because he'd come in through the wrong door. She was wearing a leopard-skin top. He leant on the desk and smiled at her - she didn't smile back.

"Don't remember, what d'you want?"

"Surely you've not forgotten me already? Rob from the Post. To see Al."

"Oh yeah," she seemed so disinterested she might drop off to sleep. Next she'd be filing her nails like girls do in movies.

She jabbed a couple of buttons on the phone and spoke into the speaker.

"Mr Allonby?"

The was a yelp down the phone in response, a single, strangled syllable.

"Wha?"

"It's me, Lauren. There's a man in the front office to see you. He's about advertising. Remember I put a Post-it in your tray?"

Another yelp, "Whatever."

Then the line went dead. She looked up at Rob coldly.

"You can go through, that means he's ready to see you."

"He's a crazy guy alright."

She shook her head and rolled her eyes at him. A moment of connection, just when it was time to go.

There was a door to one side of her desk with a managing director sign on it, you didn't have to be in the CID or anything. He knocked.

"What?" a scared angry rasp from the other side, which he took as 'please come in.'

Inside the room was smaller than it ought to have been. A couple of feet then a desk. Two green plastic chairs in front, one behind with a tiny man sitting at it. He was bald but for a scrape of hair above the neck, like a tonsure which had slipped. He had the same brown suit on as in his photo on the sign but the smile he wore on the sign had gone.

Crazy Al looked up at Rob with hatred in his piggy eyes.

"What the fuck," he demanded, "do you want?"

There was venom in the way he said 'fuck' too; you had to admire his conviction.

"Hi," said Rob. "You might remember I came to see you a while ago about your advertising account at the Post. I really think there's ways we

17

can help you to maxim…"

"Account at the fucking Post?" demanded Crazy Al.

You could tell that if this was to be a long speech and he was building up to a crescendo, then he'd started too high.

"Fucking advertising… I'll fucking maximise you, you fucking…" the pitch of his voice was heading higher still and it was making him pink.

Rob hardly knew the guy. He hadn't killed his parents or sold his children into slavery. He was like this with everyone unless they wanted to buy a door. They didn't call him crazy for nothing, they called him crazy because he *was* crazy. They called him Al because he was Al.

"And you better not have charged me for that last pile of festering shite either, it was fucking use less."

He always pronounced useless as two words, which was a nice touch, making it seem that there really was no use at all for whatever he was decrying.

"You complained, so there was a credit made to your account for part of the balance. What we need to do though is work out what we can do for you going forward.

"Going fucking forward?"

"Yes, in the next few months."

"Next few fucking months?"

He did this sometimes did Al, parroting the last part of what you'd just said back to you as though it was a question, with added expletives.

"Going fucking forward?" he said again contemplatively. He was shaking his head, lost in a moment of introspection.

"You know, for me, for this business, there may well be no fucking forward, have you considered *that*?"

He looked Rob in the eye, as though challenging him to admit that he had not. He was still pink and his face was shining. He seemed vulnerable then for a moment, needing Rob to rescue him from his private hell of fear and doubt.

"I'd never think that for a moment," Rob told him firmly. "It seems to me you're in a great position."

Al shook his head incredulously but Rob carried on.

"Geographically you're marvellously placed, right near the city centre yet on the ring road where it makes it easier to visit. You have all this new building going on in the suburbs - Merryfields and Happy Valley -

all those new estates full of new customers; it's great!"

Momentarily overwhelmed by so much unexpected optimism, Crazy Al paused for a moment, picked up his phone, put it down again. "You don't have a clue what you are fucking talking about," he concluded, morosely.

"Let's just take one thing, take where we are near the centre, big deal. We're down a slip road which everyone whizzes past ready to fill their fucking face with burgers; they're not thinking about doors and windows when they pass us, they're thinking about fucking Happy Meals. There's *no* passing trade in a business like this son, that's where you're showing your fucking naivety."

"Ah no," cut in Rob enthusiastically, "that's where you're showing your business savvy."

He left it there for a moment, just to see if he had a bite. He did.

"Go on then big-bollocks - enlighten me."

"You have the sign. It's true that you might not get people coming in right that moment to buy from you but every one of the thousands of customers at McDonalds sees your sign and is aware of your brand."

Al started smirking despite himself. You could see him thinking to himself that, when you put it like that, he really was quite a smooth operator.

"Cost a fucking fortune that sign," he allowed grudgingly out of the corner of his mouth.

"And worth every penny in all the brand awareness it brings your firm," said Rob, nodding as though his thoughts complemented and expanded on Al's own.

"And I know something else having dealt with you for the last few months, I know what your firm's greatest asset is. It's not the stock or the buildings, it's not even the workforce - it's *you*!"

Al was beginning to look a little more at peace, the colour was fading from his cheeks and he dabbed at his nose and forehead with a moist wipe from a packet on his desk.

"Yes, you are the key factor in encouraging customers to bring their business to your firm. Without your larger than life personality, without your image on that sign out there, this might be any of the other local companies which offers a similar service in the area."

"The fucking competition is intense," intoned Al.

"Yeah - Crazy Al's has it's not so secret weapon - it has you. And you know what? You need to maximise that advantage if you want to stick it to all those other bastards out there who want to take your business away from you. You have to make sure your brand is on everyone's lips. Top of mind for doors and windows in this area, not just for the people who patronise McDonalds. What about the ones who go to Burger King? Kentucky Fried Chicken?"

"So I need signs outside those restaurants too?"

"What about the people who don't even eat fast food? There must be some round here. You need to expand your brand by advertising in the local press and you need to make your own image, your own personality, the *core* of that message."

Al wiped his head again. He had on his 'Where do I sign?' face.

"I have some scamps to show you," Rob told him, reaching into his leather bag for the colour photocopies he'd run off before the visit. He splayed them out on the desk. Different shapes and sizes of ad, different combinations of the three colours, red, green and blue which appeared in Al's branding. The only thing they all had in common was a vast cut out photo of Al dominating each one, waving his cowboy hat in the air and wearing a manic grin.

"They are striking," Al allowed.

Before Rob left, he had the old bastard sign up for another quarter. There was not a thing in the world he'd rather do than tell Crazy to stick his account and spend his budget on commercial radio but there were some customers you knew were simply too scared *not* to advertise when it came to it and Al was one of those, motivated by the fear of being ignored.

When he left the office Rob was toasty warm with the glow he got when he'd done his job well. He knew he could do this stuff. He could work out what motivated people and nudge them into buying, he could weather their initial truculence and present them with options in a way which seemed attractive and compelling.

The receptionist was where he'd left her. She was on the phone so he waited, fidgeting, until she had put it down.

"It went okay in there," he told her, as if she'd asked.

She nodded and smiled dismissively, looking for something in her desk drawer.

"I was wondering if you fancied lunch to celebrate - I mean it doesn't have to be lunch, another meal, a coffee...?"

She was shaking her head slightly and looking past his left ear.

"I don't think so, I'm sorry. You're not, I mean, I'm busy." She spoke slowly as if sleepy and not fully engaged with the conversation. He realised he had embarrassed her and he was embarrassed too. He nodded as if it was all perfectly in order, sweat patches beginning to form under the arms of his dark blue shirt.

"Okay then - maybe some other time? I've got your number and I'll no doubt see you around."

She had picked up the phone again.

CHAPTER 2

'Johnno!' the blog of Robert Johnson, July 11:
"I am a child of 22. What do I know about life? What do I know about women? School was all boys, in college I was raw with shyness. This here is my first job. I think I'm doing okay so far... I don't know, you tell me?

It's not like I've never met any women. I'm a nerd, not a monk. I have female friends of course, had some at uni, we played drinking games. I knew my mother. That's about it though, if I'm honest. I suppose the best thing is probably not to be so honest.

It's a journey this, it's a voyage. What I need is a map."

That evening back at his flat, he watched a rerun of The Mighty Boosh and ate creamed mushrooms on toast. He searched through his emails where he had forwarded the web address Sam had given him and deleted the email.

Later on, while he was looking up the Tuesday night football results on his laptop, he remembered the URL and found he'd typed it in anyway: TPUA.co.uk

What was he expecting? Some kind of porn site front page maybe, with warnings not to come in if you didn't want to see hot pussy and a form for submitting your date of birth. Or perhaps a lad's mag website full of underwear models and old jokes. Instead he found a low-key, white on black web page made up mostly of lists of links to newsgroups and content on the rest of the site.

The masthead at the top of the page said Pick-Up Artists in an unfussy type but there was no manifesto, nothing to proclaim what the site was all about or make bold claims about what it could do for the browser. It was the kind of website men set up for other men to use based on information and 'fact' rather than concerning itself with the pretty diversion of fancy graphics. It reminded Rob of the sort of website non-league football fans set up with news stories, chat rooms and statistics. The only graphical content might be pictures from last week's gripping nil all draw at Vauxhall Motors, or a blurred shot of the new away top.

Still he persevered, clicking on a section which read 'PUA101'.

"If you're here for the first time then that probably makes you an AFC (Average Frustrated Chump)," read the page.

"You don't have to be this way. Many people will tell you that the key to picking up a woman is confidence. They are wrong. The key to success with women is not confidence, it is competence."

"Human beings all work in the same basic way and respond to the same stimuli. Put simply, we all want much the same things in life and go about getting them in the same ways. Knowing this will help you in your quest to get laid because if you can give a woman what she wants, if you can convince her that you have what she is looking for, then what she will want is you!"

"What we have for you here at PUA is the combined wisdom of the pick-up kings, that rare breed of men who have abandoned the time-honoured method of bouncing aimlessly from one woman in a club to another, like a pinball, constantly repelled, with no control over their destiny."

"Instead, the kings have learned the rules of the PUA and found the way to a decent level of success with women. No PUA can promise they can have any one particular woman - if that's why you've come here then you may be wasting your time. We can't promise you *the* woman but a PUA can always find *a* woman and we have found that generally, that's plenty good enough to be going along with."

Rob wasn't sure. It sounded like a sales pitch yet the site didn't seem to be selling anything, all the content appeared to be free as far as he could see. It was evangelical then, a movement he was being asked to join. He decided to read on but do so with a sceptical expression on his face. He put Skrillex on Spotify because he was trying to learn to like it and looked back at the site.

Three hours later, he was still looking and he was doing so with a notebook beside him in which he occasionally jotted down key phrases and ideas. He was hooked, not so much on the general premise of the PUA site but on the range of options it offered for dealing with the opposite sex.

He was a salesman and this was a perfect way of selling himself.

Even if it didn't work the worst that could happen - he decided - was what had been happening already. He had been an AFC and that had led to him getting blown out more or less every time he talked to a girl.

Tomorrow was Friday. Friday night meant down the pub after work and that seemed to him to be as good a chance as any to try out some of his newly acquired knowledge. It could be seen as a test or the sort of mission that was talked about often on the PUA site. It turned another night as an AFC into a night as a PUA and that was something which made him at least feel as though he was doing something positive about the boredom, frustration and occasional misery, which was his life as things stood today.

Vodka Revolution wasn't quite a nightclub but definitely wasn't a pub. It combined the worst aspects of both. The noisy barn-like anonymity of a club with the early closing hours and sense of just-got-out-of-work propriety, which surrounded pubs. It was the place people went for 'one' after 5.30pm, especially on Friday nights. It was chosen predominantly because it was a few yards from the front door of the paper; cross the road, there it was.

Quite frankly, it felt like an extension of the office to Rob, a works canteen with lager but this evening he had to stand outside for a little while and work up the courage to go in. He would have delayed longer but there were smokers outside staring at him and giggling.

He'd worn a dark shirt and dark trousers to work so he simply took his tie off and stuck it in his desk drawer before coming out and instantly looked like he'd made half an effort at evening wear.

It wasn't clothes that caused him to pause uncomfortably in the cold outside Revolution, it was the hat he put on when he thought nobody was looking. A black Australian bush hat with cream trimmings and dangling from the rim were plastic corks on strings, each one black with a white head like a tiny pint of Guinness. Its familiar harp logo was stylishly emblazoned the front of the hat in gold; it had been a promotional leave-behind, handed to him by a marketing girl in a pub at the time of the last rugby world cup.

Rob had worn it just once before, walking home through the streets drunk after the final. Since then it had sat at the back of his wardrobe but after reading the golden rules of the pick-up artist (after deciding to dedicate himself to them selflessly) he knew what he had to do.

He'd rooted around for the thing, dusted it off and stuffed it in his man-bag, pretty much without thinking about how he'd feel wearing it to the pub.

As he swung the front door of the Vodka Revolution open, he realised what he *did* feel was foolish; what had he been thinking?

This wasn't a bar full of strangers. Many of the people in here were his colleagues from the advertising department and others he knew less well from circulation and editorial. They weren't drunk either. Just half an hour ago they had been sitting at their terminals across the road with their work heads on, typing away all sour-faced and professional. Half a lager wasn't likely to put them in the mood for the twat in the hat.

It would make no sense to them. To be honest, it made no sense to *him* from their point of view, only through the zen-like filter of the PUA did it resolve itself into something close to sanity.

He approached the bar.

"Yeah?" asked the barman glancing up at him.

"Guess," said Rob.

"Fucking hell," Alan sidled up to him. "I hadn't realised it was fancy dress."

"Dress to impress," Rob smiled at him and took his pint of Guinness from the bar, still cloudy with froth.

"You better let that settle," advised Alan. "It won't come out right if you don't let it settle."

He took his pint over to where a gaggle of advertising girls stood. It was important not to head straight over to his main target of the evening. He had to put himself about a bit, show he was worthy of female attention and wearing his daft hat, he got it.

There were three girls gathered round laughing at him when Sam turned up.

"Okay I give up - why not just get 'Stupid' tattooed across your face?"

As Sam spoke, a plump Asian girl neither of them had ever met before came up and tapped Rob on the arm. She was short and pretty, and somehow looked a bit drunk already.

"My mates were wondering why you're wearing that hat?" she asked Rob.

"Stupid like a fox," he told Sam, as he turned to give the girl the benefit of his patter.

It didn't go anywhere of course. Her eyes glazed over as soon as she realised he didn't have any interesting reason for being dressed that way and after a minute or two, she touched his arm again, smirked up at him and drifted off back to her mates.

He thought about how often had that happened to him before? Girls Rob Johnson had *never* met, before did *not* come up to him in pubs and engage him in conversation. It was one of the many good things which happened to other people, like winning money on scratch cards or catching something controversial.

It was a revelation to him that making yourself look more stupid than anyone else in the room could also make you look more interesting than anyone else in the room. When he turned back he could tell Sam was impressed.

"I'm *not* impressed. I mean where does it get you? Looking like some twat off kids TV is hardly a turn on is it?"

"In the past," Rob said, taking the top off his drink, "I have been invisible. This evening, at least they can see me. Even if what they see is an idiot. It's now my job to try and correct that impression for them."

"Seems to me it probably is the correct impression to start off with," grumbled Sam.

"I have another hat at home," offered Rob. "My brother got one same time I did. I could chase back and get it for you if you want?"

Eventually he edged over towards Sue who was his target for the evening. Kerry was her gate keeper but liked him so it was no bother to get past her.

"She's talking to Eric at the moment but I wouldn't bother about that. She'd rather be having a chat with you, 'bout spreadsheets probably."

Kerry had one of those hate-hate relationships with Sue that girlfriends often have. She considered Sue work obsessed and didn't like how good she looked in the black dress she'd squeezed into in the toilets to wear to Revolution.

"She's too thin and she needs to get herself a boyfriend." Opined Kerry, who had several.

"Not Eric though, he's a pain in the arse."

Rob was feeling so confident that he gave Kerry a pat on the rump on the way past. She didn't seem to mind and made a Carry On film noise at him.

"Sorry," Rob said to Sue. "You're busy."

Bollocks, he'd only had one lesson as a PUA but it was pretty clear already that apologising for yourself wasn't the way to go. Sue cut Eric off in mid-conversation and turned to talk to Rob instead.

"You look a total prick in that hat."

"Thanks. That's pretty much the look I was going for. It's very 'of the moment' according to the men's magazines I've been reading."

"Looking at all those tits made you want to be one?"

Sue could be a handful when she had a couple of vodkas down her. You just had to ride the tiger and remember she was the boss.

"Don't let me interrupt you if you're busy talking to that guy."

He turned back to Kerry and blurted something to her about her revenue target. Kerry's face was still busy forming a 'how dare you talk to me about work' sneer, when Sue grabbed him by the shoulder and span him back round.

That worked then - one up to the PUAs - ration your attention, don't be too eager, make them realise that time with you is a privilege.

"I don't want to speak to Eric," she told him in a haughty three-drinks-in slur. "Eric is a teacher and they are invariably very boring."

Eric was staring forlornly at her arse. He gave no sign of having heard what she had said but moved off after a while spent being ignored.

"Want to hear my theory about teachers?" asked Sue rhetorically. "All that dealing with kids affects their personality. They spend their days explaining fairly simple stuff in a lot of dull detail. Not just the subject they are teaching but: 'don't get run over', 'don't get yourself knocked up' - all of that. By the end of it, they can't talk to grown-ups properly."

Rob nodded. His experiences of teachers had always left him feeling vaguely patronised, yet at the same time socially superior; maybe she was onto something.

"They get conditioned to expect you to listen as well, as though them going on about something tiresome and you sat there listening with rapt attention is their God-given right."

"Why," Rob wanted to know, "spend time with the poor bastard if you find him such an ocean-going twat?"

"He has a big cock," Sue shrugged. "And you can get me a voddy and coke,"

"Get your own," suggested Rob, wondering whether he should talk to

27

Kerry again.

"Double."

Sue turned to talk to Kerry so Rob headed for the bar.

Eric was there when he arrived and the pair ignored each other with an intensity. Rob felt a bit sorry for the guy. It's not easy to blank a man in a comedy hat. He wondered what his next move should be. The website said it was supposed to be him surrounding himself with other suitors and making it clear he was not dependent on her but it seemed to Rob this was an easier trick for women to pull off.

Like so much of this game the odds seemed to be stacked in favour of women. They got to say who they wanted and when they wanted them. They could line men up and take their pick. From what Rob had read and picked up instinctively from the tone of the thing, the PUA approach was to try to even the odds up. It was counter-intuitive for him but he had to avoid his instinct to be craven, to beg. In order to win the game he had to show that he did not care whether he won it or not, or indeed if he was even *in* it.

The notion that a woman would want him partly because he did not want her appealed to him in a perverse way but he was not sure whether he could make the thing stick. The trouble was he did want them - always and a lot. He went back to Kerry and Sue clutching a fresh pint of Guinness.

"You were going to tell me about this week's financial targets," he said to Kerry and her face contorted again into her horrified work sneer.

"Where's my voddy?" demanded Sue, a bit put out.

"They'd run out of vodka," Rob told her. "Said they'd have another delivery in Wednesday. Until then they've only got barley wine but I thought I ought to ask before I got you that."

"What's barley wine," asked Kerry, fiddling with her bra. She had big bosoms, Rob reflected. Maybe he *was* chasing after the wrong one. Big bosoms, small bosoms? Both were good but if you had one set in your hands, you inevitably wanted the other.

"It's this drink in green bottles which looks and tastes like sick," Sue told Kerry. "If he had brought me that I'd have smashed his face in. As it is I'm still going to have to deal with him for not getting my drink when I told him too." She turned her attention back to Rob.

"You," she told him. "Are a bad boy. If you don't get my drink I'm going to smack your arse and not in a good way."

"There is no bad way," admitted Rob. "I was talking to Eric, he's missing you. I'll invite him and his big cock over here if you like and me and Kerry can make ourselves invisible. I'm sure we wouldn't want to be gooseberries when you're on the pull."

"Don't you fucking dare." She looked genuinely horrified at the prospect, which pleased Rob though he didn't show it and carried on earnestly trying to set the two up for a life of conjugal bliss.

"He'll buy you a drink *and* he knows how to treat a lady, besides, I feel uncomfortable around you because you're my boss. He knows he's superior because he's a teacher," said the voice of sweet reason.

"She makes me uncomfortable too," Kerry said, nodding, "she's a psycho; keeps going on about work and that. Mind you, you've been on about it too tonight. I'm going to have to smack your arse when she's finished with you."

Rob shook his head solemnly. "Any arse smacking going on, I'll be doing it. You *both* need putting in your place as far as I'm concerned, especially Susan here."

Sue was mussing her hands through dyed blonde locks which was supposed to be some kind of sign but might just have been her finding something to do with them, as she had no drink to hold.

"Ooh - Kaz, he's developed a spine. No don't laugh, I quite like it. He's turning into a big boy is little Robbie. I'm seeing him in a whole new light tonight; must be the hat."

"Must be that you're not so self-obsessed as usual this evening, a bit more open to other people." Rob wandered off towards Sam without a backward look, though he could hear a squeak of outrage and a giggle in his wake.

Sam wasn't impressed. "You said what? Are you fucking clueless? How is that chatting anyone up, just slyly slagging them off and having it away to the bogs? That's not going to get you a shag, take it from me young man."

Rob was a bit grumpy about it, the way you are when you half suspect someone with bad news is right but are determined to cling to the wreckage of your point of view, however big the argumentative iceberg.

"Nah, you don't know nothing, it's a 'thing', it's called negging. Slagging birds off is good apparently. Though obviously, you don't want to go over the top so they hate you and that. Giving them a little verbal slap now and then keeps them keen, it's all part of the plan."

"Perhaps you could sneak up on her later when she's tying her shoelace and kick her up the arse - then she'll *really* be gagging for it."

"Hey, it was your idea this stuff, you gave me the web address," grumbled Rob into his Guinness.

"Yeah but maybe you need to look into it a bit more. I shouldn't be too critical if this is your first go, you've made a real effort what with the hat and everything. I must admit, it seemed to work."

Sam was right, Rob knew, he was doing a beginners version of what was required. He was supposed to be piquing the interest of a girl he liked, not pissing her off so they argued. Instinctively though he felt it wasn't a good idea to race back and crawl to Sue. She was used to him being submissive so maybe a show of strength wouldn't be such a bad thing in the round. He was trying to be an alpha male here after all and dominant males don't beg, so he headed off to find another woman to talk to instead.

As he wandered off he got lucky again and a couple more came up to ask what's with the hat? Although he didn't get far with them once he'd satisfied their curiosity, it couldn't do him any harm if Sue happened to be looking over. When a girl spoke to him he concentrated on smiling at her and maintaining eye contact, maybe leaning in to hear better and even touching her arm. It was stuff he would do at work all the time when talking to clients who he wanted to sell to but thinking about it, he realised it wasn't usually the way he talked to women. He would be more offhand, almost brushing them off. Perhaps he had justified this as playing hard to get but he knew it was simply a symptom of his shyness. Still, looking at it from their point of view he probably seemed aloof and disinterested to the point of rudeness.

This evening he made a game of it, scoring points for making them laugh or for getting them to touch him on the arm. Three or four women in succession he didn't know who wanted to talk to him; result. It wasn't a magic hat, it had simply been stuffed in the back of his wardrobe. He knew in the end that it wasn't even the hat, it was him. He was the same person who usually endured embarrassing silences when he tried to speak to girls, or engineered cringing faux pas on public transport.

He still didn't really know what to say to women when he spoke to them but it almost seemed now that he might get a chance to learn. He felt a tap on his arm - Sue again. She had bought herself a drink.

He was still thinking of a suitable put-down for Sam when he felt the

30

hat being dragged off his head. This wasn't a playful pull like some girl wanted to try it on, this was the kind of force you'd use to drag some bloke off your brother in a bar scrap. Wouldn't have mattered but the thing was still attached to his neck with a string. He twisted round to see Eric the educator hanging onto it with both hands, his face sullen and determined. Rob managed to get his fingers under the string and set it loose, Eric staggered back with his prize and stuck it on his head in drunken celebration.

"Now who's king of the castle?" he demanded, tangentially.

"You are mate, fucking definitely," Sam assured him. "King, queen and jack. It certainly suits you as well, you don't look an idiot or anything."

Rob was rubbing his neck and looking for a sharp exit. The bloke had clearly managed to get extraordinarily drunk very quickly which was never a reason for optimism. Plus it was clear he was resentful and probably not just jealous of Rob's natty headgear. Currently he had the Guinness hat back off his head and was shaking it around like a terrier with a rat. Rob half expected him to stick the thing in his mouth.

"Came here tonight to see Sue is all," he was saying. "We've been friends for sometime now…"

Sam cut in, "We're all friends here mate. All good buddies. Why don't you go and get yourself a drink? You don't seem to have one."

"Drank it," admitted Eric ruefully. "Drank them all."

He looked up at Rob with a beery glint in his wet eyes.

"Perhaps this bloke will get me one, seeing how he's had my bird off me?"

Rob shrugged. "She's not your bird. She's here for a good time, same as the rest of us. How about you just enjoy yourself and don't be a nuisance hey?"

He was a big bloke this teacher. Rob was betting geography and PE. He shambled over and made as if to put the hat back on Rob's head but instead grabbed him in a playful headlock. Rob felt himself being dragged down like the back end of a pantomime horse. It was a tough position in which to appear dignified.

"Can you get off me please?" his voice was muffled and a bit choked. He had a gobful of the bloke's pink T-shirt. Briefly he wondered whether to hit him. If he did so now, just once, hard and in the gut, it might surprise him enough to make him let go. After that he could move off sharpish and cut his losses. However, he sensed that was just what Eric wanted, an excuse to turn the thing into a full-on brawl. He could imagine him next morning, full of indignation down the police station. "There was a bit of playful banter, then he struck first officer."

Rob contented himself with wriggling about a little, trying to free his airway.

"If you let me go, I'll let you have a go on her." He knew this was going to make things worse but he couldn't give one now quite frankly. This sad case was beginning to get on his nerves.

"Who are you to say that?" Eric's voice had gone high pitched - Rob had definitely scored a hit.

"She's her own person. I'm a professional teacher, you're just some prole who works for her. You need teaching some manners."

The grip around his neck tightened and Eric started bouncing up and down, then span him around a couple of times like they'd invented a new dance. This was going to end in tears sure enough.

"You and me are going outside to sort this out like men."

Oh dear, what a tosser. He could hear Sam in the background making various low level threats. In a moment it was all going to go off. He couldn't see much apart from pink T-shirt, floor and the occasional shoe. Then there was a yelp and the grip around his neck went slack. He shrugged the bloke's meaty arm off him and stood up. Eric was crouched by the bar looking baffled and wet. In front of him was Sue with an empty pint glass which she carefully put down on the table.

"What did you do that for?" Eric asked plaintively.

You don't realise how much a pint pot holds until it's split all over someone. It suddenly becomes a lot of liquid. The pink T-shirt had gone red and saggy, you could see Eric's nipples right through it. Rob had suffered a little bit of splash back but hadn't done badly considering. It was all going to be alright as there was suddenly nothing to argue over. The matter had been settled and Eric would just slink away.

Then he looked at Sue.

She didn't look like the Sue from work. It was the same person overall - blonde bob, pretty, skinny, small breasted, but there was a look of cold malice he hadn't seen before. Suddenly, she launched herself at Eric with a kind of war-cry.

"You fuckerrr!"

And she was belting him. Not little girly 'you beast' slaps but proper punches like a man would throw. Eric was still getting over his soaking. He wasn't equipped for this. He slunk down under the barrage and tried to protect his face and his nuts. She didn't say much, like she didn't want to expend the energy any way other than in hitting him and she didn't show any signs of letting up either. Once he'd ducked low enough, she started kicking him too.

Sam managed to drag her back at this point then Eric got up and thankfully didn't look too badly damaged. Sue lacked the raw power to do that much physical harm but she certainly had the intent.

"Go now," Sam shouted at him.

People were gathering round. There would be bouncers here soon. Eric fled, aiming straight for the door and was gone and that was clearly the end of a beautiful friendship for Sue.

She calmed down straight away. Seemed quite chipper in fact.

"We'd better go too, before they realise we were involved. I don't want to get banned from this place."

Later, sprawled on the sofa in his flat in front of MTV, Rob started out thinking about how the evening had gone, about Sue, about the unfortunate Eric, but finished up instead thinking about when he was a kid and about his mum. He wondered whether he should tell people he was an orphan if they asked about his family, whether that would make him seem both sympathetic and mysterious which seemed like good things. In fact his father was still alive but Rob had not spoken to him since the death of his mother. There had been no major fall out or schism, it just seemed there was no further point in communication.

Her death had come as a shock, despite the long illness which preceded it. This was partly because Rob, to some extent and his father to a very great extent, had bought into the narrative woven by Rob's mother that she was in fact immortal. This was never spoken out loud, that would have seemed preposterous given the terminal bone cancer, her tiny, wizened body and weakened state. Yet it was tacit in all she did and all they did around her.

She was sick for sure but if she had returned from one of her many visits to the hospice happy and bright eyed to say the cancer had retreated like a tide, leaving her reduced and scarred but fundamentally whole, if then she had begun a slow, halting progress towards eventual recovery, it would have surprised Rob no more than her untimely death.

Next morning was Saturday. He was having breakfast in the flat around 11am when the phone rang. It was Sue. She thought he might want to take her out for a walk. Eric had been going to. It was Rob's fault, basically, when you looked at it, that Eric *wouldn't* be. She fancied Crickley Hill country park and would be picking him up outside his front door in half an hour.

Rob wondered what clothes you wore for walking. He had never really done any. Unless you counted to the bus stop, or between pubs. In the end he found jeans and a jumper and rummaged around in his pile of shoes until he found the black DMs he used to wear as a student. They were sturdy and had a tread on them and so would do.

Crickley Hill was woody and windswept. It was where people went for walks and seemed to have little other purpose other than being a corralled area of near nature held in with dry stone walls and ringed with car parks, where pensioners sat on deck chairs by the open boots of their hatchbacks supping tea from flasks.

Sue squealed the car into a parking space with a handbrake turn like they were the Sweeney and headed off at a lick up the hill. The earth was ruddy and sticky with clay underfoot; Rob's DMs were soon clarted with it and he slipped as they walked, once putting a knee down so he got a shiny red patch on his jeans.

They paused half way up the rise and sat on a bench looking out at some trees on a hillside which danced sparely in the wind. He'd read an article in the Metro on the bus which said all women are unhappy about the way they look and that smiling at them can make them feel better, plus he felt suddenly cheerful out here in the air, young and primed with possibilities, so he gave Sue a big cheeky grin, which did seem to brighten her mood.

She stopped staring at the trees and shot him a smile back, though not with teeth. He wondered whether he had managed to assuage her high level of body concern.

"I like you Robbie. You're turning out to be a good friend to me. You listen to me without doing that man thing of always wanting to come up with solutions. Men always assume that when women tell them about a problem, their job is to solve it - that's not what we want - we just want you to listen."

Rob was terrified. Friends? This was terrible news. Friends he already had. The PUAs had warned him of this, it was known as the LJBF - Let's Just Be Friends - a phrase heard with numbing regularity by

Average Frustrated Chumps everywhere. He was falling head first into the friend zone and once a woman had you herded into this pen there was no escape. You were a pal, a buddy, rather than a potential mate: game over. It seemed there was no way back.

What would make her think that? Panicked, he mentally ploughed through what little he knew of PUA lore to come up with a way to wriggle out of this; he came up empty handed. Perhaps he should just tell her? It seemed too bold, too sudden, too likely to frighten her off.

Talk about sex? It's one thing in a crowded bar full of cackling office girls and quite another on this Spartan hillside, just the pair of them blowing about like lost gloves. The wisdom he had read online suggested sex talk should be approached obliquely at first and at the behest of the woman. Instead, instinctively, he reached out and touched her, putting his hand on her shoulder he leant in and kissed her chastely on the cheek.

"I hope we can be that at least..."

He didn't think he had done too badly, there was the possibility of more, it left the door open and the touching had felt thrilling, it crossed a boundary. The worry remained though, that it was one she did not wish to cross, and that she had made a decision and he was simply being slow on the uptake, inappropriate, a pest.

He struggled to remember another technique, something which would get him on the right track; he decided to try patterning. That was a seduction technique where you describe wonderful states of mind to a girl in order to get her feeling aroused. You didn't need to describe anything to do with the pair of you, just create a mood for which you were responsible. He had a go, even though it was bracing up on the hill and not really conducive to getting aroused.

"It's great being out here together, away from everything," he'd intended to try out a seductive whisper but ended up having to shout over the gusts of wind which bullied her blonde pageboy cut and his tousled mousey mop.

"It's so peaceful and quiet. I sometimes wish I was on a desert island. Somewhere hot with white sand and coconut trees."

He stopped for a minute with a far-away look in his eye like he was contemplating fantasy island.

"I'd love to be on that island, just you and me. That would be great wouldn't it?"

She shoved the hair out of her eyes and shook her head vigorously.

"I'd miss Eastenders."

Later, as she dragged him to the top of the hill he fell towards her, forcing them into a clumsy embrace and he glanced at her eyes wondering what he might find there but direct eye contact was too embarrassing for both of them it seemed. Each had one skin too few and they fell apart again, apologising and making excuses.

"Watch your feet there darlin, you'll have us both over," she admonished.

"Yeah, sorry, must have slipped on some sheep shit, it's like glass that stuff, it's a menace."

Still, he felt quite pleased with the development since, even if it had not been what you'd call 'erotic', it at least involved some physical contact, the casual touching called Kino which his gurus on the website urged should be pursued as often as was practical, without appearing too much of a groper.

He reached out and put his hand on her arm as they made their way along the ridge. He'd intended it to be reassuring, as though he was protecting her but it felt more like the reverse, the old lady grip a grandma clings to you with, so you can help her cross the road. She did not actually shake his arm away or demand that he let her go, so he clung on.

There were views to be enjoyed back over the escarpment and down into the Severn Vale. The houses and factories of Gloucester glittered in the slender sun and from here it all had a thin sort of beauty. They could have been somewhere else, somewhere romantic where you might go on holiday, up a mountain at a ski resort say, though then they would have been disappointed that there was no snow.

"Hey, stop and take a look at that." She turned him round to face the view and he moved his arm properly around her skinny waist, where again, she did not actively remove herself from his clutches, though she did nothing to encourage him either. He could almost feel her tense up a little, she had been made to feel uneasy and the thought made him want to spring away but he resisted the urge to release her and they surveyed Gloucester's unlikely prettiness joined together, as a married couple might do, only more awkward. More in awe of each other's physical presence, like birds when there's a cat in the garden; they remained watchful, primed for flight.

He wondered whether now would be the time to try a proper kiss but it didn't seem right. She was talking about fairly unromantic topics, pointing out to him things she could see out in the elsewhere.

"There's Brockworth business park where my uncle Eric works, and see there where all the windows are glinting? That's where my gym is, the Rackets Club. Maybe we could have a game of tennis there? You any good at tennis?" she glanced at him. "No? I could teach you."

He wasn't bad at tennis as it went, least that's the way he saw it, though he didn't know how good she was of course, very, probably. County this or league that or something, lessons as a young lass from some tanned letch in tight shorts.

What had led her in her swift appraisal of his physique to suppose him crap at racket sports? Did he have thin arms or rounded shoulders, was there something gawky or mal-coordinated about the way he moved? That wasn't the guy he saw in the mirror, at least not on a good day.

"What I want," Sue told him, "is a man who is totally faithful and devoted to me, like a little puppy but I can just drift in and out as I like and he will stay the same and always be there for me." Sue was smiling when she said this but she didn't seem like she was joking. She was the sort of person who, if she got the chance, just said what she meant in a plain unvarnished way, that was it.

"That's what men want from a woman I think," Rob admitted. "You're supposed to want something different aren't you? Something mutual where you are both like part of one person."

Sue shrugged, showed her white teeth in another grin. "I don't know what I'm supposed to want, I only know *what* I want. I'm terribly jealous and I don't think I can trust anyone. I don't think people can be trusted, do you?"

He noted she wasn't just talking about men, she said 'people', she meant 'people'. Rob felt noble suddenly and wanted to go out to bat as a champion for the trustworthy segment of the human race.

"I think you could have faith in me," he said, wondering whether this was a statement his colleagues on the PUA notice board would approve of; it probably seemed needy, showed weakness. "There's people who can be trusted sexually, same as other ways, maybe they are not perfect for all their lives, but overall."

She shook her head, looking solemn. "I want perfect, I want absolute unwavering devotion but I get to do what I want."

Rob laughed, even though she'd not been joking. "You have low expectations, that's good, it will make it that much easier for you to find Mr Right."

On the way back to her car there were cows. They'd been left up on the hill to graze of course but also as a bit of a tourist attraction. They weren't the usual Friesians but huge beasts tall and wide, almost as furry as highland cattle but differently coloured. Most were black with a fat white saddle around their middle. Some were brown and cream in the same proportions. As Rob and Susan picked their way back up the field towards the car park, it felt as though their world had been invaded by giant furry humbugs. Sue's behaviour changed when she saw the great animals and their gauche overstuffed calves.

"Shit - I hate cows," she confided in a tightly wound voice. Her body language had changed too from being in charge, to wanting to be led. She fell back a step and let him pick his way through the cow pats on their behalf. He relished her vulnerability and felt an unstoppable urge to encourage her in it.

"These won't hurt you they're soft as shit," he told her. "Let's go for a closer look."

He set off in the direction of the nearest clump of cattle, a couple of shaggy black and white mothers with a gaggle of dark brown and grubby cream offspring.

"No!" she sprang back with a screech, stepping into a pat as she did so.

The crust broke and brown goo oozed around the heel of her boot. That, clearly, would be his fault.

"I don't do cows. I was chased by one as a kid. It's not funny, I'm fucking serious." She sounded it too.

Rob tried to put his arm back on her shoulder but she shrugged it off. Flustered, he resorted to some little professor bollocks about the cattle to overcompensate.

"Course these aren't any old cows, they're Gloucester cattle. They're a rare breed now but they used to be all over the hills here back in the day. They're where double Gloucester cheese comes from originally, though it's made all over the world now of course, like cheddar."

She'd zoned out and was heading for the top fence near the car park, striding ahead with a determination to leave the bovine horror behind. He scuttled after her, continuing his desperate history lesson as though it meant something.

"Erm, there's single Gloucester cheese too, though that's nowhere near as popular. I believe it's still made in a couple of spots in the county. It's single churned, rather than double churned, hence the name. I had it once... it tasted like shit."

She stopped dead. He ran into the back of her, they almost toppled but not quite.

"They're coming towards us." Her voice brimmed with panic.

He looked up and saw the truth in what she said. A couple of the animals were ambling in their direction. Whether they were coming over to say hello, or whether they'd simply spotted a succulent knot of wet grass over in this part of the field, was unclear.

Rob and Sue were a couple of hundred yards short of the fence. As far as other people went, they might as well have been alone as the nearest bunch of hikers was a family group way down towards the bottom of the long, sloping pasture. To the right hand side of them was woodland but it was bordered with a dry stone wall and topped with barbed wire. To the left of them was field, cows and more cows. The only sensible option was to plough on and aim for the top fence, yet it was from this direction that the animals came.

"Crap, shit, do something." Sue was panicked and angry.

The cows approached. It appeared they had come to investigate. Their big, furry black heads bored in inquisitively.

"Do something!" demanded Sue again. She was pushed up against Rob but he didn't think this would really count as Kino any more than it did if you clung together on a lump of flotsam after your boat sank. Feebly, he waved his free arm at the cows who stood impassively a foot or two in front of them.

"Go on," he offered. "Shoo . . . you fuckers."

The Gloucester cattle stood their ground.

"That's it," yelled Sue, springing to angry life. She tried to barge back past Rob but tripped over his feet as she did so. He stepped back and whilst trying to stop her falling, pushed her upright - but overdid it - and suddenly she was falling the other way into the pair of cows. She sprawled into them and they flustered too, like people do, backing off soundlessly but quickly heading away, so she barely grazed them as she went down.

Sue sprang up immediately as Rob went over to get her.

"It's okay," he assured her. "It frightened them off."

"You *bastard*!" she screamed, as soon as she was upright. She shot out her balled fist, catching him on the bridge of the nose. "You daft fucker!"

She turned and stalked off back to the car, vaulting the fence and disappearing into the trees at the top of the field.

CHAPTER 3

'Johnno!' the blog of Robert Johnson, July 14:
"The world can be split into those who have experienced tragedy and those who have not. Mum dying isn't something I can talk about, even here when it's just for me. But because of what happened I recognise when others are labouring under a weight of sadness. It changes your whole outlook on life.

The tragedy is always there wherever you are and it can leave you feeling angry and you don't know why. It can suddenly sap your energy so that one minute you're feeling positive and focused and the next you just can't be bothered with anything. It can make you well up with tears at inappropriate times - watching a pop video or a TV advert for washing powder.

It's always there with you, at work or on the bus, when you get up in the morning, when you lay your head down. It's the context in which other things are seen."

"I've not been doing this PUA shit long but I'm guessing that if the girl gives you a couple of black eyes that's not a good sign."

Sam looked him up and down.

"'Pends what you're into."

They were sitting at the chipped Formica breakfast bar of the café on the corner of the Promenade and Clarence Parade. In front of them were breakfast buns and cardboard coffee cups. Rob surveyed his features in the back of a spoon. It wasn't too bad. Bit of a nick on the bridge of his nose then two greenish, bluish stains under his eyes like he'd not slept for a fortnight. Soon the stain would fade through the rainbow of pain, a pale palette of purples, oranges and yellows until it was forgotten. It was nothing really, explaining it was the thing.

He'd decided to go with 'fell on my face drunk' though Sam told him this was the equivalent of 'got hit by a door' and he'd be better off claiming a scrap with a bouncer. That would give the office something to chew over; it was that or let them make up their own tale which would surely be worse.

Rob decided that - at the end of the day - he didn't really give a fuck. He had a bite of his bun and got egg yolk on his tie.

"Bollocks." Tried to wipe it with a soiled napkin.

"Did it not say anything about this type of thing on the site?" Sam wanted to know.

"Being assaulted by birds you are trying to chat up? I would think, if that happened to any of them, they'd be keen to keep a lid on it, same as I am by the way."

"Aren't you frightened she'll twat you again?"

Thing was, Sam didn't seem to be joking and looked quite concerned.

"Fucking give over."

"No, I mean it. I'd make sure you hit your targets this week, otherwise she might give you another crack round the head."

Rob was genuinely feeling a bit of an ass now. There's nothing worse than a wind-up that works. He decided to fall back on the truth rather than try to joke his way out of it - he wasn't in the mood.

"I'm not sure why she did it. Course, I know there was cattle rage going on and y'know, fight or flight, but still you might expect a few harsh words, get told to fuck off or what have you."

Sam chortled merrily, clearly enjoying the whole thing but then came over all serious.

"Look, she's clearly a fucking psycho, look how she totalled that twat at the pub. I know he was a teacher and deserved it but nobody deserves to be twatted for nowt - cows or *no* cows. She could have just run off, then given you a bollocking later if she felt strongly about it."

A bit of support - that was nice. They finished their buns in silence then went outside with the dregs of coffee for Sam to have a fag.

"It doesn't look good for the future of our relationship," Rob admitted forlornly.

Outside was a let-down of an English summer morning with a featureless grey sky and damp muggy air which clung to their clothes.

"I only know maybe three things about her personal life and two of them involve extreme physical violence."

Sam mulled it over, taking a long drag.

"How old are you again?"

"Twenty-two" admitted Rob, "but you've got to remember, that's only fifteen in man years."

Had he decided to tell Susan it was the end of the line? Sam wanted to know.

"You *are* going to give her the bad news? Tell me that one's not even up for discussion. Where's the gain?"

There should be no debate of course, he knew that. There was all sorts to loose and nothing to gain by persevering with something which was so clearly broken from the start. He would certainly lose his self-respect, he might well lose his teeth too. Plus the whole point of the PUA doctrine was that he now had options. It was never policy to chase one girl to the exclusion of others, the point was to find *a* girl, not *the* girl. The fact she had shown an interest in him should now serve to encourage other women to see him as interesting sexually. At least, that was the way it worked, or so he had read the evening before, Bud in hand, as he searched for guidance among his internet gospels.

The pair headed back down Clarence Parade towards the office. Sam almost got run over by an Aston Martin screaming round the tight bend by the Neptune statue and leapt three feet forward to avoid it, calling the driver all kinds of a mother Hubbard as he squealed off.

Yeah, it was clear cut - Rob and his Internet gurus concurred.

There was one bloke on the PUA chat line 'Sonof' who was especially clear: "If anything happens where you are made to look weak, move on. Leave her with good feeling if you can but don't hang around to be a victim - where's the gain?"

He knew this advice was sound, Sam did too. It was one date and the world's worst - kick her to the kerb. So why then was there a big solid part of him which wanted to do exactly the opposite?

"I don't really know *what* I'm fucking doing," he admitted, as he trotted to catch up with Sam who was having another fag.

"Who does?" Sam wanted to know.

Sam hung around at the back door with other fag finishers and Rob headed for the lift as he suddenly found he couldn't be arsed with stairs today. The whole idea of sex puzzled him he realised but more than that, it puzzled the world. Even though we are all owner-operators of a libido, our society hasn't got to grips with the basic facts still. The strange twee ways we avoid and obfuscate; how out of kilter it seems when someone is bold and straightforward about it.

There is no right way with sex. The only thing to do was go at it tangentially as though we were all bit parts in an underwear ad or a Carry On film. 'Carnal knowledge' there's a curiously slippery euphemism. It avoids the act altogether, as if trying to claim the issue is one of information rather than physical contact, as though it involved people whispering softly into each other's ears and passing on dark secrets in the night.

Waiting for the lift to arrive were a long-haired young lad from circulation and his little pal, a plump blonde girl who was flirting away happily with him. They nodded to Rob then ignored him.

"How old you this year then?" asked the lad.

"Twenty-one," she replied.

"What you doin' for it?"

"I'm going up the town. Going in fancy dress. Going to get a skin tight dress in nude and cover my whole body in glitter."

"Nice... classy."

The lift arrived and the three got in, the pair of them carried on the conversation as though Rob wasn't there, despite their close proximity.

"What do you want the twenty for anyway?" she asked.

"You *know* why. I want ten for the one thing and the other ten for that other thing."

"I don't know what you does that other thing for anyway, it's just pointless."

"How is it pointless? I could be going up the town on the beer and not remembering anything after - at least I remembers."

The lift stopped for the advertising floor. As the doors opened, Rob had to push past them and the girl turned to him as if noticing him for the first time.

"Hey - what happened to your face?"

It was not going to be the last time he was asked that question today.

Colin, Alan and Jude all wanted to know at once and right away. He didn't even have time to shove his man-bag under the desk.

"Bouncer," Rob told them, forgetting which story he'd been planning to use. "Or it might have been a door - can't remember - I was very, *very* drunk."

The three seemed strangely satisfied with this. The younger generation was still drinking to excess and getting in scrapes so all was right with the world.

"When I was in my twenties. . ." Alan mused.

"Aw, here we fucking go," Sue appeared from behind the filing cabinets.

She stared at Rob, made an issue of grabbing his ears and peering at his face as the others giggled.

"Nice shiner - have you told them how you got it?"

Rob rooted around for some words.

"Well, arboun... Nerm, gotadoor"

Sue turned to the others, standing tall in anecdote-telling mode.

"This daft fucker took me on a so-called date out in the countryside, ran away from some cows, tripped and whacked his head."

Gales of laughter. Sue joined in. She was brazen alright. He looked up at her from where he sat - she wasn't putting this on - she clearly believed in what she had said; it was her truth.

What about the rage, the silent car journey afterwards, the dumping him outside his flat and squealing off? What about the punch? It hadn't happened apparently. It had been written out of the world according to Sue.

"I'm sticking to my bouncer story," he joined in weakly. "I believe it shows me in a better light."

Sue headed to the swing door for the back stairs, rooting in her bag for a packet of fags as she did so. Once through the door she peered back through the glass at Rob watching her and motioned with her head impatiently for him to follow. Outside the back door she was already inhaling.

"You can take me for dinner Friday evening if you're good. Italian. I like Polenta."

He hesitated, groping around for the right words in this social situation.

"With roasted vegetables. Don't tell anyone though, about the dinner I mean, not the preference for semolina."

Finally, he managed to shake his head.

"Can't Friday night. Got library books to take back."

She sniggered at his audacity. Then had a good stare at him like she could tell what he was thinking by reading the stupid expression on his stupid face. He gave her the vacant smile he used on clients, 'nothing to see here, move along.' He didn't want her to see he was genuinely frightened of her, not just the way you are of someone prepared to poke you in the snout without a by your leave but something deeper, more profound. He was scared of her lack of empathy. He was sure she didn't get how he felt about her, or about what had happened on the hill. Either she had accepted her own version of events or rationalised it away as an acceptable lapse under duress.

Curious to hear her version of what had gone on, he felt like asking her straight out so she couldn't avoid dealing with it but there was the fear again, the warning siren telling him the matter was best avoided.

"We'll maybe get Polenta some other time," he told her. "I like Polenta too."

She blew smoke at him. "Is it only that you like?"

"I like all types of Italian food. All types of food really, apart from pineapple."

She pulled a face. "You're weird - maybe that's why I like you."

"And capers. I can take them or leave them to be honest. My least favourite dinner would be pineapple and caper surprise."

They were still standing in the chill, Sue taking a long drag and Rob feeling awkward as he had nothing to do with his hands when the door banged open and Alice poked her head round.

"Hiya!"

Sue stiffened and looked horrified.

"Hi Sweetie!" she trilled at Alice like she meant it.

Rob rummaged through his short PUA back catalogue for a thought on what to do now, then grabbed Sue round the waist and got in good and close to her. She seemed to welcome the attention and slipped an arm around his back, giving his bum a pat.

"Ooh, sorry!" Alice gave out. "I didn't know I was interrupting anything."

She tried to sound lascivious and might as well have winked but it lacked conviction and ended in a frown.

Rob said nothing, smiled a little was all. He left it to Sue to do the meek denials as he remained loosely attached to her, as though it was no big deal, contact he took as a right but could just as soon leave.

He stole a look at Alice while she was small-talking Sue. How had she

46

reacted to this unexpected development? He assumed this was the first she'd heard of the new deal. Office gossip closed down for business during the weekend and there had not yet been a big enough tranche of Monday morning for the news to spread to all corners of the advertising floor, never mind do its work in editorial and newspaper sales.

It was key he realised, indeed it was *crucial*, to let women know you were in demand. Let them see other women warming to you, his new gurus told him. It was a way of drumming up trade for your wares. Who, after all, wants anything unless others want it too?

"So are you two together then?" Alice finally blurted out, cutting across whatever Sue had been saying. She tried to make it sound jolly and exciting, like a secret shared.

Rob still kept his mouth shut and let Sue talk. He'd be interested anyway to hear her take on it. As she talked, he allowed her to draw him closer until he nestled against a flat tit. She seemed to be saying it was nothing, while trying to imply it was in fact *something*.

"It just is, what it is..."

She trailed off.

Rob shrugged. "It's early days you know? It's not like we're joined at the hip."

They stood together, joined at the hip. Sue had finished her fag. Her work ethic had her fidgeting to get back upstairs. Good. Rob was a little more easy-going about the whole work/life balance. As she made for the door she tried to drag him on gently behind her so as not to leave him with Alice but he resisted and she had to let go rather than turn it into a tug of war.

"Don't be long you, there's stuff to do up there," she chided him gently in middle-manager mode but that wasn't fooling anyone.

"Screen break," he said and she didn't bother arguing he'd just had one.

As the door shut Alice started talking.

"Caught you two didn't I? What would you have been up to if I hadn't come through the door? Wouldn't have wanted that. I mean, get a room!"

She moved in closer to him, black hair and smoky breath, buxom and beige skinned.

"How long's this been going on?" she whispered.

He leaned in as though he was hard of hearing. For someone who didn't smoke he spent a lot of time at the back door.

"There's nothing going on which wouldn't go away if I got a better offer."

She was delighted. A big white grin and a dirty laugh followed, which was the only kind she did.

"So you'd bin her if you got a chance to have a go on me instead?" she demanded cackling.

"Show me what you've got and I might consider it."

She shook her head in mock horror.

"You're a bit of a bastard you Robbie. I didn't know you had it in you."

Not long ago he'd have despaired at being called a bastard and assumed that meant it was all over. He was realising that, through the looking glass, in the world of women, being a bastard was not always a bad thing. It seemed to be something they secretly wanted, until they'd got it, then they realised they'd made a bit of an error of judgement, based on hormones or what have you.

Is it wrong just to want sex rather than to talk about soap operas or meet parents? If you didn't like the same music as a girl why would you want to go dancing with her? A lot of the stuff you ended up doing, it seemed to Rob, was all leading up to the one thing. He felt he didn't have the time and that he was being dishonest to himself and to the girl, by not admitting upfront that what he wanted was basic and primal. More primal than drum beats, more basic than dinner.

Surely though this *must* be what they wanted too? At least some of them, at least part of the time. Otherwise, how come the human race had not died out? If it was left to him it seemed it bloody might. He broke off the conversation with Alice, suddenly looking at his watch.

"You off hun?"

"Stuff to do."

He barely glanced at her as he went back inside - leave them wanting more; those were the rules.

He didn't want to run into Sue straight away now, not because he feared her reaction, so much as he wanted to let her stew. He could avoid her a little longer going through the basement of the building, through newspaper sales and then up the far stairs past the directors' offices, which he did, though he knew she'd catch up with him as soon as he sat back down at his desk.

He was heading up the final flight to the advertising floor when Louise came bursting through the swing doors heading the other way. Tall, blonde, beautiful, scary. She was remarkably young to be the ad director, thirty maybe, no more than that surely? Worked her way up, impressed as an ad rep, impressed always until the latest MD William Bean - a terse, monosyllabic Scot whose only direct communication with Rob had been to grunt at him occasionally at the urinals - had talent spotted her for the top job when you would have expected him to bring in someone less callow from elsewhere in the group.

She smiled at him did Lou. Hers was a charming and persuasive toughness, inclusive right up until to the moment she dumped you for not delivering to her sky scraping standards.

"Hello there? How's it going?" She was a Disney princess in a business suit. One it was better not to cross.

"It's a brighter day with you in it." He said and ginned at her fearlessly.

She looked at him like she'd only just noticed he was there, before that he could have been a cleaner or a doorman. She laughed at the unexpected flirtatiousness of the remark. When she laughed the focus dropped from her face and she seemed for a short while like other people, like you could talk to her about what had been on TV the night before or about music she liked.

"You're funny," she said. "Rod, isn't it?"

Though there weren't that many people in the department that you couldn't remember their names.

Down at the foot of the stairs she stopped and shouted back up. "Only kidding Robbie, you're a little sweetie, as if I wouldn't have noticed you," and she laughed again at how naughty she had allowed herself to be as she headed off to whatever was the latest meeting.

Scared and aroused, that was the way Louise made him feel, every time she appeared on the skyline. He was conditioned so now the sight of any slim blonde on Cheltenham Promenade left him with foreboding and the early stages of an erection.

It was easy to see why she turned him on, there couldn't be a straight man in creation who wouldn't feel these stirrings surely? Except maybe those who found themselves drawn to a fuller figure, who only liked buxom girls or who eschewed pale hair as a matter of taste. Still then, they must have wriggle room for exceptions? And Lou was certainly

49

exceptional.

The reason for the fear was harder to fathom. For a while he had denied the existence of it. He had focused simply on desire, nudged and guffawed with the lads in the tea-room, with Colin and Alan, with Sam and he had pretended that was all he felt. But the fear was there too.

It was something about her cool, about the way that, even when things became angry and heated in meetings and she was on the fat end of a bollocking from some other manager or a whinging from a member of her own staff, she would sail on serene as a swan. Even Wee Willie McBean didn't scare her and he frightened the crap out of everyone else. She just eyed him levelly and coolly as he rapped away at her like a little Scottish woodpecker, barking orders and questions at her in break-away nooks and corridors, meeting rooms and parking slots. She stared him out until he had finished with her, then spoke to him clearly, without hope and without despair.

"You know I'll do my best for you Bill, you know I always do."

That seemed to deflate him somehow, he was still gruff but quieter, like a terrier admonished by its owner.

Rob was still thinking about her as he washed his hands in the loos then headed back towards the advertising department with an eye out for Sue.

Louise he thought, would be his ideal woman if he could have any girl he fancied. Not just for one night, but as a proper girlfriend. Imagine that, imagine having a woman like that not only prepared to sleep with you but to identify you as her partner, as someone she needed, trusted and cared for; it was a heady notion.

She still frightened him though. When she got angry her cool turned cold and she could chill you with an admonishment or expel you into the frozen wastes with a well-turned witticism, cruel and pointed. If she thought you weren't up to the job she'd dump you without a moment's pity, haul you into the office and you were gone. Off the job entirely if you were green enough, condemned to the Siberian wastes of a far flung district office, or sent to the Forest of Dean, damned forever to chat up surly rural motor dealers, a slow, lonely death of missed targets and shoddy internal communications.

How much older was she than him? Seven or eight years? Seven years and a thousand years of experience. How did you cram all that into such a short space of time?

Upstairs Alice was thrusting her ample chest in Becca's face.

She looked up. "Oh Hi hun! I'm showing Becca my tits. We do it sometimes when we're bored."

He nodded like it was all perfectly in order.

"You should be very proud of them, they're a good effort."

She was clearly pleased. "D'you like them? They're nice aren't they?" She wandered towards him, thrusting them out for inspection.

"They're excellent. If you were as good at selling advertisements as you are at growing breasts you'd be top of the leader board all year round."

Her mood darkened.

"I'll take the pointy end of the leader board and insert it up your arse in a minute."

He sniggered and went back to his desk.

Alan, Jude and Colin were waiting there with their ears pricked up.

They had been watching him with Alice and Colin said that, from his admittedly outdated notions of young courtship, it appeared Rob might be 'in there.' The others concurred, wise as High Court judges reaching an appeal decision.

"It's tough to say," Rob admitted. "It's flirting sure but she does that with everybody, that's her. Men, women, whatever."

They accepted the wisdom of his remarks.

"In fact, if one of you lot walked past her, she'd probably show you her foof." They nodded again.

"I'd quite like that," admitted Alan. "It's been a while since I've seen one, except the wife's of course but you get used to that. We used to call it a bush."

"Noooo," interjected Jude all hot and bothered. "They don't have a bush any more these days, they shave it all off. Except for maybe a little bit."

Rob ignored them.

"That's one thing that I think's tough about being young at the moment. Because girls are so up front about everything, you can't be sure it's real. What do they really mean?"

The three wise monkeys conferred.

"It was easier in our day," said Colin.

"I'd say so yeah," allowed Alan. "You knew where you were usually, which was nowhere."

51

"If you wished to court a young lady," reminisced Colin, "you might drop your handkerchief when you were promenading on a Sunday afternoon and if her maid picked it up, you knew you could send a telegram to her father asking that she be allowed to come to supper. Always assuming she wasn't betrothed to another."

"Wow," said Rob. "What happened then?"

Jude shrugged. "You'd fuck like a pair of sex-starved Bonobos."

Five thirty, on the way out of the office, Sam had a question.

"When was your first kiss?"

"That was sweet," Rob said, "like two fourteen year old birds having a birthday sleepover."

"I mean, I don't just mean kiss, you know, proper snog, tongues, sexual and that."

Rob toyed with the idea of making something up but couldn't, in the end, be bothered.

"Seventeen," he said. "On my holiday job."

"Seventeen," mused Sam with a shake of the head, "is very late. Were you a Mormon? Was there some medical problem?"

"I'm not asking to be fucking judged here, I'm just opening up in the spirit of honesty," huffed Rob, wishing he'd made something up. "You don't get judged on Oprah and that."

"You know when I say 'kiss' it's not a euphemism for some arcane sexual practice don't you? I'm talking about a peck on the lips here."

He'd been seventeen, as he might have already pointed out. The job was in the Co-op, a big crumbling old department store in the centre of the northern town where he had been brought up. Him and his mate from sixth form college had been there together. Bo Ashton his name was.

"Bo 'cos he liked country and western?"

"Bo because he smelled of B.O."

The idea of the six week temporary employment they signed up for was mainly to clear out the cellar of the building. It was vast and dingy with a low ceiling. It crawled sleepily below the whole ground floor of the mighty Victorian pile above it.

"You and Bo together in the dark with all that time on your hands - I'm not liking the way this is heading," said Sam, concerned.

Rob ignored the implication and carried on with his tale.

The Co-op was a place out of time, even in their one hearse town. It was too big, too old, too disorganised and jumbled. Nobody there

52

seemed to care what Rob and Bo did once they had arrived in the morning so Rob and Bo did nothing more or less, just found broken old kids' bikes which had been discarded in the cellar from the toy department and screamed up and down on those, narrowly avoiding the pillars. The rest of the time they spent trying to chat up Kerry who had bad acne and worked on the till in the sports section. They'd go upstairs covered in dust and hang around like sheepish ghosts as she served customers in her tracksuit. Sure there was the acne, which he might have mentioned but she had quite a fit body. These were lean times and you had to work with what you had.

"So you snogged her then?"

"Yeah, in the cellar. I managed to win her affections, despite tough competition from Bo. He was at a natural disadvantage."

"Because of the smell?"

"Nah, he was a protestant, she was Catholic."

"You're Catholic?"

"I said I was, he was too daft to lie."

"Happy days then."

"No, she was Catholic. Hence only a snog. We both got covered in shit down in the cellar and that was as dirty as it got."

And that, he told Sam, was the problem. There was always some issue outside of lust, some reason he and any given girl couldn't just go ahead and fuck. Morals, religion, boyfriends, parents, age or consistency, ideas or class-system.

They were at the bus stop. Sam admitted it was an okay first snog story as they went, except *seventeen...*?

"Weird thing is that I hardly remember the actual kissing part," admitted Rob. Later on the bus he thought of what he did remember. The whole atmosphere of the cellar, being there with Bo racing around on bikes, cackling, the piles of powder under the pipes. They reminded him of his dad and of a tale his father told him about being a shipyard apprentice when he and his mates had made snowballs from the piles of asbestos which flaked from the lagged pipes. Big, raw, eighteen year old apprentices gambolling like bullocks and guffawing around the gun shop, happily chucking asbestos snowballs at each other, hooting with joy as the blue white powder smoked around them in a blizzard.

A scene they'd remember years later, laid up in hospital wards, wheezing and gasping like fish hooked from the sea. He was almost at his stop when his mobile went: Blue Monday by New Order which had been a favourite of his mum's.

"Yeah?"

"Where'd you run off to?"

It was Sue, he pretended not to know.

"Sorry, who is this?"

"It's me you twat."

"Oscar Wilde?"

"No, Sue," she giggled. "Where d'you go after work? I wanted to talk to you."

"Had to get off, things to do, people to see."

"You're not with that slut are you?"

"What slut?" He stood up to get off the bus and swayed down the aisle. Half way down he noticed the Spanish girl he'd embarrassed himself with a while back. She was getting off too, he let her out but ignored her completely which he hoped made him snag on her. It seemed ages ago all that spider throwing, a long time ago in a world far away. He wondered how he'd have dealt with her now? Better, he decided.

Sue was talking but he'd missed most of it.

"Look, I can't really talk now," he admitted. "I'll maybe give you a ring later on okay?"

"She's a slut," warned Sue again. Secretly that was what he was hoping. Why did things have to be more complicated than that at this stage? Why was there any need for grumbling and bollocking and slaps round the face? There was time for all of that later on.

In his flat he logged on to TPUA.co.uk and did an hour's homework. He concentrated on the section in the seduction guide aimed at patterning - the technique of subconsciously turning a girl's mind to erotic thoughts while on the surface merely holding a casual, positive conversation. Make her feel wonderful, the guide told him, then link those wonderful feelings in her mind to you.

He didn't know whether he believed this stuff, they made it seem too easy, like it would work on the screen but not in real life where you fell over your words and girls laughed at you for being weaker and more stupid than they were. Still it seemed like a plan. That was the beauty of this stuff and it was better than doing nothing. In fact it made you feel as though you were a player, rather than one of the AFC's - the Average

Frustrated Chumps who did the decent thing just trying to be themselves but never got the girl.

He'd had enough of being one of them, he was *worse* than them, he was a BAFC, Below Average Frustrated Chump.

You made the object of your lust feel those wonderful states of pleasure by describing them to her, the guide told him. Discuss how you feel when you hear your favourite music, when you dance or when you eat something wonderful. Get her to describe her holidays, the warmth of the sun on her body, the beautiful blue skies, the crystal water. That was a good one he thought, most of the girls he knew seemed like they were more horny on holiday than anywhere else, it was a place where normal moral rules did not apply, so where better to take a girl in her mind if you wanted her thinking in that way?

Just being there when she was in that mood linked it to you, the guide assured him but if you wanted to reinforce this you could do so, be subtle, self-pointing. He stood up and surveyed himself in the mirror for a while as he tried pointing at himself subtly. It was difficult to do. He looked like a school kid pretending to rub his nose while surreptitiously flicking the Vs.

What was next? Binder commands, subconscious messages which seemed even more contrived and harder to pull off than self-pointing?

"That's the way to do it, now with me it's different..." Included the command "Do it now, with me."

That wouldn't work surely? How could he pull it off without seeming self-conscious and besides, surely she'd only hear the top level sentence, not the embedded one?

He practised that in the mirror a few times too, while pointing at himself.

"That's the way to DO IT NOW WITH ME it's different."

Oh, yeah, that was working, no chance of crashing and burning at all.

The there were sexual metaphors which sounded innocent but lead the girl's thoughts in the direction of the divan. "Come over and over again to the same conclusion... feel that thought penetrate you."

Weasel phrases could be pronounced in a way to make them subconsciously sexual. 'Below me' pronounced 'blow me'. 'Thoughts flowing in a new direction' pronounced 'nude erection'.

"Bollocks" he clicked off the page in disgust and went instead to the chat forum.

"Anyone believe patterning actually works?"

There were a couple of non-committal maybes then Sonof came on.

"It can work, you just have to feel it, rather than think it."

"It all seems too contrived," wrote Rob. "I can't imagine anyone not seeing through it."

"That's because you know what you are doing in advance. The trick is to make it seem like nothing. If you sound like you're reading lines you've learned, she'll know something is up even if she's not sure what and if you drop some clanging obvious double entendre, then you're going to make an ass of yourself. Sound natural but head in the right direction. Slip stuff in gently without drawing attention to it."

"Slip stuff in - ooh, er," typed Rob.

"You're not treating this with the high seriousness it demands grass-hopper," Sonof posted sternly. "Why not just try the mood altering stuff which makes most sense to you first and save the other things for later on? You can talk about chocolate and dancing surely without feeling so self-conscious you blow it? It strikes me most of this is made up of things one would be doing at an instinctive level anyway. Have you ever noticed that, when you start getting flirty with a girl you find yourself saying things which could be taken in two ways anyway?"

Rob supposed so. Being asked to analyse phrases and responses he made without thinking was tough for him. He had a gut feeling that if he over thought what he was saying to a woman, he might end up more tongue-tied and self-destructive than he had been in the first place. But then, he had always been pretty awful with girls and this could hardly make him any worse.

"See it as a slow measurable improvement rather than expecting it to be all or nothing," Sonof advised.

"Any other skill in your life you would expect to gather gradually rather than learn it all overnight. You didn't learn to drive in a single day did you? You presumably took lessons and picked up different aspects of it on each one. Then, a while after you pass your test, you look back and wonder how something which seems so natural and easy was ever something you needed to learn? Surely it was always instinctive and never something you could stumble over and get wrong."

"How simple you make it all seem," Rob told him and logged off. He'd give it some thought, maybe cherry-pick the aspects which worked for him and mix them in with what he was doing already. He wondered briefly why he was bothering with the PUA site at all, then he remembered what he'd been like when he was going it alone.

Later that evening he went out running and it rained. A summer thunder shower, sudden, intense and unexpected. As he padded the streets of his estate in a trance, the storm came in, glowering and billowing over the rooftops and playing fields. He was five minutes out from home and could have turned back but he pressed ahead thinking he might miss the worst of it, not caring too much either way.

Ten minutes further on it came with its full force, wave after wave of rain so powerful he could hardly breathe in it unless he bowed his head. He was drenched in less than a minute and then the first lightening arrived, brilliant and alarming, like a camera flash going off in his face, which cut out all sight and the thunder grumbled obliquely beneath the noise in his iPod headphones.

Soon he had the streets to himself but for gaggles of youths sheltered under the trees, who mocked him as he lolloped by in the bouncing, flap-jacking dazzle of spray. Big drops, densely packed, he felt like he was standing under a waterfall, but without the icy cold. Then Rob realised suddenly, he was happy. There in the deluge, spitting out water and slapping as he ran with shoes full of rain, wet as flip-flops on the seashore.

He realised he was content, for nothing on this earth could make him more unexpectedly joyous than getting caught in a rain storm. He'd been planning to shower anyway, the run would still take thirty minutes; what was the harm

This was proper rain, not some niggling drizzle but a furious, devout drenching. Being caught in a thunder storm could go on his 'not expecting to like it but did' list, along with getting licked by a dog, orange sorbet in a cone and being nagged by women he fancied.

"Why orange sorbet?" Sam wanted to know the next day when Rob described it.

"It's just ice and flavour - what's to like? Where's the ice-cream in that? But it works, it really does, an angel of flavour break-dancing on your tongue. I remember when my mum used to take me to the dentist as a kid, afterwards I'd have an orange ice-cream as a treat. I picked orange because it was different from the others. It was only when I grew up I realised it was sorbet."

"Yeah, well you're definitely different from the others. Why getting

57

licked by a dog?"

"Dunno Doctor Freud, you tell me."

Sam made an 'ick' face.

"It's suspect mate... very suspect. A cat I could understand but a dog's a male thing.

"And if I'd said getting licked by a bitch you'd have understood it the same way would you?"

"From you, yes. What other explanation could there be?"

At the end of his run Rob retrieved the key to the flat from under a brick by the back door and squelched through to the bathroom. He was still under the shower when the doorbell rang. He pretended he was out for a while but every thirty seconds or so it rang again, so he answered the door with a towel wrapped round him to find Sue, under a pink golf umbrella.

"Let me in hey?" she said in what, for her, was a mollifying tone. "It's fucking tipping it down out here and if I catch a chill I'll tell Louise it's your fault I'm off."

She looked at him sternly and he did as he was told. She flapped the umbrella experimentally a few times and it sprinkled his front room with water, like a wet dog shaking.

"Oy - pack that it," he grumbled.

"Soz" she sat on his sofa, worn out leather, gold, a second-hand gift from one of the sub-editors at work in response to a notice he'd put on the tea-room wall. He'd had it free on the understanding he'd shift it and luckily he had a mate with a van.

"This settee is shit," Sue commented primly. "Any chance of a cup of tea?"

She looked around the room from her throne and spotted a framed photo on top of the gas fire.

"Who's she?"

The picture of Rob's mum had been taken on holiday by his dad. She looked plump and happy, before the cancer. She was wearing a summer dress, white with red flowers, her dark hair was tied back and there were more flowers in different colours on a cart behind her.

"It's my aunt," said Rob.

"She's a cutie - you come from a cute family."

"It's an old photo," shrugged Rob. "White no sugar right?"

She followed him through to the galley kitchen and perched her neat behind on a work top, watching him put the kettle on.

"I thought I'd come over and see you," she offered, somewhat redundantly.

He didn't reply, just hooked tea-bags from a jar.

"Aren't you going to put some clothes on?"

He grinned despite himself.

"It's only you," he told her.

"And who were you expecting? Slutty knickers? Go on, you go and make yourself respectable and I'll finish in here."

As he pulled a T-shirt on in the bedroom he wondered if she had come over here hoping to barge in on him with Alice? She'd have loved the scene he guessed, it would have given her something to get in a proper rage about rather than some manufactured row where she was made to appear petty or disproportionate.

Despite what had gone on he wasn't worried particularly. Any female attention was still a novelty for him, even from a girl where you had to watch for an overhead right coming in when you kissed her on the cheek. When he came back she had tea for him and a can of Pepsi for herself. The can stood fresh and sweating on the coffee table, misted and dribbling with chill.

"Great tea," he offered experimentally, taking a sip like a wine connoisseur.

"Stand the spoon up in it, that's the way to do it, now with me it's different because I always seem to get it too milky."

"You need to practice more at work," she grumbled over her cola. "Jude's always making me drinks but when I get one off you I know there must be a zed in the month."

"Let's not talk about work, it's doing my head in just thinking about it. Tell me about your holidays instead."

She frowned at him. "If I'd known we were going to do this I'd have brought some snaps."

"Where's the best place you've ever been?"

She mulled it over, maybe thinking it wasn't such a conversational cul de sac after all.

"Kos. You know, the Greek Island. I went there once with Dave when we were engaged. It was hot and the sea was lovely and sparkling. The people were nice, I like the Greeks, they're not too pushy, give you space."

"That was when you and Dave were all loved up then?"

She shrugged. "Kind of, we had a few huge rows when we'd been drinking which turned a bit violent. He fell off a balcony and had to have his arm in plaster. Couldn't go in the sea for the second week. We broke up not long after we got home."

Rob must have been looking horrified because she went on:

"It was a ground floor flat, he just fell over a low wall onto some sand. If he'd have watched what he was doing he wouldn't have put his arm down funny. Silly twat."

She perched on the edge of her armchair, demure and petite, took another ladylike sip of cola.

"It sounds nice," Rob offered a little weakly. "Pale sand, glittering sea. Did you and Dave have a go on the beach?"

She shook her head.

"Don't like the idea of getting sand everywhere if you know what I mean. We had a try on the balcony one night but like I was saying, it ended in tears." She looked over at him.

"Maybe you and me should go on holiday? I'd like that," she grinned and he remembered why he fancied her. Though the idea of spending hours in a Greek casualty department didn't hugely appeal. Still, he had an experiment to carry out.

"Let's just let that feeling penetrate you for a moment and create a feeling of ha-penis in you're mine."

She gave him a look like her Pepsi had turned sour but didn't say anything.

"Thinking about it, I come over and over again to the same conclusion. I can imagine us there together, the sea is blue, this guy is so beautiful, the sand's all laid out blow me, it sets my mind off in a nude erection."

There was silence for a while, the sort where wind whistles and tumble-weed bowls up empty streets. Then she looked at him over her can and sniggered into the bubbles.

"Ooh er missus. You're funny, that's why I like you. Bit of an odd bod but no-one's perfect. Come over here for a snog."

Had that worked then? He wondered as he wandered over to her. It was tough to tell. It had been a good chance to practice but it wasn't much of a challenge to attract a girl who was, it seemed, already hooked and one he was desperately trying to cut off his line and chuck back in the river. Still, he could say he'd tried the system and that the upshot of it was a girl very forcefully, almost violently, sticking her tongue into his mouth. This surely could be counted as some sort of success?

She came up for air.

"Are you not interested to know why I came over here to see you?"

He had wondered but it seemed impolite to ask. Besides, he'd been preoccupied with trying out his new technique. If he had an idea it would be that she'd come over for this, sharing an armchair and saliva. She took his silence as a cue to continue.

"I wanted to make sure you weren't eggy because of that bit of an accident when we went for a walk."

She grabbed his cheeks between her palms and moved his face back so she could see him properly.

"It's important to me that we're good hun. I think you and me could go well together and I don't want any shit getting in the way of that before we're even started."

Rob just looked at her, his face slightly squashed. He didn't want to get in a row over the thing but she'd reminded him why this was a bad idea. He'd been thumped by a skinhead in a pub once for spilling his pint and he didn't much want to go out with him either.

"So long as we're good," Sue allowed primly. "If you behave yourself I might even let you have a go." She moved around so she was sitting on his knee and wriggled about a little.

"I have an appointment first thing," Rob said, shifting uncomfortably. "It's a school night you know?"

"The boss says you can come in late. The boss insists." She homed in for another snog.

"When I was a kid," said Sue, sleepily unlocking lips with a smack, "I had an imaginary enemy."

"That's an interesting take on a well-established tradition."

"Yeah, I mean it's like an imaginary friend, you know?"

Rob assured her he had grasped the concept.

"It gave me chance to practice. She stretched her slender body, out across his lap, light and strong, she reminded him of a Siamese cat his gran had when he was a kid. Svelte and glossy, taut and petite.

"It helped me learn how to hate better. I thought that - with the world being the way it is - it's as well to be prepared."

"And how *is* the world?" Rob really wanted to know, it must be a

61

strange world the one she inhabited.

"It's a place where you get on better if you hate properly." She said succinctly.

What do you do?" he was puzzled. "When you have an imaginary friend you share stuff with - problems, jokes - you tell them things you couldn't tell anyone else in the world..."

He realised she was staring at him curiously, glassy grey eyes fixed on him.

"I imagine..." he petered out.

"It's much the same thing," she nodded earnestly, "except you despise each other, you have a bond because you need each other in a way. In some ways, the connection you get to someone you can't stand is stronger than with someone you love. That's how I felt about Alan."

"Your imaginary friend was a boy named Alan?"

"Yes - little fucker," she said with feeling."

He gave her a 'that's crazy' look and huffed because she was giving him pins and needles.

She locked in for another round of kissing but he turned his face away and stood up slowly so she slid off his lap. She was very light - a little bird - it was as though her bones were hollow. He could have picked her up and chucked her onto the sofa.

She wasn't pleased. Kept muttering obscenities and giving him meaningful stares but she didn't really take issue with him over it, maybe thought that was beneath her. Anyway, he only needed the lightest of shoves on her back to get her out of the front door of the flat. As she left she stopped at the door and told him: "I'm alright with people as long as they remember the fireworks code.

"Treat fireworks with respect, remember fireworks can kill and never, ever come back to me once you've lit me."

Later in bed, he wondered why he had turned her down. That's what it amounted to after all. She had offered to have sex with him and he had said no. She could have been here in the bed with him now and that thought made him feel lonely, stupid, horny and futile.

"Let's go through there" she'd whispered into his ear between kisses, nodding her head in the direction of the bedroom. He had ignored her but later she had said to go through again, not a suggestion this time, more of an instruction and she tugged at his arm as if to drag him along there. He had pulled her back and made a joke of it, kissing her again, squirming away when she tried to grab his crotch. They had wrestled around for a while on his creaky plastic armchair, in the dim yellow light of his urine yellow lamp shade. The TV on in the background broadcasting a soap opera with a young couple bickering querulously over a break-up. He couldn't call Sue a break-up. Not if they hadn't had sex in the first place, that didn't count as an adult relationship, only as friends.

What was all that about? This was what he wanted surely? The aim he had in mind when he did his homework on the website and made gauche attempts to turn it into action. What he wanted was sex and here it was being offered to him. He had made no provisos, no deals with himself about how things would turn out. It had been straightforward at the outset, so why complicate matters.

He had fancied her at work, in the pub. He had fancied her under the pale yellow glow of the lamp in his flat, squeaking on the gold vinyl. He knew the problem was he had been frightened, he'd bottled it. Sure, he could tell himself she was not ideal girlfriend material, with her propensity for causing grievous bodily harm to sexual partners. She was the praying mantis of the advertising department and he wasn't keen on getting his head - or anything else - bitten off.

He rolled over and looked at the bright red digits of his bedside alarm clock. 4.30am. He'd have to get up in work in four hours but he didn't feel like sleeping and the reality, the awkward, teeth-jangling locking of lips, the breath tart with fag smoke and coca cola, oh how off-key it chimed with the way he'd imagined it in solitary moments. Him and a girl, who had Sue's face for now, but could have a thousand other faces, sitting close together, their shoulders touching maybe as she lent towards him to look closely at a magazine on his lap. Eyes meeting. A gathering together. No dented sensibilities or pranged morals, no emotional car-crash.

Then he did what he always did sooner or later, he had a look around for positives and - as was his habit - he found some. A fumbled, half-cocked sexual experience which fizzled out in disappointment and confusion was still a sexual experience, plus he'd had a proper offer and the fact he'd chosen to reject it on health and safety grounds didn't mean all was hopeless.

He'd found his way down the pot-holed B road to where he wanted to go once, so surely the signs would make more sense to him the next time around? Maybe he could give Sue another go? Nothing has been said which he couldn't take back and he wasn't considering asking her dad for her hand in marriage - find 'em, fuck 'em, forget 'em was the PUA way.

What about work though if he dumped her? She'd still be his boss - that would be awkward. Yet wouldn't it be anyway? He'd have to reject her, maybe he already had, he wasn't sure, he'd have to ask her. He sniggered to himself, thought briefly about having a wank, better get some sleep though, yeah.

CHAPTER 4

'Johnno!' the blog of Robert Johnson, July 17:

"I know I don't really have a choice and that I'd take whatever, but let's pretend for a moment that I did. Who would I have if I could choose: Susan, Alice or Lou? I'm honest here - here if nowhere else. I would have them all. Even Sue, who really I don't want and scares me.

Actually though, they all scare me, each in their own special way. I can't meet any of them without feeling frightened and aroused at the same time. Maybe that's bad and it means I'm looking in the wrong place but at the same time, that sort of strength of feeling is something I haven't had before, perhaps because I have avoided it. It's easy to avoid people, even when you are around them and I think that's what I have done up to this point.

Life rolls by more smoothly if you just watch it on TV rather than live it. Times I have had to roll my sleeves up and get personally involved, those have not always gone well in the past. I think part of me, the part which doesn't write things down or think them through, has decided I would be better off as a spectator rather than a competitor. I don't know whether I agree with that though. You can't lose if you don't take part, that's true but then you can't win either and maybe I need to give myself a chance at winning?"

Colin was at his desk peering at the editorial of Gardner's World.

"Runner's World, Gardener's World, if they produced Sad Bastard's World you'd have a lifetime's subscription," opined Jude.

"I am a forty year old man," Colin huffed, nose still in the dahlias. "My reading matter is commensurate with my vintage."

"You're forty-four," said Jude, fiddling in her drawer for a Lady Grey tea-bag. "Runner's World my arse."

Colin flicked placidly to an article comparing varieties of broad bean.

"Where's the third stooge?" Rob wanted to know. The place seemed incomplete with only two of them bickering, he was used to the full set, wise monkeys, magi.

Jude bent over the desk for the mugs, olive drab T-shirt flapping.

"By Christ," said Colin with feeling as she shuffled off. "She's not wearing a bra again. Should be bloody banned. Nipples like chapel hat pegs, you could hang a wet duffle coat on 'em." He drifted back to his runner beans.

There was a crash and assorted swearing from the glass fronted offices to the rear of the room. Lou came tearing out, glossy blonde hair flying. She strode up to Rob's desk and barked a question without acknowledging him.

"Where's Sue?"

"Out on an appointment I think." He was alarmed to see her like this, cross little snarl around white teeth and eyes flashing. Alarmed and a little thrilled, though it was probably best not to give that impression.

"You'll do then," she said. "Come."

She stalked off again and he stared after her.

"Wash that boy and bring him to my tent," deadpanned Colin without looking up from his magazine.

At the door of her office she turned back and rapped, *"Well come on,"* before banging back through the door.

He knew what was up. Sue had forgotten the 'Going Forward' planning meeting which was held fortnightly. He glanced at her screen and there was a calendar alert for it but that wouldn't do her much good now. She'd be gutted to have missed it as she loved a good meeting did Sue and liked to give the impression of being every bit as capable and on the ball as Queen Lou.

As it was, she was out trying to do a deal with some ring road cowboy over ads for white goods, carpets or sofas, missing one of her favourite head to heads of the month.

Every so often, during her work related stream of consciousness ramble around their pod of desks, she would talk about something which happened at 'Going Forward'. It would be some nugget or other which clarified matters, or a shiny new idea for making things better.

Occasionally as a treat, she would stroke Colin, Alan, Jude or even Rob himself by promising that she would bring up some passing notion of theirs to Lou and the team at 'Going Forward' awarding them full credit of course. It was an important meeting in the fabric of this place because it fostered the notion among the middle managers that they were all thrusting executives, forging their way towards a director's office.

Rob didn't want to go. At this stage in his life he had no real aspirations towards high office, or even middle management come to that. He had yet to find out who he was, never mind what he wanted to do with his life. Besides, he found those meetings uncomfortable and awkward. The few times he had been in them, he had found himself swamped in the baroque, meaningless office kant which characterised them and seemed to act, for so many of the swiftly promoted junior managers who attended, as a substitute for any real intellect or understanding of the business.

Unfortunately, he had no choice and followed Lou through the door; at least it meant he could spend some time close to her.

The room was dominated by Lou's desk in pale wood and around it were a couple of faux leather sofas, plump and taupe, where the other attendees of the Going Forward meeting already nestled, somewhat uncomfortably.

There was Jayden from motors, short and black, smiley and well in with the management, always ready to stay late and ingratiate himself with a lavish complement. Nessa, the nervous middle-aged copy control manager who hid behind a frizz of greying hair and contributed nothing to meetings but was efficient at her job and made sure the pages left the building on time. And finally Leon, the property manager, smooth and catty and gay, made you laugh even when you were the butt of the joke, which was usually.

Rob stood awkwardly in the doorway, Lou was already behind her desk but he did not know whether he had to be invited to sit down. He had an unfortunate tick born from a deep-seated desire to keep checking he had zipped his fly. He was tormented by the dark fantasy of horrified bystanders in the office, or a bus queue looking down to see his underpants exposed like a flag of shame. Sadly the result was that he appeared to grab his crotch at random intervals, as if listening to Michael Jackson on his invisible iPod and dancing along in a low-key way.

It was a disconcerting habit from the viewer's perspective and heightened by the fact that Rob never seemed to find trousers to fit around the crotch. They were always too snug and though his endowment was unremarkable, what he did have was always prominently displayed.

"Why do you keep grabbing your cock?" demanded Lou.

"I er."

"Well stop it, it's like being at the zoo." She looked down at her agenda as if she'd forgotten about him.

Then, more quietly and without looking up again she bleated, "And sit down, are you not stopping?"

He squeezed in between Jayden and Nessa. Jay winked at him and gave him a supportive smile. Nessa moved away from him and closed her legs together as if scared he was about to jump on her.

"Right, said Lou briskly, consulting her agenda. "Building for the challenges of tomorrow. Rob. What's your action strategy for that please?"

He pretended to cogitate, though frankly he was baffled. The sofa was desperately unsuitable for business use. Once you were in it your posterior sank so far down into its nether reaches, you were wedged in and had nowhere to balance your notepad.

"I thought we'd just get on and do it."

He'd hoped this would be both vague and positive enough to make a good impression but she shook her head and tutted tightly through thin lips and tapped her shiny pen on her expensive looking leather folder.

"You need to engage with the problem more holistically."

She seemed despairing of him but before she could offer more business wisdom, there was a sharp single rap on the door which opened a crack and the MD, William Bean, poked his angry red head through the gap as though he was too busy to push it all the way open.

Lou perked up immediately, she sat bolt upright in her chair and gave her biggest, toothiest smile. The others preened as well, sitting as straight as they could with their behinds consumed by the sofa, all bar Nessa, who sunk down even further and hid behind her wire wool fringe.

"Hi Bill," Lou trilled brightly.

"When's the wedding supplement appearing in-paper," he demanded without pleasantries.

Lou replied smoothly and without flustering, her speech was still larded with jargon but became oddly coquettish.

"We still have to facilitate solutions with a number of stakeholders." She played with her pen and grinned at him as if he'd told a joke.

"I'd like to block it in the diary for June 13, which I accept is later than you anticipated."

He scowled at her as if she'd told him she'd just scratched his BMW with her keys.

"We have an exciting window of opportunity here," she went on, voice level and enthusiastic. "A chance to really lay down the predictors of beaconicity with this project. Going forward I could see it rolling out group wide!"

He looked at her blankly for a moment with his shark's eyes glazed, then barked gruffly, "Agreed," before his head popped behind the door like a crab retreating behind a rock.

Lou was instantly and absurdly elated. Her eyes gleamed she punched her small tight fists in the air in triumph. The others whooped and yeahed along with her to a greater or lesser extent, with Jayden and Leon taking the lead. Lou looked around for someone to celebrate with and found a baffled looking Rob.

"Yes," she crowed. "Fantastic, we've been given the green light for that."

Rob scratched his nose frantically to anchor her feelings of happiness. That way when he repeated the gesture later on, it would bring her echoes of that same feeling of elation. That's what his gurus on the PUA website claimed anyway.

"That's really exciting," Lou insisted, against all evidence.

Leon was nodding like a dashboard dog.

"We've got the go-ahead. It's going to be a fantastic product, I can't wait. Make sure you all give feedback on that to your teams."

The others tried to rouse themselves into further thin celebration of their own over the opportunity to take slightly longer than planned putting together an ad supplement. Rob scratched his nose again for good measure and Lou beamed at him.

There was a portentous crash at the door and Sue burst through without a by your leave. She was struggling to remain composed but failing, telegraphing her emotions like a cartoon character, first alarmed to be so late, then horrified to see Rob sitting in her place on the snuggly sofa.

"Apologies for my late arrival - something vital came up."

"Nice to see you this afternoon," deadpanned Lou, making a big Marcel Marceau mime out of looking at the time on her watch, as Sue sat her skinny bum rather primly on the edge of an occasional table and roosted like some caged bird. She looked uncomfortable and ready to fall off, bracing her legs to stay there, trembling slightly with the effort, trying to look nonchalant.

"It's so lovely you could make it," Lou went on smoothly, "but a shame to lose Robbie. He's been entertaining us by grabbing his testicles and picking at his nose - it's been a joy."

Robbie. He liked that. That was like a pet name, she had obviously been giving him some thought.

"Yes, he's a sweetie," Sue said briskly, turning her attention to him, "but you can get back to it now. I'll take over here, there's one of your clients on the phone to Jude. Come on now, hop to it, those targets aren't going to hit themselves."

He managed an ungainly exit from the sofa, using Jayden and Nessa's shoulders as handrails. Jayden braced against him and did his best to lever him out. Nessa was clearly mortified by the physical contact and sank further down into the leather comfort blanket.

"Cheers J - Nessa. Thanks everyone." He looked around the room and saw Sue was nodding impatiently to tell him that was enough now. He made for the door and Lou leapt up and darted across to open it for him in a show of old-world courtesy.

She showed him through, elaborately as though she was his flunky, then followed him out said, "Well done Robbie, your first Going Forward. You've got the makings of a manager I'd say. There's hope for you yet and I like your cheek." She looked sternly at him. "But you're very young," she shook her head as though this was an insurmountable obstacle, "and you have a lot to learn."

She was grave and pale and beautiful - he looked back at her wide-eyed.

"I want to learn, if you teach me I'll do whatever I'm told."

Her face clouded briefly and he wondered whether he had over-egged it and she would consider his daring to flirt the most appalling, inappropriate cheek. Then she laughed and leaned in towards him so that, for a moment, he thought she might actually be planning to hug him but she just placed scented, manicured, finger ends on his chest and

70

pushed him away playfully saying, "Go and get some work done," before turning her back on him, all long legs and toned rear.

He'd not even made it half way back down the office to his desk before his phone started cheeping away in his trouser pocket, like a fledgling needing food. A text. He fished the phone out and squinted at it, baffled. He'd never really embraced texting or the terse shorthand his generation used on Facebook. It was a girl thing it seemed to him and not something he took to easily. Though it seemed like the place you ought to have a presence if you were trying to find available women, so he persevered gamely, though not without dropping the odd bollock.

He fiddled with the phone, trying to make it reveal its cache of messages, pecking away at the keys with thumbs too big for the job. For a long time he had believed the initials LOL stood for Lots of Love. So he used them regularly in emails to friends and family: 'I was so sorry to hear about your gran dying - LOL - Rob.' He had been mortified when his cousin Laura told him LOL meant Laughs Out Loud."

The text read: "What U doin for lunch?"

He perched the edge of his rump down on the corner of a desk he was passing and stopped to read it again. It read the same, thing was he couldn't quite work out who it was from. The sender's name appeared to be Petal. He didn't know any petals. Knew a Rose, couple of Daisies and a Clover that was it for flower related acquaintances. Laboriously he texted back: "Nowt."

Rob sat and waited, even though Janice from copy control - upon whose desk he was sat - came and perched back in her chair. She was quiet and mousy. Got on with her work even though he was intruding on her personal space. She shifted her novelty rubber sheep further up the blue grey surface in case he rocked back and squashed it.

Another text came back: "Want to go out wiv me?"

He pondered for a while what sort of faux pas it would amount to if he admitted he didn't know who she was. He assumed 'she' but even that was a gamble. Rob decided to ask Janice. She flushed behind her specks and pretended to have something big going down with her personal organiser until she realised he wasn't going to get distracted and wander off.

"Well I don't know" she settled down to give it some thought. "I suppose it might leave you a bit pissed off if you were asking someone out for a meal and they didn't know who you were but then the idea that

71

someone's in demand isn't a bad thing." She shrugged, embarrassed to have said something which wasn't work related and went back to her organiser.

He texted back: "WHICH ONE ARE U" he seemed to have got it stuck in upper case. The reply ignored his question entirely. "cu back door 12.45"

Back at his desk, the three wise monkeys were on top form.

"So have you not done it with our Sue then mmmh?" asked Alan, peering owlishly over old-fashioned oversized specs.

Rob, embarrassed, indicated the negative with a shake of his head and pretended he had a form to fill in. "Where were you earlier?" he asked, in a doomed effort to change the subject.

"She must be at least somewhat interested," Colin mused. "Unless she's just not interested in sex full stop, rather have a nice cup of tea etc."

"He's not on her any more," Jude chimed in, grumpily. "It's that Alice one now isn't it? Unless I'm losing track."

"Oh well, her?" Rob put in, "She's like a photographic negative of Sue she is. Very interested in sex. Probably even find something disgraceful to do with the cup of tea."

Turned out Alan was late because he'd had to pick up Sue in his car as hers had broken down but by the time she got back out of Going Forward, the officially approved story was that she had rescued him.

"And if Louise asks," Sue told him, "look grateful."

Rob headed off to his mystery lunch and when he got there was pleasantly surprised to see it was Alice and it was curry. Wrinkled prawns stared back like tiny parentheses on his plate. The waiter was slender, polite and graceful, dignified through years of treating drunks with polite deference.

"Don't really fancy Indians," admitted Alice tucking into her steak and chips.

"How come?"

"Not sexy enough. No big bums. No attitude."

"Seems a bit tight on a whole race of people, didn't know big bums were a good thing anyway."

"Oh yes," she nodded enthusiastically. "Not fat you know but men need to have an arse to be sexy, it's a well known fact."

It seemed strange to be in an Indian restaurant during the hours of daylight. It seemed odd to be in one sober. They were evening after-the-pub places as far as Rob was concerned and the one she had chosen, at the top of Montpellier, tucked between the O'Neills Irish pub and a fru fru shop selling lamps and stuff, was a very Indian Indian indeed. It was all dark flock and maroon with the curtains closed so it could have been Friday midnight rather than a sunny Tuesday 1pm.

"What *do* you like then?" he asked her in the interests of research.

Alice leaned forward, all the better for him to look down her top. She laughed a dark, dirty laugh and the ruby in her tooth twinkled. It didn't matter so much what Alice said, it was good to be in her presence. She radiated an energy which gave him warmth. The glow of her tan, the gloss of her skin, she smelled of coconut some days, vanilla and cinnamon on others. She was a cargo of rare spices and plump curves, not just in those obvious places - buttocks, breasts - but her calves, beneath her leggings, the seductive sweep of her upper arms.

There were magnets at her core which compelled him to stand closer to her than was polite, to reach out and touch. She welcomed this contact with a murmur, gurgle and a cluck in the throat of animal approval.

"What would you like?" she whispered to him, her legs touching his under the table and he nearly told her, until he saw she was holding the menu.

He kind of wondered why she had brought them to an Indian when she clearly couldn't be all that fond of Indian food, given her choice of steak and chips. There were lots of restaurants in Cheltenham, something for everyone you might have thought. He didn't want to ask her outright as it might appear as though he was criticising and he was keen to avoid the petty arguments with girls which seemed to have dogged and frustrated his relations with women since his teens.

Here in this dark, out of time place he felt she could have whatever she wanted; what was it to him? He would rather have her happy, engaged and sharing with him, than defensive and angry.

"I know what 1 like" he glanced down again and she cackled some more.

"How's your curry?" she said. "Mine's a bit hot."

It was odd, that she thought steak and chips was a curry but what the hell. She could think haddock and mushy peas was a non-vegetable thali as far as he was concerned, so long as she kept not minding when he looked down her top. She squinted at him like she had a bone to pick.

"What did you mean when you asked who I was on your text?"

"It could have been any one of my other women," he deadpanned.

She laughed but it wasn't convincing.

"Besides - your phone says 'Petal'. I didn't know you were called that," he added quickly, mouth full of kheema naan.

"Oh yeah, it's a nickname, after the petals on my tat," she looked over her shoulder trying to catch sight of the thing on the base of her spine, which was half hidden anyway by her slightly too short shirt.

There was a plumpness around her hips, a vague roundness to her belly and she had no chance of being dismissed as not sexy due to lack of a behind.

"When did you get it done?"

"Couple of years back. I weren't drunk or nothing. I thought they look great, still do. People say 'what about when you're sixty?' but I don't live my life for when I'm sixty."

He nodded. That was something they could agree on. He wouldn't have a tattoo but he did like them on women, particularly there on the base of the spine.

"It gives you something interesting to look at when you're on the job," he said without thinking much about it.

If he'd filtered that one though his super-ego before it popped out of his gob, he might have decided against it but it was a big hit. She laughed so much she spat bits of chip out - he didn't mind.

"I've not had a proper look at it yet," he added.

"You'll get your chance if yer a good boy," she teased, pleased with herself.

"There's a girl round the corner from me," he remembered, "she's got hers done in the same place as yours, only hers says 'Dad'. That's not right is it?"

Alice wrinkled her nose. "I can see how that might be a bit off-putting. There's some things you don't want to be thinking about at a time like that and I'd say that is probably one."

She paused for a while then added thoughtfully, "This is loads better than my last date."

Rob was gratified to learn this was considered a date.

"Was he boring then?"

"Nah," she shook her head and talked through the chips. "Boring's good, boring's a relief with all the strange men out there. He was some

Swedish guy who poked me on Facebook. We went for a weekend together and he turned out to have about a million issues with everything, food, he was addicted to sleeping with strangers, turned out he was still living with his wife and kids on and off."

Rob thought this news through.

"I mean, so called addicted to sleeping with strangers, that just translates as 'a man'. I'm more interested in the food thing," he said, tucking into his naan.

"Oh yeah, I mean, apparently, he used to be huge, arse like a double-decker. He slimmed down but it left him with more issues than Kleenex have tissues. He couldn't eat anything which had been touched by a human hand, which started off as sandwiches and finished up as pretty much everything."

"That is weird - I do like my grub."

She nodded gravely.

"The sex thing was bloody weird too though. He'd been working as a holiday rep out in Tenerife, so he got to shag a long string of strangers but he said he couldn't shag me 'cos he *liked* me."

She coloured and hid behind her drink. "I'm embarrassed now."

"It's a rough one," Rob admitted. "Don't see how it's something for you to get embarrassed about though."

"You kidding?" she grumped. "I'd bought new knickers and everything."

The waiter came for their plates.

"That was great," enthused Alice.

"The company was great," agreed Rob, all smiles. "We should do something else together."

"What you got in mind?" she was coquettish which seemed to be her standard setting.

As the waiter eased a jug of water into the centre of the table, she reached over and patted the taught black polyester seat of his trousers and muttered an approving, 'good lad'. He looked at her, clearly quite shocked.

"If I forgot my purse, could I come back and pay you later on?" she barked at him cheerily and gave him a grin big enough so he could see the ruby in her tooth.

He sniggered nervously and said "You not forget" and shook his head, sounding like he had suddenly lost his command of the language which had been tip-top a little earlier. He sidled off but Rob noticed the leer he shot back over his shoulder - part puzzlement, part lust.

Rob didn't ask, just looked over at her and she gave the grin again, even wider and ripped off a big chunk of naan to have with her steak. The waiter was back again fairly sharpish, presumably finding this table more interesting than others where he didn't get goosed. He had come to relieve them of the aluminium stand of pickles, which had come with the popadoms. He leant over to get them, three burnished cups suspended from a central stand. He moved more cautiously this time but she didn't grab him again, instead she bent forward too, so that with a small adjustment of his head, he could look down her top, which he duly did.

"What's those?"she said, not pointing at anything in the first instance, which obviously caused some confusion in his mind but then gesturing a tanned hand towards the pickle containers.

"Mango chutney," he replied, pointing at the viscous marmalade in one. "No, that one?" she took his hand in hers and moved it over so the tip rested on a pot containing a red-brown paste bulked up with chunks of green peel.

"Lime pickle," he said shaking his head and chuckling. "Very hot." He mimed waving the heat away from his open mouth in case we were unaware of the concept of hot.

"How hot?" she challenged him, still keeping her hand on top of his.

"*Verrry* hot, you just need a little."

"Could you eat it?" she made eye contact.

He thought about it "How much?"

"All of it?"

He thought about the prospect, smiled to himself and said, "The chef here once ate a whole pound of raw green chillies in a five hundred pound bet with the manager. His mouth closed because of the acid but he kept pushing them in because he needed the money. You can do things if you have to."

She smiled at him again, flash of ruby, stroked his hand.

"Do it then."

He laughed again, his nervous laugh and shook his head.

Later when he came with the bill she simply ripped it up and winked at him. He smirked like they had some kind of understanding and she palmed him something, a piece of paper.

In the street she was cackling.

"Did you give him your number?" he said, affronted. "Thought you didn't like Indian men."

"I should have made him eat it," she said, sounding cross with herself. "I could have done. I could have *made* him stand there and eat the whole fucking pot."

She could make me eat the whole pot too Rob was thinking, how dangerous to have such power without responsibility. Suddenly she stopped and span on the ball of her foot. She sprang into a canter and headed back through the red and gold door of the restaurant before he had time to do more than flash her a Cro-Magnon frown.

By the time he'd mustered the energy to follow her, she was mired in conversation with the waiter again over by the bar. He was backed up against it and she was leaning in towards him, staring at him, they were both laughing, he a little hysterically and he was shaking his head.

Then she stopped and trotted over to the nearest empty table, gathering up a tray of pickles and giving Rob a grin as she did so. Back with the waiter, she handed over the pot of lime pickle and a spoon. She watched him intently and during a brief pause - where he was probably wondering how he had found himself at this point - he began shovelling it down, more or less enthusiastically.

The first couple of mouthfuls seemed to go down fairly easily but after that the pace of his attack slowed significantly and he broke out in beads of sweat. A few more mouthfuls and he seemed in real discomfort. He began clutching at the collar of his shirt and made choking noises as he tried to get the rust-coloured gloop down his throat. He managed one more mouthful, lifting the spoon tentatively towards his lips and depositing its load gingerly on his tongue but just as he reached for another spoonful, a change came over him. He paused with the spoon in the air, silent and flushed, as though his entire body was coping with things inside, that those in the outside world could not comprehend. Rob looked at his face for a bulletin on how his body was dealing with the assault, not well apparently. His grin dissolved and his brow furrowed. Flustered, he weighed up the pot and Alice's embonpoint, before signalling with a shake of his head that he could do no more. He tried to smile but looked embarrassed and defeated.

Alice grabbed the pot from his trembling hands in triumph and rage. It was still more than half full. She didn't even bother with the spoon, she scooped at the red green gloop with her fingers, manicured purple nails digging in, shoving the mulch between her lips and bright white teeth. Again and again she shoved it in, eating it hungrily like prison rations until, within a minute, the pot was empty. She flung it down on the bar with a bright clatter barking a laugh of triumph at her vanquished opponent.

"Lightweight."

The other waiters and a few customers had turned to watch and, once she'd scraped the pot, she got a muted round of applause.

"Oh God" he said shaking his head and rubbing his stomach. "Oh God."

"I knew I could do it," she beamed at him, turning for the door. "Call me."

Out in the street a second time, heading back to work.

"What if he rings the number?"

"It's Sue's number, she smirked. "Sue might like him."

"I'm no good at this," he thought. "That was a masterclass in how to play these games and it came from a woman, who can't lose by virtue of having what men want anyway. All she has to do is stand there and be female but she knows the stuff, the teasing, the touching, the negging, the kino. She knows instinctively what I'm trying to learn. How could I seem anything other than a big clumsy child to her?"

CHAPTER 5

'Johnno!' the blog of Robert Johnson, July 18:
"I know I'm young. I like to think I know my limitations, the big gaps in my understanding. Sometimes people talk about stuff and it just feels like it's going way over my head. Other times they say things which, though I might not understand the detail and only pick up the gist, seem deliberately intended to confuse.

I might be a bit naïve but I can see when people are trying to hide behind pretending to know something. It's what happens in Going Forward and it's what I'm trying to do as a PUA. Why can't people be honest, with themselves and with everyone else? It would make things a lot easier in the world if people would just say what they mean. It's because we can't trust each other I suppose, we are all too scared of getting hurt. People need to be braver. I know I do."

In the days, not long gone, when Rob Johnson had appeared permanently single, woman avoided him as though he had a particularly unpleasant kind of B.O. but once one woman expressed an interest in him, others followed. There appeared to be a pack instinct, beyond that, a need to poach men who were already taken. Perhaps this was about affirmation, the need to be told a particular man was worth securing in order to make him worth pursuing for yourself? It's like a screening process, Rob thought, as though you have to have a C.V in order to secure an interview.

He was now discovering the many ways of making it seem as though one had a relationship beyond a friendship or flirtation with a particular girl, even if you didn't. What *told* you a couple were together in any case? It wasn't as though you ever saw them in bed together, it was just the way they were with each other, the things they allowed to be known, the things their friends claimed to know.

Though he had known Alice and Sue for eighteen months or more, it appeared one didn't seem to get all that interested in him, until the other did. Now they were both offering him their attention, what further opportunities could be on offer? Perhaps this was not going as badly as he sometimes thought.

Sonof: Do you ever think about the woman's point of view? I mean, consider her as a person, what she might be thinking?

Rob: All the time. I think that might be my problem.

Sonof: ?? :-/

Rob: You know, because I think of women as individuals and complicated, I struggle to accept there are ways of appealing to them, as if they were all the same.

Sonof: They are all the same mate, no question about it.

Rob: And what about men, are we all the same?

Sonof: Well, you tell me?

Rob: Oh yeah, okay, I take your point.

Friday night was for beer in the Revolution, Monday lunchtime was for bacon sandwiches in the Cabin but Sunday afternoons, like this one, were for football on Plock Court.

Plock Court was in Gloucester which made it a pain in the arse for Rob transport wise as he had to get the 94 bus from Cheltenham Promenade and walk a bit from Oxtalls roundabout, through the grounds of the University of Gloucestershire, down the cinder path past scabby allotments with their gangly bean stalks and creosoted sheds and onto the back of Plock Court.

It was a huge sprawling complex of sports pitches, carelessly cared for by the council. Sometimes it was flooded, sometimes invaded by caravans of gypsies with their febrile dogs and feral kids but often enough a usable space to play soccer where you could simply turn up on the day with a number of other like-minded souls to hoof a ball around in clumsy abandon for an hour or so, which, at the very least, made you feel more virtuous afterwards when you trooped down the pub.

This was a place Rob and his co-workers could get on for a game even though the proper Sunday league sides were playing and they had only a rag-tag mob of half-interested office blokes with shirts in assorted club colours and the traditional jumpers for goalposts. There was no way onto the Astroturf unless you'd booked and many of the proper marked out pitches were in use for proper league matches with referees and what Colin and Alan still persisted in thinking of as linesmen, but there was always room somewhere on the vast sprawl of green.

Somehow the pitches always seemed to be muddy, even in the summer and the mud was red clay which meant that, by half-time, the players were ruddy with warpaint, like a lost Amazonian tribe.

It was a nothing match each and every week between themselves depending on how many turned up but it was always hotly contested and it had become a fixture Rob - like many of the others - did not want to miss, whatever the state of his nascent hangover in the hours before kick-off. Not only did plenty of players turn up each week, enough for a game at any rate, but there tended to be a smattering of supporters too. They were generally friends of those on the pitch who'd come to offer lifts, or on the promise of a pint after the match, were there to cheer ironically at the cack-handed attempts at set piece plays and thrill at the sky-high, rugby match style, final scores.

There was always some sitting on damp grass to be done before the match started, rooting around in sports bags for boots caked with dried mud from the week before and battered shin pads to stuff down socks. There was glugging of orange squash from sports bottles and there was the inelegant ballet of blokes stretching underused muscles in half-remembered warm up routines.

The matches featured a range of ages from late teens to mid-forties and often a there were one or two female players as well as male. Ability ranged from not bad, to bloody woeful but there was no shortage of enthusiasm or indeed aggression, with some matches descending into ill-tempered scraps with wrestling, half-hearted punching and inevitable jeering about 'handbags at dawn'.

This Sunday when Rob bundled up at about quarter past one there were already half a dozen or more would-be players hanging around on the grass waiting and by the time he'd peeled out of his trackie bottoms and got his boots on, there were a few more; three blokes from editorial he didn't really know, Colin who was the oldest there but could still just about get round the pitch with his legs strapped up like Robocop, a couple of young lads from circulation, Sam of course and Sue who played a feisty midfield general role and was always responsible for most of the two-footed tackles. Jayden was there too from advertising with Mike and Gareth, two of his lads from motoring.

No one was much use at football when it came down to it except maybe Mike, who got the odd game for one of the local league sides. They were mostly the sort of standard you usually saw in pub league and five-a-side teams, where they usually played. They all liked this because it was easy going for the most part and their short-comings were generally overlooked.

Team picking was an ad hoc affair. Sue tended to pick herself as captain and she had grabbed two or three players, including Mike, before it was clear they had started. Rob didn't notice as he'd been having a look round to see if anyone had turned up to watch and was surprised to see Lou, who hadn't been before, sitting beside Jayden's kit bag all polite smiles and floaty white skirts like she was having strawberries and cream at Henley regatta. She was talking to Alice which was another surprise and Rob guessed they'd all driven over together. He wondered whether there would be room for him to get a lift back given he'd come over on the bus.

Alice waved weakly at him when they made eye contact, she didn't look well. Wan beneath her perma-tan, she was standing by what could be assumed as the by-line, given the grass was a little longer than the so-called pitch. She seemed in need of a sit down and rested herself on Lou who was given to coming on these sorts of occasions erratically and without warning to show she was part of the gang and not too big to fraternise with the little people.

This would mean today counted as team building and they would have to be on their best behaviour - bollocks.

He waved at Alice and blew her a kiss, she was too under the weather to return it with anything other than a watery smile so – horrifyingly - Lou thought the kiss was for her and frowned back over at him to let him know he'd not so much crossed a line, as triple jumped over it setting a new county record.

'Shit!' he thought to himself succinctly and moved his skippy, jumpy warm-up over to the other side of the pitch where Jayden and some of the others were stretching.

The game began in a huddle of decisions with Sue and Jayden swiftly picking what was left of the players. Rob wasn't keen on this part which brought back painful memories of being among the gaggle of tail-enders against the school wall - the bed-wetters and mummy's boys, the fat kids and asthmatics - yet he consoled himself with the fact that these days he was never last to be chosen.

He had always been technically poor at football not having grown up in a football family. His dad played golf and his two older brothers were away at college and out of the picture by the time he got old enough to fancy a kick about with them. At school he assumed he was useless at the game and so it came to pass that he moved over to playing badminton as soon as he was able and didn't kick a ball again until he left uni and started work. However, once he'd settled into his role in the display department, he realised that regular football games were part of the ebb and flow of office life and a good way of making friends out of your colleagues.

He'd played the first few games with a degree of trepidation, expecting as 'of old' to be brought low with crunching tackles, left lying winded in the mud with taunts of 'spacca' ringing in his ears. Yet strangely, that wasn't the way it worked out. He found he had grown into himself and was possessed of a size and fitness which made him hard to knock off the ball and tough to make a fool of. He had pace to get past people, seemed to be able to think more quickly than many of them as well as move with more agility. If he did get hit with a late tackle or clumsy body check, then it was often the other person who came off worse rather than him. He found he had time to place passes, to move into space and receive them too, he even found himself scoring the odd goal.

It was a minor revelation for him this belief in the power of his body, never before had he viewed himself in physical terms, he'd always been a mind first, served by a functional body which he needed to keep fed and watered. Now though, he was able to enjoy what his body could do, take pleasure in the way it moved, compete with others and win. At school he had been a little over-weight, chubby rather than fat. That had dropped away during a university career fuelled mainly by Bran-flakes and orange juice, admittedly supplemented with regular supplies of lager. Now he felt at home in his body which invariably did what he asked of it and often gave him more than he had expected in terms of swiftness, strength and stamina.

It was a scrappy start to the play with most of the players not really noticing the game had kicked off and Sam had the ball up the right wing and into the net before Rob (left-back) had moved from the spot where he had been contemplating Alice's unexpected attendance.

Colin, the goalkeeper, yelled some choice remarks to him regarding his parentage and mental capacity and Rob mouthed apologies and gave a shamefaced thumbs-up to Colin, who was already covered in mud having dived fruitlessly for Sam's shot as it slid in the bottom right corner. A couple of minutes later it was three nowt thanks to a brace of stunning strikes from Sue, one from around the half-way line. There were full-throated appeals from Colin that this one had been over the bar but in the absence of any bar it was a tough call to make.

Shortly after play resumed Rob had the ball rolled in front of him by one of the lads from editorial so he forged ahead, managing to barge past Mike and performing a clumsy nutmeg on Whoever from newspaper sales which won him a muted cheer from the terraces. Rob saw Sue bearing down on him from defence and out of the corner of his eye glimpsed Sam tracking back down the wing. Ignoring pleas to switch it and pass into space from his exasperated team-mates, he decided it was time to hit and hope so he hoofed the ball with a fair amount of welly in the general direction of the opposing goal. It smacked the kid from circulation (keeper) right in the face and went in, though there was a fair chance it rolled over one of the jumpers for goalposts on the way in. There was a bitter five minute discussion in the centre circle over whether it had indeed been a goal, though the game had to be halted anyway while circulation kid dealt with his nosebleed and in the end, the white smoke rose from the roof of the Vatican and the verdict arrived; Rob's goal stood.

"Yes," he hissed, punching the air. "Never in any doubt. Played for and got."

"Pass and move," grunted Colin, with satisfaction, "S'like the Dutch team of the '70s - total football."

3-1, exciting stuff.

By the point they decided it was half-time as they were knackered, the score stood at 14-11 or 12, no-one was sure any more. Rob strolled over to where Alice was sitting and peeled his sweaty shirt off, throwing it on the grass and flopping beside it.

"Urgh, you *stink!*" She wrinkled her nose and flashed her jewelled grin.

"Fresh male sweat is supposed to be an aphrodisiac," he countered,

84

adopting a hurt voice. "Suck up those pheromones and think yourself lucky love."

She laughed then and threw his shirt at him.

"You'd need a shower before I'd want to have a go."

"We could have one together."

She cackled again, this was all going swimmingly.

"You want to make sure you don't get injured playing that," she said with mock concern. "It looks rough."

"Yeah well, I might suffer for it later on but I don't live my life worrying about what will happen when I'm sixty. I don't think you should do that, do you petal?"

She nodded thoughtfully. "I've always thought that - that's very true that is. I like it when you call me petal."

"It would be great if we were in a big bed of petals. All sweet-smelling, soft, beautiful colours - we could wrap them round us like a duvet." He scratched his nose.

She moved a little closer to him on the damp grass.

"That sounds lovely. What sort of flowers should we have the petals from?"

Rob was stumped, he didn't know many types of flower.

"Rose petals, he said at length as her tattoo looked like it might be some sort of stab at a rose.

"All different shades and types of scent. All sweet and perfumy." He had another little rub at the side of his nose.

"We could roll about in them and make ourselves smell like roses," Alice said sleepily - I'd like that."

A shadow fell over them. He looked up to see Sue smiling down.

"Hi. Can I join you?" She didn't really have the option to take her shirt off, so it hung limp and red with mud over her shoulders. She was mopping her damp taupe hair with a towel from her bag. A couple of full-blooded challenges had rendered her left leg clarted with mud from the knee to the shorts. One of those two-footed tackles which Gareth was still trying to limp off, had led to a hotly contested penalty.

She sat down next to them, assuming permission. Somehow it kind of killed the conversation. That said, Rob liked the idea of being flanked by two women with whom he had a romantic connection, it was like being a gorilla, sitting out there in nature, his big silver back glinting in the sunshine, surrounded by girl gorillas who were his suitors; maybe later they would mate. He looked about to see if anyone was watching and thought he fancied Lou might be.

Another part of him knew though that this was socially awkward. The whole tone of his conversation with Alice had been personal and having it interrupted meant they suddenly had nothing to talk about.

"Match is going well," offered Sue. "We're kicking your arse."

"It's pretty even," Rob insisted woodenly. "Could go either way in the second half."

Alice seemed dismayed. "You mean there's more? I thought that was it. When do we go to the pub then?"

Sue chuckled indulgently at her naivety. "Football matches do tend to have two halves sweetie, it's in the rules."

Alice shrugged unperturbed. "Don't really like footie, I just came for the crack and to support Robbie."

She reached out to give his leg an affectionate pat but missed and ended up slapping his arse, once by mistake then again harder to show she hadn't done it by accident and finally she gave it a bit of a squeeze.

"Ooh, nice muscle tone, have you been working out?"

Rob tried to think of something witty to reply with but was stalled by Sue who leapt to her feet and dragged him up with her by the shirt. She was surprisingly strong for such a small slender package and she overcame his inertia quite easily so he was forced to hop onto his feet after her.

"Right - second half then. Some of us have exercise to do." She looked down at Alice who had fished a pouch of Maltesers out of her bag.

"Don't eat too much chocolate sat there hun, it gathers round the hips."

"Least I've got hips," Alice responded, shoving a handful of the small round chocolate balls in her gob. "You run along and play footie with the other young lads and make sure you don't wear out little Robbie too much for me though. I might need him later on."

Sue shrugged: "Yeah, whatever. Has he gone on to you about a desert island yet? That would suit you I think - great place for a diet."

The second half was a scrappy, bad tempered affair, made so mainly because Sue was in a towering temper and hunted down Rob every chance she got, steaming in with reckless tackles, high and hard. Rob didn't know which bit of her was likely to hit him next, only that it would be gnarled and bony and hurt like fuck.

It was difficult to figure out how such a slender frame could make such a significant impact. Yet she did and on one occasion, her two-footed take off brought her so high that, as he stooped to avoid her, she caught him round the neck like a boomerang and took him down with her in a painful muddy bundle. After that he had to go and rest by the side of the pitch for a little while, limp and winded.

He was back in position but still a little dazed and out of the game when she came charging down the wing at him again, abandoning her so-say position in the centre of defence for another foray on goal with the ball at her feet. Rob hoped for a moment that Gareth in midfield might take her out for him but she dropped a shoulder and eased past him, digging a sharp elbow in his ribs as she did so.

Wary about taking her on again he back-pedalled and was relieved to see her shaping up for a shot on goal. He stood and watched as she knocked the ball a yard or so ahead of her, then took one, two, three strides forward and rattled it through the air like an Exocet. He caught a glimpse of the ball frozen on his retina as it left her foot, blurred and dizzy with speed. He was still processing that image and wondering which corner of the net it was heading for when the ball hit him square on the nuts.

The thing must have been doing a hundred miles an hour when it struck him and it was a direct hit. He had no time to do anything by way of mitigating the connection and hadn't even moved his hands down to the favoured 'wall' position.

He wasn't aware of what had happened as such, only of an instant pain, intense and unexpected. He bent forward in an exaggerated bow and air wheezed from his mouth wordlessly as he toppled forward on the grass.

Sue trotted up and chipped the ball again from where it lay in front of his face and it sang into the open goal as a concerned Colin came forward to check his condition.

21-13.

"Thank you," said Sue sweetly, as she turned a pert rear on him and headed back to her own half.

"Christ almighty!" soothed Colin. "I'll see if I can find you a bag for those."

Rob played no further part in the game. He lay where he had fallen for the longest time as play resumed around him, then realising Sue would probably trample him given the chance, he rose gingerly to his feet and limped to the side of the pitch where he rested, prone on the grass with a cool can of cola pressed to his groin.

As he lay there, making no noise but for an occasional involuntary whimper, Lou came over to take a look. She seemed to be on even more of a different plane from him than usual. She wasn't lying down, she wasn't covered in mud and she wasn't clutching her groin.

"How are you?" she asked in a measured voice, like a visiting royal greeting the hoi polloi.

"Been better," he admitted with a grimace.

"That looked very painful," she admitted, by way of conversation.

"You really have no idea," he replied, aware his eyes were watering. "These aren't tears by the way it's just..."

"It's okay to cry," she soothed. "You mustn't think you're being tough by holding it in. It must have been a blow to your pride as well as anything else. I do hope there's no permanent damage."

As he scoured his scrambled brain for something worthwhile to say she headed off back to the gaggle of spectators who seemed to have lost interest in the match in favour of checking him out.

There would be no lasting damage. He examined himself in the pub toilet cubicle as he changed into a T-shirt and jeans. Bit of swelling maybe, some localised chaffing. Nothing some Savlon and TLC wouldn't remedy. He went out to the sinks and sloshed himself clean of the red mud from the pitch and dried himself by sticking his head under the hand drier.

Then he slipped out into the Wetherspoons beer barn where they had gathered for post-match refreshments - ordered himself a pint of lager at the half deserted Saturday morning bar and found himself a stool by a tall table underneath the enormous model of King Kong which hung from the roof.

How's it going?" Sam wanted to know, breezing past on the way to the loo.

"Well, y'know. About the same as usual," Rob admitted. "Birth, school, work, death. I'm still on the work bit at the moment, it's quite a long bit."

"I don't know now," Sam said, sounding slightly impressed, "seems to me you've got options. Alice. Sue. Even Lou seems to be showing a bit of interest, though she truly is way out of your league. You're a *player* my son!"

Rob shrugged and tried not to show he was flattered. He fiddled with the empty bag of dry-roasted peanuts.

"It's like that game: shag, marry, avoid," suggested Sam.

"Yeah," Rob allowed, folding the shiny peanut bag into smaller and smaller squares.

"Alice is a shag. Lou's a marry."

Sam nodded in agreement. "To be honest, when blokes play that game it should just be called shag, marry, 'cos avoid doesn't really come into it. What about Sue though, you forgot her." Sam squinted over to where Sue was sitting. She was side-on to them, round a table with some of the other players. She had a tracksuit bottom wrapped round her waist like a short skirt and her bare legs were crossed.

"She has got the most amazing legs," Sam exhaled in awe. "They're gorgeous aren't they? I tell you, I would..."

Rob flicked his nut bag sculpture at an empty pint pot and missed.

"Yeah," he said, "and Stalin had a great moustache. Really thick and lustrous but sometimes - and I *know* this is a sad thing - the bad in people outweighs the good."

Sam wasn't listening to his wise words, instead there was something off over the sticky dance floor which seemed to have taken precedence. Rob followed the stare and found Lou swanning over towards them.

"Trouble at three o'clock," said Sam with a note of panic. "Not keen on socialising with the ice maiden. I'll leave you to her and go 'n wash all this crap off me."

Gone without so much as a 'see ya' but at least it left a space for Lou to slink into as she approached, elite and unruffled, calm and serene. Regal, that was the word, which was ironic really as that was also the name of the beer barn they were in. There was an element of a royal visit in Lou's appearances in the pub, the way she worked the tables, gave of herself for her people. "Hello I'm the Queen and what do you do?"

"Hiya Lou-Lou," Rob chirped at her with a cheeky grin as she approached and she couldn't help but grin back at him, warming up suddenly, leaning in towards him with her elbows on the table. As she did so, he found it hard not to look down her top, did his best to avoid it, failed.

"Thought I'd better come over and see how you are," she soothed.

"That seemed like a terrible incident, you could do yourself a serious injury like that."

It was if she was warning him in case he'd been considering getting hit in the balls with a football again sometime soon.

"I can assure you it won't be happening again. I'm wearing a cricket box in future."

She laughed, "It must be sore."

"Not really, just feels like my testicles are tiny nuggets of Semtex which have exploded."

She nodded sympathetically. "Well, I'm sure we can find someone to give them a rub for you."

Rob thought about asking if she was offering, decided that was going way too far. Even Lou-Lou had been pushing it, he could see why Sam was scared of her, she was a walking cold front and even when she thawed a little, it was on her terms and you knew she could turn the temperature back down to absolute zero on a whim.

"I don't see a queue forming," he settled on - though he knew this was wrong - he was supposed to be giving the impression he was a player, not some loser who couldn't even get any female sympathy if he got his sack crushed.

She seemed to respond to his modesty, clucked a bit, put her hand out and stroked his head, told him he seemed to have plenty of girls interested in him as far as she could see.

She was still doing this and consequently he was purring, when Alice arrived.

"Oh hello. You two seem cosy."

She sat down on the seat next to Rob and stared at the space where her drink should be.

"Oh sorry, didn't know you were coming over," he mumbled, embarrassed, as though he had been caught doing something wrong by his mum.

Lou clearly found Alice turning up something of an energy killer too as she stopped stroking Rob's damp head quick smart and made brisk conversation about how these gatherings were good for morale before excusing herself to mingle.

"Stuck-up bitch," grumbled Alice after her once she was out of earshot. "What she needs is a good seeing to. That would loosen her up a bit.

She didn't appear to have a drink of her own but she helped herself to his pint, draining about a third of it in one long thirst-quenching swag.

"Has she not got a boyfriend then?" Rob did his best to seem like he was just making conversation.

Alice turned a mocking look on him, picked up the beermat and flicked it as his face. It bounced off his nose.

"Yeah, you'd have a go wouldn't you? You'd bloody *love* a go on her - she'd eat you for breakfast."

He tried to pretend that ending up as Lou's breakfast wasn't an enticing prospect. It turned out Alice had intended the breakfast comment to be a kind of temporary parting shot because she stalked off to the toilets without another word. Rob watched her go, she had one of those hip swings some women have, the ones that make their bums sway as they walk. That's great, thought Rob, that's a force of nature.

He was looking for a few moments peace to gather his scrambled thoughts and tend to his bruised package but pretty much as soon as the dark wood of the loo door had swung shut on Alice's twitching derrière, Sue was clacking over with her heels clip-clopping off the floorboards. It was as though they were all engaged in a particularly fraught game of musical chairs. She must have been watching, thought Rob, keeping one eye on them from where she'd been flirting with Jayden a couple of tables along.

"Wanted to check you were okay?" Sue offered without preamble. She scrambled onto the bar stool next to his tall table. The stool was a little too high for her and made her look like an adolescent as she hauled herself into position - cute.

"Yeah, I'll survive. Bit sore to be honest but you know?"

She wasn't really paying attention, then cut in with, "I'd watch out for that Alice if I was you," she spoke hurriedly and seemed to be struggling to control her emotions. "She's trouble, you *think* she's nice, she's clever, but you'll see. She's a right trollop. I don't even like going in the toilets after her 'cos she's got real bad granny fanny."

She paused for breath and took a huge gulp out of the oversized glass of chilled Chardonnay she'd brought with her for company.

Rob was at a loss for something to say. Granny fanny certainly didn't sound that appealing, though he wasn't entirely sure what it was.

"Listen," Sue went on, her tone softening. "We don't seem to be getting on as well as we were." She reached out and touched him on the cheek, dropped her hand down and took his glass from him.

"What's this? Ooh lager," then helped herself to some of that to complement the flavour of the wine.

Rob flustered at the accusation, immediately put on the spot. He knew he was supposed to be playing it cool and not giving too much of himself, spreading himself around and making his attention seem like a treat but at heart he was the same sweet, slightly daft kid he had been a few weeks before and he was, in essence, a people pleaser.

"Aren't we? I mean, I thought we were getting along fine. You came to my house that evening and everything was... nice."

He accepted the pint glass back and took a drink from it himself, his mouth seemed suddenly dry.

"Mmm," allowed Sue, "but we were getting close. I thought we had something special me and you. Remember that afternoon on the hill? You were my Heathcliff."

He'd never read Wuthering Heights, or even seen it as a TV drama. He'd heard of Heathcliff, sure. He knew he had something to do with the moors and romance but that was about it. He wasn't even sure whether Heathcliff was a goodie or a baddie.

"Ugh, thanks, yeah. Ooh, have you seen that ad on the beermat for wearing a condom?"

She didn't look at the beermat he was holding up for inspection, or seem to register the big dopey grin on his face.

"That's how I want us to be Robbie. I don't know what you want to be bothering with that Alice bint for when we are getting along so well."

Her glance shot over his shoulder and he knew without asking her what she'd seen.

"So...," she said, suddenly hurrying her pitch. "You're coming over to mine Saturday morning. I have a couple of manly things I need you to do around the house for me." She tried to make the last bit a seductive purr but it was on fast-forward. "Okay? Good."

Alice arrived at his shoulder.

"Oh hello. Nice of you to pop over and visit us!"

Sue smiled like licking a lemon.

"I came to see Rob, just to make sure he hadn't forgotten about Saturday."

"Saturday?" inquired Alice, bustling back in-between Rob and Sue, tits first.

"Yeah," Sue replied, nonchalantly playing with her wine glass, strangling the stem and scribbling on the misted bowl. "He's coming over mine, we've got a date, haven't we Robbie?"

Alice glanced at the side of Rob's head. He was studying the condom ad on the beet mat.

"Oh no," Alice was shaking her head, "I'm sorry. We can't Saturday hun. He must have forgotten, he's coming over to my folks' place. We're having a barbecue."

They both smiled at each other again, all teeth, then looked at Rob.

"Um," he stared at the beermat for inspiration. The cartoon man with a prophylactic on his finger and his cartoon girlfriend casting him a despairing glance.

"Maybe I could do the barbecue" he looked at Alice with a nod, like they had all the barbecue thing worked out in advance, hoping this dumb show would placate her for later re: Sue's 'date'.

"Then," he switched his attention to Sue, "after that I could pop over yours and sort out that job you need a hand with."

It seemed to him like the wisdom of Solomon but neither of his friends seemed best pleased with the compromise. Both appeared to be gearing up to hand him a bollocking once they got the chance. Given that and the fact that between the three of them, they seemed to have finished his pint, he decided now was probably the best time to leave them wanting more.

"Got to go, there's a programme about dinosaurs on the Discovery channel I need to see," and he grabbed his bag, flashed them a wink and more or less shot out of the place, hand-slapping and hair-ruffling his fellow players on the way out.

That evening at home, with his laptop on his knee, he filled in a page of his PUA journal, reflecting on how the campaign had gone that day. It had not been an unqualified success, sure. The only real measure of success could be getting laid, which was after all the final aim. But things appeared to him to be going well enough. He had wanted female attention and now he had it didn't he?

CHAPTER 6

'Johnno!' the blog of Robert Johnson, July 19:
"What do women want? And, more importantly, does It matter? After all, as far as I'm concerned it's what I want that counts and how I make them give it to me."
The more I study the way of the PUA, the more I realise I've been going wrong all this time by being too nice. I've cared too much about what women want and how to give it to them. I've wanted them to like me but what I really wanted was for them to fancy me! They can hate me if they want, so long as they fancy me as well."

That evening in his flat, after his run and a shower, he ate beans on toast and studied the next stage of his PUA training. Good traits to foster included patience, persistence, sensitivity to how your target woman (also known as 'the mark') feels and responds, finding opportunities in situations where you didn't expect them and being comfortable talking to any new woman.

Rob resolved that he would work on those, especially the 'being comfortable' bit, rather than sweaty and shifty eyed, which was his default setting with women he hadn't had time to get to know.

Apparently, he also had to be confident, have a good sense of humour, smile a lot, be well groomed and as good looking as he could manage given his natural limitations. Oh, and he also had to foster the ability to create feelings of romance and emotional connection.

The list was a mixture of things he could work on improving and others which seemed far beyond his control but it helped to know where he was going, even if he didn't have the bus fare to get there.

There was more advice about what to do with a girl once you had her attention. One piece that stood out for him was the idea that it was best to minimise pointless smalltalk and instead focus on questions and conversational gambits aimed at leading her to a state of arousal. Anyone can chatter about work or TV. Anyone who can lead a woman to an erotic mental space is a rare dude. He had to learn how to be that special person.

On top of this, he recapped on the key ways to behave when he was in the presence of the mark. He learned to mirror her physical gestures, notice and repeat back to her the special words she used frequently and emphasised her so-called 'trance words'.

He had tried some of this out on Alice at the football today. He needed to create good feelings and then anchor those feelings with a gesture he could repeat later on to recreate the same effect. There was a lot to remember: don't argue with her, be understanding, rephrase key things she says and feed them back to her to show your empathy, keep good eye contact, touch her.

It felt as if by concentrating on one aspect of what he was supposed to be doing, he would let the rest slide. He was a balancing act trying to keep a circus ring full of plates spinning and he envisioned every one crashing to the floor as he rushed around trying to service them all.

Palmistry, the website informed him, combines patterning and the touching known as kino with devastating effect. You touch, you lead her the way you want to go.

Ask her: "How do your friends describe you?" Then use her answer as a transition into a palm reading. Hold the hand, comment on the soft skin. She sees a truly emotionally responsive person, so sensitive, so highly sexed. Don't let go of her hand when you are laying it on thick like this. Stroke it, caress it. The way you are with her is, as always, as important as the words you say. Remember, 90% of communication has nothing to do with what you say.

Tell her: "People don't really know each other until their bodies get to know each other."

When you begin the reading, simply repeat to her the information she has already given you. Dress it up changing the language somewhat so it is not an obvious and direct repetition. Talk slowly with a little showmanship and a lot of empathy. Slip in sections of what she told you, she'll forget where the information came from and simply assume you chime with her, you understand her innermost thoughts. Her hopes and dreams are yours too.

The other technique is to tell her things that, frankly, anyone will agree with, things which describe all of us, or at least mirror the way we would like to describe ourselves. Fine examples include that you can be lazy sometimes but only when it comes to matters you don't really care about. You are sensitive to what others say and do, though you might not always admit it. You have a deep-rooted need for the approval of other people, especially when you have done something well. You tend to be a bit more honest than many of the people you meet. You have a very generous and giving nature and can be unselfish, though, if you're honest about it, there are times when you have acted selfishly.

Rob scrolled down and studied a diagram of the hand showing the main lines for palmistry. The fate line cutting the palm in half vertically, the life line tracing a looping arch round the ball of the thumb. The brain line and heart line parallel like rail tracks running at a diagonal arc across the centre.

He looked at the smaller lines for marriage and love and the sun line, whatever the hell that was. He looked at his own hand for comparison and was alarmed to find he didn't appear to have a life line. Shit, did this mean he was dead?

His mobile rang out the 'A Team' theme, he hated it but didn't know how to change it,

"Hey?" he asked.

"S'up?" It was Alice.

"Hiya hon, what you doing?" he asked her, pleased to hear from her, thrilled she'd taken the trouble.

"Having a bath," she made splashing noises for verification.

Rob was concerned. "You want to make sure you don't drop your phone in the bath, you'll electrocute yourself."

She laughed a hollow, echoey bathroom laugh of mockery down the line.

"No I won't you knob, it's a moby not a bar fire, I'd just knacker my phone is all."

"Hmm, I'm not convinced. Have you got bubbles in your bath?"

"Huge piles of bubbles that smell of lavender. Got bubbles all over me, all over my knockers like a dress."

"Are they tingly?"

96

"Hey steady! You're not getting off on this are you? You perv." She giggled a bathroom giggle.

"Yeah," he admitted frankly. "You carry on telling me about your bath, I'm just going to go a bit quiet for a while."

Raucous laugh, he had to hold the receiver away from his ear.

"I bet you are, you'll be having a sly shuffle while I'm doing it."

"Well how do I know you aren't doing the same thing. Where's the soap?"

"It does though doesn't it!" she parroted the punch line from the nuns in a bath joke and cackled uncontrollably for the longest time. Rob wondered whether to go and make a cup of tea. Finally the mirth subsided.

"So, are you coming to dinner with me tomorrow then like you promised? Remember, if you back out, I'll have to hunt you down and kill you."

"Sounds like an offer I can't refuse." He rested the phone between his shoulder and ear and tried to use the laptop to access the PUA advice on telephone seduction.

"Good. At mine at ten o'clock. We've got to pick up some stuff for the barbecue."

"Barbecue? I thought you lived in a flat?"

"I do. It's not at mine you numb-nut. We've got to pick up stuff and head over. Okay now sweetie the water's getting cold. I'm either going to have to get out or take a piss in it to warm it up. Ten o'clock. Don't be tardy. Laters!"

Yet he was tardy. Blame his age, blame the times. He was never any good at getting up promptly, even when he didn't have a hangover to sleep off. His body clock seemed an hour or two slower than other people's and the only way he made it in to work on time often enough not to get fired, was by having two alarm clocks set to go off half an hour apart and half an hour early.

He turned them off at weekends so it was 10am before he'd even rolled out of bed and gone 11 by the time he rolled up outside Alice's place in a panic.

Her flat was just round the corner from Cheltenham's preposterous neo-classical Town Hall, on the third floor of an Art Deco style block called Cambray Place.

The complex looked expensive, it was walled and gated, had private parking and a snooty air. He wondered briefly how she ran to it on the crap they got paid, even if she made her bonus every month which they tended to make sure was damn near impossible.

There was a lift but he eschewed it and bounced up the stairs until he burst out onto her landing breathing heavily and scaring exclamations out of a gentle old couple in church clothes coming the other way arm in arm.

He hammered on the door and when Alice opened it, her eyes were glinting and her small brown face was flushed with either passion or anger and he could more or less guess which.

"What time d'you call this?" she barked at him grumpily not making any move to let him in her place.

He was on the point of blurting out an abject apology, breathy and contrite. He had some half-cocked excuse planned about needing air for his tyres and it being better to be safe, than on time but he paused for a couple of breaths and his training kicked in, 'Hey great' he thought, 'Like a Ninja.'

He shrugged - smirked.

"You should be grateful I turned up at all. Got other stuff I could be doing of a weekend." He'd no clue what the response to this bit of cheek might be, door in the face most probably. It felt odd doing it, making himself that disagreeable ran contrary not only to common sense but to his day job as a salesman when eating shit and making the client feel good at your expense were a daily chore.

He shut his mouth and waited resisting the urge to take it back or dilute it with an ingratiating grin. Alice breathed in sharply as if she was getting into cold water, then thought things over for a moment and became more resigned and graciously so.

"Hmm, well you're a bastard, shouldn't have expected anything else really after all, you're a man."

She turned and went into the hall with him following. He gave her a sharp rap on the rump as he did so and she yelped and giggled.

"I promise to do as I'm told now I'm here," he said with penitence, gracious now the battle was won. "You're the boss after all."

"Well clearly I'm not," she chirped, suddenly quite cheery now. "Since you won't bloody come when I tell you. We're going to be late now."

He nodded. "I mean I'm more sheepish than a sheep about the whole thing, honestly, but you know what? We'll be fine." He had no evidence for this but felt sure of it anyway. It was a sunny day, they were young, fine was the very *least* they would be.

Luckily Alice had stuff ready she told him disappearing through a white door in the white hall and into the white kitchen. 'Stuff' was bread rolls, sausages from the fridge and a couple of bottles of red wine. She loaded it into a Tesco bag while he went looking for the loo. He found instead her front room, where it was clear she did most of her living.

The place was a tip. Not dirty really, but award-winningly messy. If there was a flat space there were knickers on it, or CDs, or magazines with pictures of girls on their undies on the front. Why did women's magazines do that he wondered? Put pictures of sexy women on the front. He could understand it for men's magazines. The women were a big draw and everything else came a distant second. Surely Marie whatever and Just the other should have photos of blokes in their Calvins on the front?

It just went to confirm his fondly held belief that all women have a secret lesbian side.

"You alright?" Alice asked, coming in behind him. "Thought you'd gone to look for the bog."

"I did but then I found this. Have you been burgled?" He sounded mock concerned. She laughed.

"Life's too short for sticking the Hoover round," she told him.

"Don't do housework though I do have a maid's outfit, which I might let you see if you're a good boy. Now where's my fucking car?"

She found it in its private space, a Ford Focus in a goldy, pinky metallic girl colour which was probably called champagne. She'd bounced it out onto the road before Rob was even properly sat down. Her driving was ferocious, all urgent acceleration and stamping on the brake and clutch. The first five minutes of the journey took some getting used to as they wound their way precariously through the town's near deserted Sunday morning roads.

Once, she leapt through a red light, another time she stopped suddenly explaining it was to avoid a bird as she gestured vaguely down the street where, fifty yards or so further on, Rob squinted to make out sparrows playing in the kerb.

When things calmed down a little he sought to make conversation. Thought through what might be a good line from a PUA point of view;

99

warm her up, make her feel like he was the sort of soul mate who could answer her emotional needs. In the end he gave up and instead brought up an issue which had been on his mind for a while.

"What do you think of Jayden?"

She thought about it, checking her lippy in the rear view mirror.

"He's a solid professional, a good sales executive and an experienced middle-manager."

"Erm, no. I meant do you fancy him?"

She fiddled with her hair, one hand on the wheel.

"Hmm, he's had mixed reviews."

He persevered, "You'd have a go though right?"

Alice gave a little Mona Lisa smirk. "Who's to say I haven't?"

Rob was immediately consumed with sexual jealousy, that most pure and potent of emotions. He battled to come up with a witty rejoinder, a phrase which would at once convey how unconcerned he was with the news, whilst making Jayden appear diminished and Rob, by contrast, more attractive and urbane. He came up blank though and found he was too upset to say anything.

Alice jammed the brakes on for no apparent reason and Rob, who had neglected to wrestle with his seat belt, nutted the windscreen.

"Crap!"

"Oops, sorry. It's just you reminded me, sausages! I forgot the Cumberland sausages - they're in the fridge."

She performed an eight point turn with cars honking and fellow motorists making wanker signs at Rob as though he was in the driver's seat rather than rubbing the egg under his hairline."

"So, are you saying you've actually had him then?"

"I'm saying I've forgotten the fucking sausages and we're late enough already."

He followed her out of the car and paused in the communal porch watching her behind bounce back up the stairs to her flat. Then he stood motionless and silent with an old lady watching him as he waited for her to return. The lady had a wicker shopping basket with a tiny Yorkshire Terrier in it; the dog growled at him.

"Tinker doesn't like you," the elderly woman informed him, matter of factly.

Back in the car, Alice was all brisk and businesslike.

"Even less time now and I've got to concentrate on the driving."

Squeal of tyres and smell of rubber; Rob had his belt on this time.

"It's a simple enough question. I'd tell you." He tried to repress a whining, pleading tone, distinctly unattractive, which he heard was creeping into his voice.

"What, you'd tell me if you'd had Jayden?"

"Anyone you want. Just ask," he challenged her. "That's fair. I get one, you get one."

Alice thought about it, cornered at speed, throwing Rob towards the window so childhood rides on the Wonder Waltzer popped unbidden into his mind.

"Hmm, okay then. Have you had Sue?"

"No," he said firmly. "Have you had Jayden?"

"Yes," she retorted, equally firmly, "and so has Sue."

They travelled to the outskirts of town where the road banked steeply up the Cotswold escarpment, the houses thinned to a scattering on each side and there were fine views back over the racecourse. Alice took a sudden turn to the left, barely bothering to slow down and rattled down a concealed driveway through deciduous woodland. There was a breakfast cereal crunch of loose shale under the wheels and grey squirrels darted for the trees ahead of them on the track.

Alice was chattering about some work related matter and Rob was still mute and sullen. He wondered dimly where the hell they were, out in the suburbs with their sausages and he waited for a gap so he could ask Alice, who seemed to have developed some kind of circular breathing system which meant she didn't have to pause even for the shallowest gulp of air.

"And she sez... 'ere we are."

Screech of brakes, a sideways drift and a gravel waterfall in front of them.

"Impressive house!" he admitted, gawping at it and indeed it was. Not only in scale but also, he quickly realised, in its awfulness.

The front elevation of the house was vast and blocky and looked as though it had been built from pale yellow Lego bricks. There was a portico sticking out at the front like it had been added on later with pillars and a mammary style dome in the roof mimicking a cut-price St Pauls.

Overall, the building appeared to have too many windows and way too much glass. It was impressive in its scale but ugly too, in poor taste

Rob thought, though he didn't consider himself any great arbiter of architectural standards.

He knew crap when he saw it though.

"It's... certainly something," he breathed as he followed Alice beneath the pillars.

Heavy front door, old wood, oak maybe, something from a reclamation yard. Inside was an entrance hall of great size and scope, the floor shiny white marble or something doing a good impression, walls with tall arched windows and a nice view of the garden.

A central staircase wound its way to the upper floor and Rob looked up into the dome he'd seen from outside. There were gold swirls on it and plaster cherubs frolicked.

Here on the ground floor the central feature was a white marble fountain, perhaps from the same reclamation centre as the door. It was a three tiered wedding cake with flower petal style bowls increasing in size. There was pink water cascading down from one layer to the next and red flower petals in the pools. The fountain made a tinkling sound which echoed around the hall. The whole thing reminded Rob of a house from a Hollywood movie; opulent but sterile.

"It's quite a place," Rob admitted quietly. "You sure we're supposed to be here? I mean you have an invitation right?"

"Oh yeah, yeah", Alice replied nonchalantly.

She stepped behind him and slipped his green canvas jacket off his shoulders then headed over to a door to the rear of the stairs to a cloakroom, she dropped off her pink fake fur too.

"Hey hun, I'll go stick this food in the kitchen," she looked back over her shoulder. "Be back in a minute with a drink for you." She made a mwah noise and blew him an elaborate kiss. "Laters."

He waited lost and lonely as people moved around him, lots of faces he didn't know, the sound of gaggles from around the fountain invaded his ears. Finally, after much scanning of the crowd, he found someone he recognised. A ruddy head with a puzzled expression under a comb-over of sandy hair; it was Crazy Al of Crazy Al's windows. Noooo, thought Rob, the last thing he needed was to have to socialise with that nutcase. It would turn the whole afternoon into work and what the hell was he doing here anyway? Was this some work-related thing of Alice's business contacts? It was the only way he could rationalise what they were doing here, surrounded by tacky opulence and middle-aged businessmen.

He tried to edge back behind something to obscure himself, a terracotta maiden holding a conch shell in the classical style seemed favourite but Al's rheumy blue eye had fallen and rested on him.

"It's *you*," stated Al, blankly. "It's ages since I saw you."

"Yeah well, you know how it is. Time flies like an arrow, fruit flies like a banana." Rob shrugged.

Al's brow furrowed as he digested this non sequitur. It seemed to fuse something in his brain that created an electrical bridge of neurons which short-circuited him altogether for a moment, so he stood stock still with his mouth open like a robot unplugged. A silent tear of sweat worked its way down his pink brow.

"Ha, Ha?" He offered tentatively, as if to test out whether it had been a joke.

"Very good, yes. You kids, I don't know. You're so fucking smart hey?" Then again, quietly to himself. "So fucking smart."

Rob hid his face in his hands for a moment and grimaced. Show no fear, that was the key, in sales and in life. It was like dealing with a big dog.

"What you doing here then?" Al was suddenly curious, he asked with a sideways squint as though it was an accusation and he half expected that Rob was a modern day Raffles, mingling with the nouveau middle-class in order to spirit away their Sky Plus boxes and X-Box 360s.

"Here with a bird," Rob replied casually, showing no fear.

"Oh aye?"

"Aye!" he nodded.

"What's she like?" Al's tone was playful, borderline lecherous. He didn't exactly dig Rob in the ribs with his elbow but he might have done. This seemed like a conversational gambit which might pay off.

"Hot," Rob mouthed.

"Aye?"

"Dirty."

"Aye?"

"Yeah well, you know what it's like at my age Al, if I can call you Al?"

Al didn't say he couldn't.

"You have to take what you can get. I'm a young guy Al, I'm sure you remember, I mean, it wasn't that long ago!"

He was patronising the old fucker now!

Al listened, tucked into his glass of chilled white.

"And she gives you what you want does she?"

"She's a very giving person Al, if you know what I mean. Of course, I have other options, if you know what I'm saying but you wouldn't want to miss out on a bit of what she's offering."

He felt free, felt released from the fear which had grabbed him when the man first appeared in front of him. This was all going very well. The party span on around him as middle aged men and women cackled and talked too loud about nothing at all.

"In fact later on, we might have to see if one of the rooms upstairs is free in this God-awful mess of a house and you know, be very giving."

Al nodded sagely. "God-awful, aye?"

He was a much more charming and attentive man than he seemed in his professional environment, Rob thought. Perhaps he had misjudged the guy. You couldn't really claim to know someone unless you had socialised together, taken a drink in each other's company as equals rather than in the stilted hierarchy of the salesman-client relationship.

"Yeah I mean, she's gagging for it if I'm honest. Can hardly keep her knickers on." He was warming to his theme now and felt quite sorry for poor old Al really. The old boy was probably decidedly horny at the thought of him and Alice having a romp, probably had a wrinkly dyed blonde wife somewhere who was too busy down the tanning salon to give him any.

He wanted to warn Al against any indiscretion when Alice returned but as it turned out he didn't have time. She had reappeared at the far end of the vast white reception area and was making her way towards them with drinks and snagged slightly as she went on her way past groups of people who knew her and wanted to exchange a few words.

Still, it would be okay. Al was a guy, admittedly a *crazy* guy but still a guy. Rob was a guy. They were guys together bonded by the Omerta of manhood. Alice was puffed out from weaving through an obstacle course of plump forty-somethings.

"Hi Robbie. Hi dad."

Rob's mouth lolled open. He looked back hopelessly at Crazy Al.

"Who do you think you are?" Al inquired, his voice quavering with angst. "Who the flying *fuck* do you think you are?"

Rob froze like a lamped rabbit playing dead. His camouflage was crap in here though, they could all see him, the guests, Crazy Al, Crazy Al's daughter, the object of his lustful affections.

"I er... I dunno." Rob looked at his feet. "I dunno who I am."

It felt like the first honest thing he had said.

"Well I know who you are!" Yelled Al, jovially.

"You're a cunt!" and with that, he leapt at Rob, with surprising speed for a big bloke and grasped him in a clumsy bear hug. Al was laughing but his grip was fierce. The pair of them danced a cheek-to-cheek tango across the white pot tiles, bemused guests scattering as they did so.

Al kept up the laughing, loud, high and abandoned. Somehow he found the wind for that as well as for shoving Rob around the place like a prop forward but then, Rob hadn't really found his game yet. He was still baffled, off-kilter, his natural balance kept him on his feet.

"Come on then lad," Al was wheezing, "let's see what you got then, come on son, let's wrestle!" Superficially light-hearted he sounded, though Rob could hear his voice straining with menace underneath. Then that laugh came again, starting deep and gruff but with a high, bright finish.

Rob still said nothing, shocked as he was, backpedalling and grunting under the weight of Al's comedy assault. Al was playing it for laughs still, at least as far as the other guests were concerned. He was whooping with merriment, even as he bundled Rob around the reception hall like a tackle dummy. From his reaction, you could take the thing to be good natured high jinks, a laddish display of machismo.

Finally buckling under the pressure and still grim faced and mute, Rob dropped to one knee on the marble floor, which sent a sharp pain shooting up his leg, so he said 'ow' in a small distracted voice like a kid waking up. He certainly felt like saying more but Al loosened his grip and Rob entertained hopes that his ordeal might all be over, so he kept his own counsel, placed his hands on the cold floor to regain his balance and strove to sort out his scrambled thoughts, his brain presenting like a fragmented hard drive.

The reprieve was short lived. Al wasn't releasing him, merely changing his grip and the stocky, crimson-faced ginger lunatic came at him again for a fresh hold, this time grasping Rob's head under his sweaty armpit and dragging him back onto his feet again in a clean jerk.

If previously Rob had been able to say very little, what with having the breath squeezed out of him by a compact, yet surprisingly powerful

105

maniac, now he found he couldn't speak at all, as his windpipe was coming under significant pressure, even breathing was proving a chore. Each gasp of air was at a premium and he found himself being dragged around the room again after the cackling Al scuttling behind him, bent over like the back end of a pantomime cow.

Rob's head remained uncomfortably low in the shorter man's grip, as Al conducted a one-sided conversation based on light banter.

"You up for it then lad hey? You nearly had me there, you wee tosser you! You scallywag!"

The two blokes continued rough-housing, indulging in some strange kind of horseplay. From his unique and peculiar vantage point under Al's arm, Rob could see the crowd parting to let them through. Party-goers stood aside in the half-filled room, as they careered through and watched in amusement, joining in with Al's laughter, perhaps a little bemused. Then again, this was Al after all, the crazy guy.

Rob couldn't pin-point the exact moment he lost his temper. He'd had enough and it was clear matters weren't going to be sorted out unless he took decisive action but there was more than that, there was a sudden irritation, the realisation that he didn't have to put up with this humiliation, that he had a right to make it stop.

As their runaway train trundled towards the centre point in the room where the fountain gushed its pink, rose-scented, champagne, Rob stood up but before doing so made sure he had a hand firmly supporting Crazy Al's crotch. He planted his feet on the marble and lifted Al off the ground, hoisting him into the air, his legs waving like sticks, Farah slacks flapping impotently. Al let out a wheezing squeal perhaps because Rob made sure to give his nuts a good squeeze as he picked him up but he wasn't in that position for very long.

He was heavy and Rob was tired. Tired in his mind, tired in his body and tired in his heart. Without ceremony he dumped Al in the big bottom basin of the fountain and watched pink water slosh over the sides onto the floor.

Rob stood there, watching Al flap like a starling in a bird bath for a short while as laughter rang out around him, full and throaty now rather than the nervous giggling which had gone before.

Al seemed to be panicking, the water was only shallow, the depth of a washing up bowl, yet he gave the impression he might put in the effort to drown anyway, so Rob grabbed his arm and hauled him out, landing him wetly on the deck like line-caught sea bass.

He sat down next to Al and observed him wearily. Al eyed him in return, puffing and panting while struggling to formulate words.

"You big daft fucker, you daft fucking sod," Al relapsed into more heavy breathing. Something in his eyes suggested he might be contemplating round two but Rob knew very well that if he tried anything he would be getting another cold pink bath.

Suddenly Al disengaged, he'd lost interest apparently. Flushed and knackered, yet seeming strangely exhilarated, he lay on the pot tiles by the fountain like a toppled statue of Buddha, vermilion petals sticking to his face and his soaked Hawaiian shirt.

"Dad loves to wrestle," explained Alice, seeming only slightly strained. Then, louder for the gallery, she added. "He loves to play fight, he's just a big daft kid is dad!"

"I'm gasping for a fag." Al insisted, getting up. He wandered off, got sidetracked on the way to the garden by a bloke wearing the shade of an occasional lamp on his head for a lark. Al laughed like it was the birth of slapstick - Charlie Chaplain, Stan, Ollie and Harold Lloyd all rolled into one. Purple-faced and winded, spit-flecked and pearly with sweat, Al finally made it to the front door.

Rob shrugged. "Nice to meet your dad," he said. "This is supposed to be a barbecue isn't it? Any chance of a burger then?"

"Hmm," said Alice vaguely, eye's tracing the path of her departed dad. "I better tell the cleaner to come and mop up this water but yeah, let's go get something to eat - you must be hungry."

It was as if all which had gone before was traditional pre-barbecue entertainment, the sort of thing designed to leave you with a keener appetite for your hot dogs. Rob gave up trying to rationalise it and followed her into the main body of the house.

In the front room there was music of a kind wafting through hidden speakers. Vague and bland it seemed to be made by an insipid choir. Characterless American voices singing sanitised middle-of-the-road hits.

"Christ," Rob grumbled. "This assaults my ears." Alice seemed genuinely miffed.

"We used to listen to this on Sundays. It's one of daddy's favourites.

"Did he listen to this while he wrestled people?"

"It's charming," she insisted distractedly, as if hypnotised by the dreary sound. Rob shook his head to wave away the headache which was growing behind his eyes.

"It's as though they captured a bunch of catalogue models, herded them together into a recording studio and made them sing."

Alice shook her head and made a face like she was straining to hear.

"It's gorgeous, it's like angels singing. You've got no taste."

He smirked at her and bumped hips. "I like you."

She grinned. "Yeah well, other than *that* you have no taste."

She grabbed him by the arm excited, suddenly upbeat and apparently forgetting the unseemly scramble she had just witnessed between Rob and her father.

"Come on, let me show you where we're having the barbecue. She turned a serious face up to him. "They have a lovely garden, really lovely."

It was too. It didn't fit the house at all and seemed perhaps to have been left over from an earlier property that had been bulldozed to build the current monstrosity. It was formal in layout, a long lawn with clipped box borders and with a rectangle of silver fish pond down the centre. Alice dragged him across to survey the fat Koi flitting dreamily beneath the surface. Gold and black and the bright orange of boiled sweets.

"They are lovely," Rob murmured, surprised at his delight, his lack of cynicism faced with a pond of fish.

Alice nodded gravely. "They are a great age and worth a lot of money." Sounded like something she was incanting from her childhood, remembered phrases and rituals which take on a spiritual significance as you grow old with them.

The barbecue was a more recent addition to the garden, stone-built and standing to one side of the lawn. There was a guy in a chef's hat tending the gas flame and flipping burgers.

"I would have thought that would be a job for mad... for your dad?" Rob said, gesturing towards the cooking.

"No, he has a chef," she replied nonchalantly.

It was a warm afternoon and people were sitting on the grass with paper plates piled with burgers and chicken pieces. There were bowls of coleslaw, bottles of beer from a well-stocked fridge beside the barbecue. Perhaps this wasn't going to be so bad after all now he'd had his confrontation with the biggest sumo in the dojo. Maybe he could relax now and concentrate on Alice? Alice and ribs, Alice and a glass or two from the big glass bucket of mint-coloured punch people were helping themselves to in ladlefuls. Alice went to get a couple of glasses while Rob sat by the pond surveying the flow of distant fish.

Lost in them he was but he sensed someone behind him and turned to see Louise standing in the sun. She was wearing a white summer dress and looked lovely, classy he thought, even with the money floating around this place, perhaps because of all the sordid money, she looked too good to be here, too pure and special.

"Hi?" she asked him.

He didn't respond except with a grin, partly caught by surprise, partly remembering he should not be too eager, no leaping to his feet and bouncing round her like a puppy; stay cool, survey the fish pond.

"Caught any?" she asked him.

"Mmm, they're a bit too quick for me. I'll have a hot dog instead."

She was obviously holding out because it seemed uncool to ask but eventually she relented.

"So what are you doing here? I didn't think you had an invite?"

She sat down next to him, her white dress reflected in the pond.

"Invite?"

He stretched out on the lawn, open and at ease, he didn't care whether she sat down next to him but he certainly wasn't discouraging her either. They were like lions at a waterhole he thought.

"The invite from Al's company. It was just for senior people."

He shrugged. "I'm connected."

For a moment she looked impressed then her face hardened a little and she said. "Of course, you have his account, he must have thought it was good business to invite you too."

She looked a bit smug, back in control, she was showing him who was top dog. He laughed and spoke slowly, remembering that it doesn't matter *what* you say, it's *how* you say it that counts.

"I tend to make a good impression on most people I meet. I like them - they like me. You should get to know me better, then you'd see. He reached over and gently lifted a wisp of her blonde hair from off her cheek and placed it back behind her ear with the rest.

She grinned and made eye contact.

"You think you're cool," she teased.

He paused for a moment, tempted to justify himself, tell her he was pretty damn cool actually, these days at least but he caught himself in time and instead smiled and relaxed. He had demonstrated higher value to her simply by being here unexpectedly. She was impressed he had got an invite to what she obviously felt was quite a sophisticated event, without her patronage or the golden tickets for a select few which had come through the office. His work was done - he did not need to be defensive.

So he smiled again, made eye contact with her, said, "I think you're cool." Then he reached over and took her hand. She gave it to him without too much fuss, amused, compliant. He lifted it to his lips and kissed it. She laughed, all warm and inviting; she moved in a little. Alice appeared in his eyeline behind Lou's golden head as it bobbed forward towards him.

"Oh, hi," Alice said, strained and rather alarmed. "What a thrill to find you here."

Lou turned her head, unconcerned.

"Hello sweetie, nice to see you too. It's like an office team building session here! Is there anyone who didn't get an invite? I haven't seen the cleaners yet."

Rob felt the urge to explain and started out with the intention of glossing the whole Alice's dad is Crazy Al thing for Lou but he'd hardly got a, "Well you see" out of his mouth, when Alice dived in, dragged him to his feet in a surprisingly meaty grip and insisted shrilly that there were people she wanted him to meet.

"Hope you don't mind hon, we'll catch up later - byee!"

Lou did seem to mind a bit actually but it would puncture her air of superiority to admit it, so she demurred and started dangling her fingers in the water as though her whole plan had been to have a sit down on the grass communing with the Koi.

"You can get listeria from putting your fingers in a pond if you don't wash your hands after," whispered Alice in another snippet of received family pond-wisdom as she marched Rob away. She didn't seem too unhappy at the prospect of this fate befalling Lou.

She headed purposefully down the lawn towards an arch in the hedge. Rob followed her through it to more garden, herbaceous borders, mature shrubs, the distant twinkle of a greenhouse winking at them in the sunlight.

Alice headed left past a purple Buddleia swarming with Red Admirals and there in the shade of an Acer tree was a summerhouse. It was coated in flaking white paint, had a pagoda roof and leaded windows. It was pretty, though dissolute and past its prime.

She led him in holding his hand. He felt as though he were being shown somewhere secret and special, as if behind the door there was going to be a snowy forest and a talking lion offering him a pawful of Turkish Delight but there was just white-washed brickwork, cast-iron garden furniture and some crude abstract paintings on the walls.

One showed a crying clown in the style of Picasso, another was of a mobile phone melting in a cartoonish hand. They were daubed in acrylics and seemed to have been painted with passion at least, you could see the finger marks were the fevered artist had decided a brush simply wasn't enough to convey the intensity of his artistic passion.

"Who the fu...?"

"My dad and I would leave it there if I were you."

She didn't seem too angry at his attempted opener and smiled as she sat him down, leant over him and breathed warm words in his ear.

"You're funny. You always say the wrong thing but it's endearing sometimes. You remind me of my first real boyfriend, the first one I lived with."

"Mmm? That's good then I suppose. Who was he? What did he do?"

"He was a clown."

"That's bad. I know mistakes have been made, but still."

"No, he was an *actual* clown, he ran away to join the circus in the end. Left me living in a leaky caravan in the Forest of Dean. I didn't want to go home and admit to my parents I'd cocked things up, so I hauled water down from a spring on a hill and shit in a bucket for six months until dad got me the flat in Cheltenham."

"That's a touching tale, it's like Dickens, rescued from poverty by rich parents."

"Yeah well, it was good some of the time, at the start anyway. We travelled round Europe in an old bus with a couple of mates doing circus skills and smoking breeze blocks of cannabis resin."

"Like that Cliff Richard film, except for the blow."

"What film?"

"The one where they go round Europe on a bus and he finds himself erotically drawn to the charms of an adolescent boy who turns out in the end to be an adult woman."

She stood up, shook her head, baffled and opened the door.

"No, you've lost me. If you wait in here I'll get us some drinks,

111

maybe a plate of food. We can have time alone together."

Then, before he had chance to form an opinion, never mind a repost, she was away past the butterfly bush again and he was alone on his own. Not despondent though, far from displeased at the turn matters were taking.

The way he saw it, being alone together somewhere where she felt safe and at home could only be a positive move, so he sat on one of the black ornamental iron chairs in the summerhouse and waited patiently. He vacantly surveyed a spider plant sitting on a small marble table in the corner and avoided thought beyond being vaguely pleased about his progress with Alice and terrified at the prospect her mad father might at some point reappear intent on two falls and a submission to sort out their differences.

He was still sitting, staring at the tendrils of the plant when he heard Alice reappear and looked up with a grin to find it wasn't her at all but an impish blonde girl aged maybe thirty who he thought he recognised but couldn't quite work out from where.

"Oh... hi," she was surprised to see him clearly and seemed a little sheepish about something. She grinned apologetically and he resisted the urge to apologise for being there.

"Can I help you?" he asked gravely as though he was a doctor and she was attending his surgery.

It wrong-footed her, she flustered a little and her cheeks coloured.

"Oh I er, you got me, this is where I slope off to for a sneaky fag. I'm not supposed to be having one."

"They're bad for your health."

"Oh I know," she tutted. "but you have to have some fun don't you? You won't tell on me will you?"

He weighed it up. "Yeah well, you're a bad girl but it's not my problem if you're off the rails."

She smirked as she lit up. "Yeah, I'm a real animal."

Where did he know her from? Ah, then he had it, she was the girl from Crazy Al's place, the receptionist. She'd been a bit of a cow to him he remembered but she seemed okay now. Different circumstances maybe? Still, they were cosy here, just the two of them, sharing a secret and the circumstance presenting him with a chance to try out some of what he'd learned as a PUA. He just needed the nerve, the right techniques and he could go in for a quick close - he'd finally have something to report back on the site which amounted to a small success of sorts.

"What were you doing here anyway?" asked Crazy Al's blonde taking a voluptuous drag on her fag.

"Waiting for customers," he told her, "I'm a fortune teller."

"Ooh, really?" she leaned in and seemed genuinely interested. She was wearing a tight white T-shirt with a low neck and a pair of black jeans. She was his type he decided... actually, they were all his type.

"Okay then let me show you, can I borrow your hand? Promise I'll be gentle and you can keep the other one for smoking your fag."

She handed over her left hand demurely, palm down.

He took it but looked back at her, all serious face.

"Is this the hand you use to write with, your dominant hand?"

She shook her head, amused.

"I didn't know we were going to take this so seriously."

He ignored her invitation to levity and continued with quiet dignity.

"I'm going to need your other hand in order to get a proper reading."

She switched fag hand and gave him her right not quite bored with the theatre of it, still happy to play along in the absence of anything better to do. He looked up at her dyed hair and mid-brown roots and her brown neatly plucked eyebrows too. Her eyes were an unnatural blue, probably contact lenses. She had a tan which could be sunbed, or, this time of year might even be real. He felt incredibly attracted to her, so much so he found his tongue thickening in his mouth with lust so he was worried he couldn't talk properly. He cleared his throat, grabbed a gobful of her bottle of lager, which tasted sourly of fags.

He looked directly at her again and stared deeply into her eyes, as if searching for something in her, or for some inner-peace which would allow him to proceed. She sniggered but kept her hand held out. He turned it lightly to look at the palm and coaxed the fingers out loosely and caressed the flat of it with his finger as if brushing away cobwebs to get a better look.

He furrowed his brow in concentration and traced his pointing finger along the long line. "You see this line here? That's your fate line. You see how it breaks here, about a third of the way along? Know what that tells me?"

She bent her blonde mop down to look at her palm with renewed interest. A strand of her hair fell in front of her face, he pushed it away for her. As she leant towards him he could see down her top but he strove to concentrate on the important matter of the palm, glancing up only occasionally to stare into her eyes.

"That tells me your life is heading for an important change. That you are going to alter your course in life."

He began nodding gently as he said this and she nodded a little too, perhaps without realising it. She said nothing though, concentrating instead on what he was saying.

"You will stay on your chosen path until about thirty, maybe a little later and then you'll change course and, you know what? I think this new course will be what you wanted all along. You are a kind person, passionate, giving, I can tell that from the strength of your heart line here but this kindness means you are sometimes easily led by others. You're a people pleaser, you want to do the right thing but your palm tells me the time is coming when you will find a new passion, or maybe go with the thing you should have been doing in the first place. Your future holds change but you shouldn't fear change I don't think you do, do you?"

He looked back up into her eyes, caressing her hand gently, stroking it as though it had done well. When he looked back at her he was alarmed to see the change which had washed over her demeanour. Gone was the sophisticated, slightly mocking attitude she'd had when he first took her hand. Instead she was focussed and serious, even a little damp-eyed with emotion.

"You got that right." She nodded, a little surprised maybe but sold on it, sold on him.

"I do think you are right about my being led and I have felt that it is time for a change, that I ought to be making more of myself. I *am* a people pleaser, that's very true, *very* true. I need to be needed but I know I have more to give, more love, more kindness. I feel I should be nurturing, giving that love." She looked grave but then brightened up a bit and smiled at him.

"Tell me what else you see."

He looked back down at the palm and moved the tip of his finger slowly across it.

"This isn't a prediction about the future so much, this is something which has already happened to you, is that okay?"

She looked a little taken aback but nodded.

"You see the heart line that I showed you before? You see this other line here going across? That's your life line. Do you see the way it touches your heart line here, right near the base of your hand? What that means is back when you were a girl something happened to you. It means that early in your life something happened which meant that you, though you were still a child yourself, had to take on some of the responsibilities of a grown adult. That you had to grow up quicker than perhaps you should have done and almost give up part of your childhood. Can you think what that could be?"

He sounded full of concern as he told her this bit, all soft voiced so as not to intrude, like a counsellor or a priest maybe. She thought for a moment then nodded again.

"I think that would be the birth of my little sister," she said firmly. "I'm sure that's what it is referring to. She was six years younger than me and a real baby even when she was old enough to stand on her own two feet. My parents always expected me to look after her, always. As though I was her mother rather than just her big sister. It was always: 'Belle, why's Susie crying?' and 'Belle, make sure you take your sister with you if you're going out to town.' It was a total drag but you know... I didn't mind too much, I'm good with kids, I always have been."

He nodded. "I know I can see. I can also tell you're a very nurturing person and I can see here," he traced her palm, "at your fate line and here, at your head line, that the new you, the one which is coming very soon, will be very involved with children, young children, a *baby* maybe?"

This was clearly a hit, she took a deep breath, she had forgotten her fag.

"I don't know for sure yet whether it is your child, as yet to be born, or perhaps you will be working with other children but there will be infants in your life. When someone has an experience early in life where they give up part of their childhood, it means something nice is in store for them later in their life, a bit like yin and yang. You get back what you have earned and you have that nice surprise coming for you just around the corner."

"That's amazing," she admitted without irony. "I'm quite moved by that you've nailed me. How do you do that?"

He caressed her hand, then, feeling brave, he bent down and kissed her nicotine scented finger tips.

115

"You have to be sensitive," he said. "I mean attuned to the way the hidden world works. I don't think it's something you can learn really you are either born with it or not, that kind of sensitivity. It's how I see you are open, passionate, positive. How I know you're a dreamer but positive too and it's how I predict you *will* be happy in the future."

He wasn't looking at the hand now but back into her eyes.

"Thank you," she said and leant forward to kiss him on the cheek. He kissed her back, first on her left cheek, then on her right and feeling a willingness and no resistance, he moved over and kissed her on the lips. She moved in towards him and kissed him back - his eyes were closed.

Suddenly, there was a hefty bang – oh crap, the door – he opened his eyes to find Alice standing over them, plate of food in one hand, beer in the other and a foul look on her horrified face. There was silence, emptiness. It was one of those frozen moments when people sit stock still in the apparent belief that this will render them invisible.

"I better be going," said the blonde. She turned to Rob. "See you round."

Alice stared at her as she left, "Yeah, see you Mandy, I think dad's up at the house. I'm sure he'll be delighted to know what you've been up to with my date."

Mandy pushed past her, mouth smirking round her fag. For a moment they stood together angry with each other, all ripe and pouty. Rob knew he was supposed to be feeling subdued because he'd done a bad thing but he was only a man and he couldn't help feeling inappropriate again.

When Mandy had gone Alice turned back to him. "Nice, I mean that's really classy."

"I didn't know," Rob gasped honestly. "If I'd known she was your sister I might not have..."

"Yeah well, don't stress it 'cos she's not my sister, she's my *mum*." Alice stalked off, slamming the door behind her so hard that one of the glass panels cracked.

Rob leapt up and shot after her, at least partly because he didn't fancy getting blamed for the smashed window.

"She can't be," he said in her ear, panting a bit because she was travelling at a fair lick back up the garden powered by the internal combustion engine of her indignation.

"I mean I know botox and that, it's amazing what they can do these days and her tramp stamp and false nails and whatever, but she's no way

116

old enough to be your *mum*."

"Okay – step-mum," but that doesn't make you any less of a sex criminal," she huffed and he had to let her go because there were people and it looked like he was pestering her.

He let her gain a twenty yard head start and set off after her. As he chased her up the garden, he more or less crashed into Crazy Al and Louise coming the other way. She was doing her best to flirt with him, hanging off his arm and staring up into his eyes but he seemed to be in his own mad world. He was muttering to himself and pushing his ginger wrap-over back into place.

Rob was hoping to avoid them but it wasn't happening. As he moved to detour round the pond, Louise hailed him. He could see she was finding Al hard work and here was her opportunity to ditch him.

"Hi Rob!" It was too sunny, too bezzie mates. Usually she was keen to show him who was boss but it didn't feel like that now. Trouble was, Rob didn't feel like capitalising on it because he didn't want to get too close to Al at the moment either, not close enough for a half nelson say, or a flying crucifix.

"What you doing?" asked Louise sounding desperate. "We're just hanging out aren't we Mr Allonby?"

Crazy made a 'mnur?' noise like someone had just woken him up. He glanced sidelong at Rob and recognition dawned.

"Hey? How's it going?" he demanded gruffly. "Where's she at?"

"I was just off to keep her company," Rob said, hoping this might segue to a quick exit. He was heading off when Al lunged at him.

'No, not again,' Rob thought, feeling a bit sick but Al grabbed him in a manly embrace and gave him a cuddle, patting his back.

"You're alright you, you're a good lad. We had a right laugh before wrestling didn't we eh? A great laugh, I got fucking soaked mind." His breath was sweet and fruity with whiskey. He leaned in and stage whispered into Rob's ear. "You look after our Alice or I'll fucking kill you." He patted Rob's rump affectionately.

Louise stood back during all this, completely baffled and feeling like a bit of a spare part.

"I didn't know you too were so close," she teased bleakly, trying to crowbar her way back into the conversation. It had been a golden opportunity to leave yet here she still was watching them transfixed as they cuddled. Rob managed to extricate himself, grabbed Louise by the

117

arm instead and pulled her over to him. She came willingly and giggly, with wine.

"You've got a lovely garden," he told Al. "Lots of plants and that, nice summerhouse."

Al leaned over conspiratorially. "There's rats under that summerhouse, rats big as Scottie dogs. I had to poison the big hulking bastards."

Louise tutted, she seemed to sober up quick. She was a veggie, a greenie and she nagged now and again about recycling paper in the office. Rob nodded approvingly which gave Al renewed impetus.

"They were gambolling about on the lawn here like kittens. Hanging about under the bird table waiting for the starlings to kick scraps off for 'em. Big plate of poison I put out – bright blue it was. Next morning they'd had every scrap, dragged the plate into the bushes to have a go at it in private and that was the last I saw of those fuckers."

He was quite triumphant, puffed up and pleased with himself.

"Great stuff," Rob rejoined enthusiastically, get rid of the scaly-tailed buggers."

Louise simmered. It was clearly a moral dilemma for her, given she was trying to suck up to Al, a valued advertising contact with deep pockets. She threw Rob a furious look which seemed to imply he should have been on her side, even without knowing in advance what that was. She drew away from Rob. He had casually draped his arm round her hip and she wriggled out from under it.

He glanced over her blankly like he didn't care.

"I think it's horrible you would harm a rat – it's probably more frightened of you than you are of it."

Rob frowned. "Yeah, but my urine doesn't carry Weil's disease!"

Louise couldn't avoid a little squeak of horror and Crazy chuckled to himself like no-one else could hear.

Rob shook his head, as if baffled by what had come out of his mouth.

"I haven't used that chat-up line for a while. I remember it going down better."

Al choked on that one then leant over on tip-toes and ruffled Rob's hair like he was some young scamp caught scrumping apples.

"Yeah, I'd er, better get off," Rob stumbled, unable to think of even the most trite excuse for chasing off up the garden in pursuit of Alice. He caught up with her at the side of the house where he stumbled upon water butts, a Russian vine and a small white dog tied to the downpipe fizzing and apoplectic with noisy rage.

"Fuck off Hamish," she was saying, "or I'll drop kick you over that fence."

"I'd better watch out then, he joshed dryly, or I'll be over there as well.

"You bloody will you bastard, getting nasty with my mum, well, practically my mum and to think I was going to let you have a go on me. You can have a tug now 'cos that's all you're getting."

"Hey," he put in and thinking it through, felt genuinely ticked off about this one.

"You get to shag Jayden and whoever else most likely and I'm supposed to just let it go, be all mature about it, no biggie. But I look at another woman, okay maybe more than look, but definitely *less* than shag, and you kick off like it's Wuthering Heights!"

He was pleased with his literary reference. She pursed her lips and did the tongue poke the website told him meant bad news.

"Hmm, well yeah but it's nothing you know? *Less* than nothing. It's just like blowing your nose having sex with someone you don't care about. I think it's a bit mental of you to keep going on about it."

She fidgeted as bit like she was at least having the good grace to be a bit uncomfortable about the whole thing. Not that, he realised, he had any right to a stake in her past, yet he did feel upset about her and Jayden; he wondered her and who else? He felt a tart pang of jealousy - it wasn't an emotion he was used to dealing with.

She blew fag smoke and managed a smirk. She looked tough and tarty and made him want her again.

"I mean that's nothing at all compared to say, an abortion. It's nothing I remember much about even, though there was something about him made it memorable."

He turned away towards the side gate which lead to the front of the house and she shovelled past him to stop him going, though she'd seemed keen for his departure when he wanted to stay.

"I don't want to know the details," he told her, aghast. "What makes you think I'd want to know? Anyway, *what* abortion? That must have been horrible for you."

She shrugged. "Two so far. That's no big deal either really, any girl who tells you she's bothered by it is lying. I just meant that there's shit that happens which is bigger than just a few quick goes on someone in the disabled."

"Disabled what?" he was baffled.

"The disabled toilet. You know, the one at work. Everybody does it there. Don't tell me you haven't."

He didn't tell her.

"Look, I've got to go. Sorry again about wrestling your dad into the fountain and French kissing your mum - It was an embarrassing episode all round – let's never speak of it again."

She laughed and relented a little.

"Well, you don't have to go. We can go in the library if you like and do shots of Sambuca - they always make me horny." She bounced her bosoms off him. It worked but he *had* to go, he'd promised. Anyway, if he changed his mind now he would feel defeated, conquered, as though she was in charge. Did it matter if he got to sleep with her, that was supposed to be the final aim after all? He thought of Jayden and decided it did.

"I don't know if it would be such a good idea me hanging round with your young milf around the place. You never know, she might get restless in the middle of the night and fancy a bit of rough."

Alice snorted, "You aren't rough, so get that out of your head. *She's* rough. Soon as mum and dad got divorced she was all over him, a bit before n'all probably."

"Where's your real mum now?"

"Living in a villa in Portugal, skin the colour of American tan tights and always pissed. She shags waiters and rings me in the middle of the night to cry down the phone and tell me how happy she is now she's not with that bastard."

Rob nodded appreciatively. "The good life eh. Some day, if you stick with me and play your cards right, that might be you."

She laughed. "You're a class act." Then, a bit more serious, she turned to him and came in close, looking up at him.

"Stay. Please, I want you to."

He wondered about wheedling out of it but realised he didn't want to.

"Okay, look if you can clear it with your old man, then I'll do it."

"I can wrap him round my little finger," she told him, holding up the finger to demonstrate.

As he followed her back up the side of the house, she shot him a look over her shoulder.

"Anyway - tramp stamp? If you don't like my skin illustration you better look for a chick who's not got one."

He pulled a 'whatever' face.

They stood in the back garden by the vast and baroque conservatory – it truly was the biggest and most elaborate Rob had ever laid eyes on.

Alice grabbed a couple of beers for them from a passing waiter.

"I'll make sure Al's fast asleep before anything happens," she promised. "That's if anything's going to, you've been about as bad as you could have been since you got here."

"I can always leave... Sue's expecting me to go round and do chores, she's going to be upset."

Alice tongue poked again, then hair stroked and sidled up to him.

"I'll give her something more than that to be upset about. Just wait and see what I'm going to do to her little boyfriend. She won't want you when I'm finished with you."

Rob was genuinely scared. There seemed to be a common thread running through the stuff he was learning about women - they were *scary*. He'd never been frightened of them when they were aloof and unobtainable, same as you aren't frightened of tigers in the zoo until you jump into the cage with them, then they aren't just pretty, they smell feral, they have teeth and they satiate appetites.

Alice laughed at him.

"You look horrified! You're okay? I won't hurt you, you want me to be gentle with you honey, hey?"

Rob put on his too proud to beg face. "I won't respond to that. It is beneath my dignity."

That's how Rob came to be standing in icy darkness at 3am at the top of Crazy Al's marble staircase wearing only his Superman boxer shorts. There were a few minor details to clear away before he reached that point but these could be easily handled. Al was sweet-talked by Alice, who also threatened her step-mother with exposure and disgrace in blood-chilling terms Lucrezia Borgia would have been proud of.

Alice's young man could stay for 'a sleepover' Al called it, as though they were both 12 and Alice still lived at home. The pair of them were too drunk to find the car, never mind drive it back to town so they made no complaint. It was agreed Rob would take one of the first floor guest rooms. Alice meanwhile got the much larger downstairs bedroom with en-suite and dressing room, which looked as though it might have been originally built as a granny annexe.

The other guests left slowly and drunkenly, topped up with booze and burnt meat. Louise first tried to drag Rob away with her, ostensibly to save him from the faux par of overstaying his welcome but when Al waved her away and said Rob was going to stay behind to try his malt whiskey collection. She gave Rob such a soulful look of jealous longing and he felt sure she was his for the taking. The early evening was an embarrassment to be sure. They sat in the snug as Al called it, a little room with a full bar in the corner with oak panelled sides and leather bar stools. It even had optics with mirrors behind them and horse brasses on the walls; the whole Rose and Crown experience. Rob almost laughed at the tackiness of it all when he went in but could see the gruff enjoyment on Al's ruddy face and realised it wouldn't be a good idea. Al made him drink whiskey which he hated, then asked him to tell the difference between various sorts which all tasted like petrol to him.

After a couple of drinks, Alice sat on Rob's knee and he sneaked plenty of looks over to see whether this made Mandy jealous - if it did she hid it well. She didn't sit on Al's knee, just snuggled up to him on a big leather chair. Al swirled his straw coloured liquor round his stubby crystal tumbler and held forth on its contents.

"This one's an Islay, you can taste the peat and the seaweed on the beach. It needs a little drop of water to open up the flavour."

It tasted as bad as all the others, maybe a little worse. Rob was feeling both drunk and nauseous but also horny, as Alice was fidgeting in a way which had that effect on him.

Al had the demeanour of a practised drunk, his manner hardly changed as he downed tumbler upon tumbler of straight whiskey. His speech was slower perhaps but not slurred, he didn't stumble on trips to the loo, or crash down with clumsy abandon in his leather chair upon his return as Rob was wont to do. All that changed perhaps was the quality of his conversation which became a little coarser and more combative, his laughter a bit harsher, louder and more braying.

After one such bellow of red-faced laughter at some flirty put-down Mandy had aimed at Rob, he leaned over and grabbed Rob so firmly by the knee he almost yelped.

Crazy Al fixed Rob with a rheumy eye and said, "In the world today, there's two types of men son, those who talk bollocks and those who have them. Which sort are you hey son? Which sort?"

He patted the knee and leaned back into his chair nodding to himself, pleased with his great saw of wisdom. Rob found himself nodding too and heard the girls murmuring drunken burbles of approval and admiration at this salty aphorism.

Al was obviously pleased with the reaction, "And you can write that down son, you can write it down and take it to the bank."

He looked at Rob expectantly, as though he actually anticipated that he would whip out a notebook and scribble it down. When it became apparent this wasn't going to happen, Al looked a little crestfallen but cheered himself up by pouring them another quadruple whiskey.

"Irish this time son, feel the burn. I like 'em all though, we have Catholic tastes in this family son, Catholic tastes.

"What, young boys?" Emboldened by the booze, Rob felt it was okay to have a go at a quip.

Al spluttered on his dram and Mandy tutted and rolled her eyes.

Alice leaned over from where she was perched on the wide leather arm of Rob's chair and whispered in his ear, "We are Catholic you knob, no paedo jokes."

He knew then that the longer he stayed down here, the more likely he was to say something bad they wouldn't have forgotten by the morning. It was time to go, no doubt about it.

He nudged Alice in the ribs a few times to let her know he wanted to get off up the wooden stairs but she didn't take the hint, she was getting stuck into the malt with apparent relish. There were another three generous tumblers full of petrol before Alice decided independently that it was perhaps time for bed.

"Got to get off," she whispered drunk and sleepily as if to herself. "I'll show himself up to his room," and she tousled Rob's hair lazily.

There's something exciting about being in a strange house with new people. Rob was caught up in this and though he hadn't enjoyed the whiskey it had certainly done its job, assuming that job was to make him feel more divorced from his own body than he had done since smoking too much skunk in college. These two elements combined made the whole arrangement seem alien to him. Half the time that made him want to go with it as passively as possible, the other half he felt spooked and paranoid, worried Crazy Al and Mandy were whispering about him when he went out to the loo, concerned his spillage on the seat in said

123

loo would be considered a massive faux pas.

So when Alice announced it was time to go he was greatly relieved and went meekly on his merry way.

He was all ready to tumble up the wooden stairs to Bedfordshire, probably holding Alice's hand and dripping along after her but the moment they left the lounge bar she did a quick left into what looked like an office, pinned him against a filing cabinet in the darkness and stuck her meaty tongue down his throat. He could feel her metallic stud rattling around in there and panicked about getting his teeth chipped but she pushed her breasts up against him which were sizeable and firm and squashed only under significant pressure. She started grinding too but that didn't have quite the effect she might have hoped for, since he was tucked under a duvet of drunkenness and almost entirely oblivious to the erotic potential of what was going on. It was just a chore to be undergone before he could get to bed, like cleaning his teeth or setting the alarm.

"Mmm," she said breaking for air. "You're a good kisser. Since you've been a good boy this evening and not dunked my dad or felt-up my pretend mam, you can meet me down here later and we'll see what you're made of."

"Just flesh and blood," he whispered forlornly, "I am merely a man like any other."

"Yeah, well we'll see how much of a man" she said and reached down with a firm hand to investigate - somewhat roughly - which did the job where her earlier attempts had failed. Satisfied with this and grinning to herself, she took him up to his room, kissed him again at the door and slammed it behind him, shouting, "See you in the morning then," plenty loud enough for the rest of the house to hear.

Rob made an effort to get his trousers off. Rolled them down as far as his knees, toppled onto the bed and fell asleep where he lay.

In his mind, he conversed.

Rob: I'm finding women easier to talk to I think.

Sonof: You had trouble talking? Anyone can talk. Too much talking can be part of the problem.

Rob: Yeah, maybe, I dunno. It feels like progress to me. I've struggled with it. Mostly, if I fancy a girl, it screws me up so I can't even do basic stuff properly; talking, walking, breathing, they all become an effort.

Sonof: Yeah, not breathing though. Must be a bit of a turn-off, unless

124

you are hoping to get a sympathy shag by falling unconscious.

Rob: Do you think that might work?

Sonof: At this stage I wouldn't rule anything out.

Rob awoke in cold and darkness, jerked from sleep by the loudness of his own snoring, consumed by the feeling of dread which sometimes came over him for no good reason. He could not remember where he was, nor why and he assumed something terrible and life changing must have happened for which he was in some way at fault. He spent a little time in silent assessment of his body, moving fingers, toes, arms, legs, running a hand over his face, his torso, his genitals just to make sure nothing was broken or missing. At length he was satisfied he was whole and unharmed, which probably meant he was not in hospital. His head was dazed and fizzing with wasps, he had the start of a headache grumbling at him from the place his spine joined his skull and his mouth tasted like a graveyard for small mammals.

He deduced he had been drinking alcohol, waking alone somewhere strange after a forgotten night on the booze. Perhaps he was in police custody? This particular thought alarmed him and his stomach turned. He belched whiskey fumes and the medicinal scent acted much like Proust's tea and Madeleine cakes. Memories surfaced from some distant time: childhood; last night. He remembered Al, purple-faced and spit-flecked with laughter, head back and gasping for air at one of his own jokes. He remembered wrestling, remembered moist lips, breasts, though he couldn't quite remember whose.

Something was nagging at him, it was the reason his body clock had raised him at this ungodly hour from sleep.

He peered down at his Seiko watch, a familiar old pal. He couldn't see it in the dark but knew its battered case and scratched face well. Outmoded and unfashionable though it was, it had an inscription cut into the base metal on the back which read, 'Christmas 1996, love mum', so he wore it and tonight, was exceptionally glad he did because unlike modern watches, it had a button he could press which lit up the display in a thin urine-coloured glow, bright enough for him to read the time: 3.00am.

That opened other avenues in his baffled brain and although many of the major routes were closed for essential maintenance, a thought made its way round his synaptic branch lines and eventually found a connection to Alice. He was at her parents' place and was supposed to meet her at 3am. That was it. So nothing *too* bad then? The memory of the fountain business filtered through too, but that was nothing a mop couldn't fix. Everything was fine and he sank into a warm bath of relief.

Hey, he wasn't even late for the date; result.

He sat up in bed, head swimming, swang his feet round onto the carpet and pitched forward, when his jeans - still lassoing his ankles – unstylishly tripped him up. He flipped his trainers and socks off which were still fountain-damp, then removed the equally moist jeans and made his way to the door in pants and a T-shirt. On a whim at the door, he peeled the T-shirt off and threw it back on the bed figuring if he was going to the trouble of turning up for this, he wanted it to be pretty clear he wasn't expecting a game of cards. He felt he'd missed opportunities the previous day by taken things too slowly and hadn't pushed his agenda enough. He was mad with himself for not trying harder but before him lay an open goal, this was a chance not even *he* could miss.

He wished he had condoms and made a mental note to carry some around with him in future... Alice would have some surely, she certainly needed them from what she'd been telling him.

The door opened smooth and noiseless, the hardwood floor in the landing was tight and new and didn't creak. It was dark, of course, but there was a big arched window at the end of the landing through which a little moonlight dappled. It illuminated his way down the hall to the left turn which led to the big marble flight of stairs and the ground floor where Alice's room lay silent and waiting. He wondered if she had woken too and was sitting up in bed anticipating his knock, giggly, excited. This got him turned on despite the fact it was cold and he reckoned the central heating must have gone off at midnight.

He padded cautiously down the corridor, squinting into the vague light, dodging an occasional table with a huge vase perched on it and banging his head painfully on a row of metal coat hooks. He reached the end of the hall and turned onto the stairway which opened out onto the marble-floored atrium. It was lighter here because of the glass dome and the white floor below. Through the panes the fountain glittered, the whole scene was pale and eerie, cool and frosty, a fitting abode for an ice princess but the princess he was heading for was warm and giving, buxom and pliable.

He stepped onto the cold marble stairs and stifled the impulse to gasp as the chill gripped his feet. He felt out for the carved oak banister, reassuringly sturdy beneath his palm and for some reason he counted the stairs in his head as he tentatively descended; one, two, three... seventeen, eighteen, each one the same as the last, smooth and cold, regular and even. As he went past the halfway mark, an excitement grew inside him. The butterflies in his stomach were active and he fought a raging impulse to snigger out loud.

What he was doing, what they were about to *start* doing, was outrageously naughty. This was living, this was what being young ought to be about.

He could see next to nothing, though the house was not entirely dark, the silvery shards filtering through the double-glazed dome complete with stars winking bleakly though the roof-light. Thankfully, he could make out the vaguest outline of the flight of stairs leading down to the ground floor stretching away in front of him.

The first few steps took him an age to dismount. He paused after each one, holding his breath to make sure he hadn't disturbed the sleepers upstairs but as he descended, each step was so solid and silent, he became confident and surer-footed and started to make quicker progress.

When he thought about what he was doing, his stomach squirmed with excitement, he couldn't remember feeling this alive since he was a kid. A memory fleeted through his consciousness of being with gangs of mates out on the wasteland near where he lived, running wild and feeling like there was nothing more to life than the pure enjoyment of it. He stopped for a moment to relish being in it, inhaled the room-freshener scented air and felt the night wrapped around him.

He relished the feeling and the thrill of it made him reckless. He took two or three more stairs at a trot, his bare feet slapping on marble tiles, then one more but this one felt very different. Something was under his foot as it came down with his full weight, something warm and furry, like a slipper left on the stairs but it crunched under his foot like a bag of broken crockery. There was a sound too, the mound under his sole wheezed unnaturally with a high, hopeless whine and a frail cracking.

What the hell was it?

Though he couldn't work it out, it was sickening and it filled him with alarm. For a moment he stood completely still, his weight bearing down on the bag of fur. Then he leapt away, down the last half dozen stairs to the ground floor and over to the nearest wall where he patted desperately for a light switch. He couldn't find one at first, then began to panic but figured if he put his hand inside one of the doors there would be a light for whichever room it was. It worked, he'd found the bar. He used its jolly English pub glow to find a chunkier light switch on the white wall of the atrium and the whole place lit up suddenly and alarmingly, all bright lights glaring at once and to make matters worse, the bloody fountain started up spurting pink spray which sounded unnatural and noisy in the silence that surrounded it.

Rob dashed back over to the stairs, hoping he'd somehow imagined what he had felt but no, there it was, about six stairs up, a white shape in the centre of the pale step. He bent down to see what it was. The dog. The West Highland terrier which had been tied to the down pipe at the side of the house when he'd threatened to leave. And now, how fully, roundly and deeply did he wish he had walked out of the gate as intended.

The miniature yappy thing was silent now, its eyes fully open as if in an alarmed state, his small pink tongue poking from the corner of its furry mouth.

"Shit." He said. There was nothing else *to* say.

He felt like crying, the whole episode seemed deeply unfair. He was angry at something and realised it was the dog. Furry little fucker. How dare it?

He forced himself to look at it again, it didn't seem dead, perhaps it was only having a nap with its tongue out? He poked it gingerly with an icy big toe but it showed no signs of life. He shuddered, must have crushed the breath clean out of it with the whole of his weight coming down.

God – what now?

He thought it through for a few moments, surveying the dead dog. Maybe he could do what they'd do in a sitcom, dash out and get an exact replica dog which would fool everyone into thinking it was indeed Hamish... until it unexpectedly had a litter of puppies. He tried to think where he might find a 24-hour pet shop. Shit, there really was nothing for it but to go and see Alice as planned.

He headed off rather less surreptitiously than before. By the time he stood at her door, he didn't feel angry any more, just sad and as deflated as the dog. He felt the way he often did when he was copping flak at work for something which wasn't his fault. Tentatively he tapped on her door, shivering in his boxer shorts. There was no answer. He tapped again a bit harder, trying to make the rap seem businesslike rather than playful with the sort of sound that said, 'I've just trodden on your dog,' rather than 'let me in for some recreational shagging'.

There was a sleepy whisper from inside.

"S'that you?"

"Yeah, it's me. Are you decent?"

She opened the door in her bra and pants.

"I hope not."

He was supposed to be on serious dog homicide business but he couldn't help admiring her body, this was the best view of it he'd had so far and the best he was likely to get now he'd squashed her puppy. What a shame, what a bloody waste.

"Come in then, I've got something for you." She made it sound enthusiastically filthy.

"Mmm, yeah," he held the door as she tried to pull him into her bedroom. "Look, I've got something for you too. I'm really sorry about this, you can't imagine how fucking sorry to be quite honest."

He took her hand and led her, puzzled and compliant, back through the marble hall towards the foot of the stairs. He'd thought maybe they would scoop the animal up in a coat and take it out and hide it in the wooded approach to the house. It would be taken by foxes, go down as 'escaped and lost' rather than trampled on by an oaf. He didn't have the forethought to warn her properly and only gave her a 'watch out' so when she saw the dead bundle she screamed, rich and throaty, more of a bellow really. Unsurprisingly, it echoed all up and down the centre of the house, bounced off the glass dome and came back again.

"Shit, no!" He wondered whether to put his hand over her mouth. "You'll have everyone up," but just as he said it, there was an inevitable commotion at the top of the stairs and Al appeared, wild haired and ashen, his red comb-over dangling down over his left cheek.

"What the flying fuck's going on here then?" he demanded, lumpenly. Mandy was behind him wearing something skimpy. Alice looked down at the dog then threw her head in the air and wailed, "Daaaad!"

Her face crumpled and she began to cry, not quiet stifled sobs but a rage of tears and straight away Rob was alarmed and embarrassed by this sudden show of extreme emotion, especially as it was all his fault and there was bugger all he could do about it. He stood staring at her, horribly transfixed and sneaked another look at the dog corpse then back at her.

There was a storm of emotion, tears flew from her eyes horizontally. There was snot. Wailing. Rob felt he ought to comfort her, or at least to be seen to do that. He wanted to cruise in smoothly and put his arm around her, let her and Al and Mandy know he was there for her in the depths of her despair but he was standing there naked except for his Superman boxers and felt terribly vulnerable. He found he could not move, only stare despairingly, pleadingly, at her, hoping she might catch his eye and take from it his heartfelt desire that she should protect him from the consequences of what he had done.

Al's eyes bulged, his mouth hung open, he flew down the stairs on winged slippers.

"What's the matter angel? What's happened?"

He shot a glance at Rob, pregnant with malice then turned his attention back to his angel. He was halfway down when she spoke again, bubbling, broken.

"It's Hamish."

"Hamish? What's happened petal?" they met in a hug at the foot of the stairs, he wrapped her up and she buried her face in his fleecy beige dressing-gown. She was smothered in the fabric for a few moments then blew her nose on it quite loudly.

Rob, alarmed, under-dressed, guilty as Judas and frozen to his nipples, could barely suppress a wheeze of mirth. He tried to hide it in a cough, one which might show he was overwhelmed by the emotion of the occasion but Al shot him the look again.

"What's the matter with the little fella then angel, has he gone missing again? He'll be alright, like a bad penny he always turns up does little scruff!"

There was a shriek from the stairs, it was Mandy on her way down, eyes wide, blonde hair everywhere like Lady Macbeth.

"He's there!" she pointed a silver varnished nail.

Al turned, saw the crushed body laid out on the cold marble like a cadaver. He made a lowing noise replete with disbelief, shock and grief; his curious song rang out long into the broken night.

CHAPTER 7

'Johnno!' the blog of Robert Johnson, July 21:
"You are alive, you are a source of energy, like electricity. You have light and heat which draw people to you and make them want to possess you.
You attract them simply by being what you are. You have no need of them, you have no need to perform for them or make them want you. Just do what you do.
They need you like they need a diamond ring or a poem or a flower, simply because of what it is. Let them learn you like a poem, let them covet you like a diamond, let them pick you like a flower."

"So, good evening then, overall," Sam said.

"Yeah," Rob sighed then grinned, looked at Sammy over the pub table and laughed out loud at the bizarre mess he was in.

Sam slurped at a pint of Guinness and frowned thoughtfully.

"How'd they take it then, when it all became apparent that Hamish was no more?"

"Mmm, well Alice was as bad as you might think then a bit worse. Randy Mandy was a gem over it though, she was crying and that but she said I wasn't to know that Hamish sometimes liked to sleep on the stairs, which I thought was very even-handed of her considering."

He took a gobful of cider and shuddered as if the back bar of the Retreat had suddenly become unseasonably chilly. The Retreat was a laid back, studenty place, an old hippie of a bar, worn but still cool with Bauhaus art prints on the walls and indie pop on the stereo. There were cute young bar staff and cute young clientèle. It was the sort of place a brightish young thing like Rob should feel comfy with his fashionably cropped hair and studied air of unconcern, but right now he would feel ill at ease in his mother's womb.

"You're still freaked out by it though aren't you?" Sam asked semi-sympathetically, pushing back ginger fringe and hiding a smirk. Rob thought - not for the first time during his précis of the previous night's events - that Sam was enjoying the whole thing immensely.

"Yeah, I am. I can still feel the bones cracking under my foot."

Sam grimaced. "Poor Hamish."

"Yeah, poor daft little fucker more like. All the comfy warm places to sleep in that big house and he had to pick the effing stairs."

Theirs was a lunchtime pint, a rare treat in these days of lunch being for lightweights, and booze at lunchtime being for dipsomaniac dinosaurs.

"So what you going to do about Alice?"

Rob had been putting off that decision. He was still numb from the fraught hour standing in his boxer shorts watching the Crazy family weep over Hamish. Al tenderly wrapped his lifeless body in a shroud made from a tea-towel that Mandy had fetched from the kitchen featuring scenes from the English Lakes. Nobody actually said to his face it was all his fault, if not an act of murder, it was surely manslaughter due to negligence. Eventually, everyone went back to bed.

There had been much talk of 'the accident' and at one point Al turned to him with mad red eyes and said to him 'if only you had looked, if you'd just *looked*' in the way you would if someone had just mown down your child in their speeding car. Rob felt about as bad as if he had done.

He told them he'd woken up parched from the whiskey and not knowing the layout of the house, decided to head down to the kitchen for a glass of water. It was an innocent enough excuse and they bought it, it didn't matter after all, the damage was done. Hamish was laid out in the conservatory in his dog basket, ready for the burial service in the morning. Alice said nothing. She was still crying as she headed off to bed. Rob said sorry a few more times to Mandy, she gave him a hug and pressed her big round bosoms up against him before he headed back to his room. He felt inappropriately horny and guilty all at once; he didn't sleep much.

In the morning, Alice said nothing during the drive back into town.

She dropped him off at the communal front door of his flat block and drove off without even a wave.

"What you finding out about the fairer sex then, would you say?" Sam wanted to know.

"I'm finding they're all screwed up."

"Yeah?" said Sam. "You are too."

"How so? I'm a normal, well-adjusted example of early manhood."

"All this stuff with your mother for a start. You need to come to terms with it mate and move on."

"It's done, it was hard but it's all in perspective now."

"Denial ain't just a river in Egypt baby."

Rob ignored this cue to spill his innermost demons and went to the bar for an ill-advised second round instead. Sam demurred only slightly and tucked into the fresh pint, stopping first to admire the shamrock traced in the cream.

"Then there's Sue to consider," Rob went on. "She was in Going Forward most of the morning but when she came out she made a big fat deal of ignoring me. I can't imagine that she'll be all that delighted about me blowing her out for Alice."

Sam shrugged. "Yeah well, say it was for work, that it was all about Al. Skinny blonde bitch is so obsessed with graft she might even believe you and even if she doesn't, there won't be a lot she can do about it however much it gets on her pert little tits 'cos she knows she would have done the same if it meant cozying up to a client as big as Crazy Al."

"Killing his puppy," intoned Rob, "does not count as 'cozying up' to him."

"Yeah, yeah, but she doesn't know the stupid dog's dead does she? Alice won't have put out a press release on it, she's on a day off today anyway, isn't she?"

"Mmm," Rob agreed.

"Then there's Lou," Sam went on, halfway down the new pint already. "What are your intentions towards our glorious leader young man?"

Rob sighed a long hissy sigh. "Oh I don't fucking know. I mean I fancy her of course I do, but then I fancy Sue and she is well scary. All three of them scare me if I'm honest in their own unique and special ways. They'd all have me for breakfast. Well, that's what you're hoping for anyway, keep your eyes on the prize."

An inordinately loud rock track came on the stereo, something old and raucous which meant they couldn't talk.

"What the fuck was that?" Sam wanted to know when things had simmered down to another song with tremulous guitars and a banshee wail.

"Iggy and the Stooges, Search and Destroy," Rob parroted.

"And what the fuck is this?"

"Cocteau Twins, Sugar Hiccup."

Sam made a 'how?' face.

"My mum had a big record collection, probably the same one the old geezer who runs this place has got."

"So then, Sue. You go and see her this aver and tell her you had some serious sucking up to do at the weekend with a major client. Leave out the dead pet bit. Lou, you need to sort out. I heard she was right up your arse in Going Forward this morning, banging on about what a fine upstanding young fellow you are and how she has you earmarked for great things. The story I heard was that when she said 'great things' she went all Mae West, Sue had a cow moment and Jayden and that lot all did a dirty laugh."

Rob looked despairingly at a Klee print on the wall. It was a giant golden fish surrounded by other, brightly coloured fish in red, purple and blue. Rob felt like one of the tiny fish in the background, doubtless about to get gobbled up by the huge gold one which was the centre of attention.

"What's the problem mate? You're getting what you wanted aren't you? Hot female attention likely to end in a shag and Lou - let me remind you - is very hot indeed."

Rob stood and picked up his brown leather jacket ready to go, that was sometimes the only way to get Sam out of a bar.

"Yes she *is* hot but that's not right, is it? Senior managers aren't supposed to be hot. Their moral turpitude is supposed to be mirrored in their physical repulsiveness."

There was a curious atmosphere at work that afternoon. Sue made a big deal out of not talking to him even though she was sitting across the desk from him for most of it. She hid behind her monitor, pale and angular, didn't flirt round the side of it, or slide her bare foot under the desk until she found his leg as she had been doing the last few weeks.

She wore her glasses because she said her contacts were irritating her and her eyes were indeed red and tired looking. The specs were obviously a few years old, unfashionable and slightly school-marmish. They made her look vulnerable. Seeing her there exposed in the ridiculous specs made Rob feel sorry for her and guilty. He was feeling guilty about almost everything else so this just added to the pile.

When he went to make tea he had to pass Alice's department, Leisure Advertising. It had an array of desks or work pods as they were supposed to call them and although she wasn't around (thankfully) she had clearly been busy texting all her mates to let them know the depths of his depravity she'd been dragged to over the weekend. This was clearly evident because they either ignored him, or threw mortified looks his way as he walked past, then whispered about him loudly as he headed off up the office.

During one such pass, he slowed down and had a look at Alice's frowsy mess of a desk, with its geranium hand cream from Neal's Yard, its multi-coloured Post-it notes, moist wipes, lip-liner and various shades of highlighter pens scattered over it.

He was thoroughly alarmed to see a small red frame just under her monitor with a little photograph of Hamish staring back at him, all cheeky faced and wet nosed.

"Hey, what you looking at?" demanded one of Alice's close personals from the next pod.

"I really don't think she'd want you going through her stuff, do you? It's a bit... stalkerish." She pulled an 'oh no, he's a stalker' face.

He hadn't been going through anything, not unless you can go through stuff with your eyes but he felt it was incumbent on him as a PUA not to show too much weakness at a time like this, so he affected a sort of sneer and carried on with his tray of mugs.

"He's such a bastard," the girl told her mate with great satisfaction as he left.

Well, that's good then. Good that he was a bastard, even though he hadn't deliberately hurt the animal and wouldn't have, not for anything. As far as Rob was concerned, he hadn't even been careless.

Then it was back to his desk and Sue's stony silence.

"Here's your tea Sue." ... grunt...

Jude, Alan and Colin, the three wise monkeys, were courteous but quiet and seemed to realise he was in the dog house. They all thought it best not to incur Sue's wrath by palling-up to him too enthusiastically this afternoon.

"Cheers mate," said Colin for his coffee.

"Thank-you hun," said Jude, when he passed her a peppermint tea, she squeezed his hand too.

After a while, with no social stimulation, he was willing to do anything - even his job - in order to make things more bearable. He rang clients he hadn't spoken to for a while to try and take his mind off things. They were reliably rude, or their secretaries were, though he did pick up a surprising bit of business, 'which just goes to show', he thought, 'that you get back what you put in'.

This was also something he was learning rapidly as a PUA. Now he had become fully involved in the world of women, in their spats and schemings, their hatreds and behind-backs, he also realised you should be careful what you wished for.

Later, when Sue had gone out on appointment taking her little black cloud with her, the three wise monkeys were on good form.

"You know that mad bloke Bernie who pushes the empty wheelchair round town?" asked Colin. "He's a salutary lesson about what happens to a man without women."

"Nyeah? How?" Jude wanted to know and had her her head in the drawer where she kept her chocolate raisins.

"We might moan about you in our ear all the time, like a particularly irritating Jiminy Cricket but without you we would all have beards like Bernie's with birds nesting in them and body odour that would stop a rhino."

Alan nodded. "They're not just blokes with tits are they?"

Jude was touched "I'd like to thank you on behalf of my sex. That's the nicest thing you've ever said about women, though admittedly it's coming off a fairly Lenten shortlist. Perhaps now you'd like to tell me what men do for us?"

Colin and Alan ruminated silently for a while. Alan sharpened his pencil into the bin, Colin played with the small rubber sheep on his desk, an advertising leave-behind from a sister paper in the Forest of Dean.

"We lift heavy items," Alan said at length, "and we sometimes do simple DIY tasks around the home, though not me."

Sue was grimacing when she returned to the desk, her tongue poked out in distaste.

"I hate it when men stare at me, like I'm an animal at the zoo, a chimp in a cage, or like I'm one of those lads' mag tarts, oiled up for them to gawp at and think about - it's disgusting."

She sat down, all prim and straight-backed.

Jude put in, "When you get to my age you just get ignored. Middle-aged women might as well be invisible for all the attention we get. No one gives us a second glance, it's like we aren't there any more and that's disgusting too, the way they treat you."

Rob was baffled. "Women say they hate getting stared at by men when they're young, then that they hate getting ignored by them when they're older. Surely you have to be positive about one or other? They can't both be terrible, right? Either you're happy to get the attention, or delighted to be out of it. You can't hate both. When do you win?"

"You just don't understand," Sue said airily.

"Never have, never will," confirmed Jude.

Rob saw Louise three times that afternoon. Once on the stairs, where she seemed to want to stop and talk to him but he scurried past with a cheery, "Hi." The second time she definitely did want to chat because she was walking past his desk nonchalantly on a tour of the troops and came to a standstill leaning over so he could see down her pristine white blouse. She was opening her glossy mouth to speak to him but thankfully his phone rang and it was a client so he saluted her with his pen and she moved on again with a fixed smile.

He didn't really know why he didn't want to talk to her today, it just seemed like one more thing, which he could do without for now and besides, keeping a girl at a distance, denying them your attention, letting them make the running, it was all good as far as the PUAs went.

The third time they encountered he couldn't avoid her. She called him into her office, or at least her secretary did and when he got there she was slipping her black and white houndstooth coat over her skinny shoulders.

"We're going out," she told him over her shoulder, "to the Retreat."

As he listened to Lou talk all about herself and her day, it occurred to him that she reminded him (in subtle yet powerful ways) of Sue. On second thoughts, he thought, perhaps it was actually the other way around, with Sue reminding him compellingly of *Lou*.

Each had starved and trained themselves to an ideal glimpsed in the magazines Rob read over their shoulders, a pair of Spartan twigs just this side of scrawny with hard stomachs and bony arms which left these

137

tough girls fragile and shivering under office air-conditioning.

Then there was the way that Sue was growing out her dyed blonde locks to match Lou's longer, softer and more feminine shoulder-length look. Sue's lipstick had changed too from dark, almost Gothic shades, to light pinky browns which made Lou's glistening lips look like such a coveted pair of jewels.

There were other things too, ticks and habits the two had in common, a slightly brusque dismissiveness when the conversation drifted from the point, a willingness to use the business flirt when necessary. Lou had this and Sue seemed to be cultivating it. When Wee Willie McBean the MD stopped at her desk to bark terse questions about the bottom line earlier in the afternoon, she had been all over him like a cloud of Highland midges, giggling at the jokes he hadn't made and insisting Rob get him a brew even though he was patently keen to bugger off back to his office and left it on her desk without taking a sip once she'd printed him off the figures he'd asked for.

Furthermore, Lou and Sue both relished the slightly behind the curve brand of business jargon which they trotted out at meetings. 'Blue sky thinking... not fit for purpose,' and of course, 'Going forward.'

Everything was going forward in the world of Sue and Lou.

Had Sue even *been* 'Sue' before Lou was brought in to head up the advertising department? She'd been head-hunted from their sister paper in Bristol twelve months earlier and Rob tried to remember she was known as 'Susan' when he started working there? It was evident to him that Sue loved Lou so much, she was probably trying to become her.

Across the conker-dark pub table, the same one where he'd sat with Sam earlier, Lou grinned at him with American white teeth and brushed an invisible blonde hair away from her face.

"I was very impressed by you at the weekend," she told him warmly and he couldn't deny it gave him a bit of a thrill when she said it. He tried not to show it though and sipped his fizzy water so as not to seem too much of an alkie in front of her. When he didn't respond, she felt compelled to, in order to expand on the compliment.

"The way you charmed Mr Allonby, got yourself invited to his home and fitted in so well with the calibre of people there; it's made me see you in a whole new light."

Rob was trying to think who Mr Allonby could be then it dawned on him that this was Alice's surname. He used the information and worked backwards; Alan Allonby was Crazy guy! He didn't want to talk about that right now and thought it best to change the subject, wave it away. It might even make him look suave.

"Did you know," he asked her, "that all Polar Bears are left-handed?"

"No," she admitted, unfazed, "I did not know that. Did you know I used to be married?"

Rob gaped like a goldfish spilled from its bowl and tried to hide it in a gulp of mineral water. The bubbles went up his nose and he had to sneeze into a napkin.

"Well, you told me something I didn't know, so I told you one back," said Lou. "I was maybe your age when I got married. I wish I'd known back then what I know now."

"I wish," said Rob recovering, "that I could throw a snowball and shout catch."

She laughed, which released the tension for him and for her it seemed. He didn't know why she suddenly wanted to talk about her divorce. He had known, of course, the whole office knew as an entity, as an organism but he didn't like to think about these types of life events, it was all a bit too grown-up and made the issue seem less of a game.

He knew her husband had been called Alasdair, that he was a solicitor at one of Cheltenham's big legal firms, that they had been love's young dream for the first year or so but that things had cooled. Not long after she arrived at the paper, she removed his photo from her desk and started going on nights out with the senior management team, rather than rushing home to the Montpellier flat she shared with her husband.

They separated, had a no-contest divorce, each taking out what they'd put in Rob heard, no kids, no mess. The amazing thing was she'd thought he didn't know about it.

She looked at him earnestly. "How do you feel about people sleeping with other people while they're married?"

It seemed like a genuine question. She wasn't trying to tease him, they were talking seriously, communicating like grown-ups. This was terrible, thought Rob. He knew that from a PUA point of view, it could be disastrous.

He did not want to be her friend, her confidante or her counsellor - he wanted to be her lover.

"I don't know what I think," he said at length and he didn't.

"You know what?" she asked, "I don't know either. I thought I did

139

once but that was in another lifetime and things are different now." She looked around the Retreat. "Life is like that painting on the wall."

"Which?" asked Rob. "The one with the big fish?"

"No, not the Klee, the other one, the Kandinsky."

He must have looked blank because she took his face in her hands and pointed it at the painting she meant. Her hands smelled lovely, there was something fresh and floral about them, freesias maybe. He wanted her to hold his cheeks for a while longer so he could smell it some more.

"You have a cute little round face, like an otter," she said.

He didn't think this was a very dignified remark so he ignored it and applied himself to the painting.

"It's called 'Several Circles'," she said. Kandinsky invented Abstract Art you know? Artists don't usually invent a movement all on their own, they generally had help, like Picasso had Braque for cubism."

The painting seemed to him to depict a scene from space. There was a huge black hole to the left of centre and it was sucking planets into it, some huge dark ones and other smaller ones in pretty bright colours, pinks and lilacs, yellows and reds. There were so many planets they overlapped some were so tiny they were barely bigger than pin-pricks, dwarfed by their big brothers.

"It seems a little confused," he said.

"There's so much going on," she agreed, "and everything keeps getting in the way of everything else and we're all heading towards a big black nothing anyway."

"Deep," Rob smirked. "Cheery."

She looked crossly at him. "You're going to get such a slap in a minute, well you would but I suspect you'd probably enjoy it too much."

"No look, you're the boss and I'm like, fascinated by your philosophy of life and that, so do go on."

She pouted like she didn't want to, then did anyway.

"I thought I could impose my moral certainties on another human being but now I realise none of us has the right to do that, it doesn't work and it just leaves you frustrated and unhappy."

"Women think too much," Rob said.

"We do," she agreed gravely. "Or maybe we think the same amount as men, just about the wrong things."

"We think about women, sport, women, music, work and women," Rob said, helpfully.

"Have you got a woman?" she asked him.

"Sorry?"

"You heard. I see a few things, I hear a few things but I'm not sure how much is gossip and how much is true so I'm asking you honestly – have you got a girlfriend? A lover? A partner?"

Rob looked at his watch. "Is that the time, we ought to be getting back 'cos I've got a sales call booked in this afternoon and you've probably got an important meeting about statistics or something."

He'd hoped she would laugh again but she looked at him sternly instead.

"You don't have to tell me of course, it's your life. I've learned not to expect to control people. Hey, d'ya wanna know why I dragged you out here, aren't you curious?"

"Killed the cat."

"Hmm, well, I want you to come with us to the Going Forward symposium at the weekend."

'The what?' Thought Rob silently but there was something more pressing he wanted to ask her about.

He paused for a moment. "Tell me about him?"

"Oh!" she mocked. "I have to tell you all *my* personal information but yours is top-secret is it?"

"You're like the planets painting, I'm like the big goldfish," he said. "All on my own, ignoring the other fish, that's the way I roll baby."

He'd called her baby... and hadn't got the sack!

"He was just a guy I met when I was in my first job at Cavendish House," she said. "I was in sales, he was with the law firm they used. He seemed so much more mature than me, he'd been to uni, he knew more. I was thrilled to have his attention.

"What were you selling?"

She didn't want to tell him but did so anyway because he sat silent and looked into her eyes.

"Perfume. I was one of those perfume counter girls but don't tell anyone. Now I'm big and important it wouldn't look good, it shows you know! But it's not *where* you've come from, It's where you're *going* and that's why I'm inviting you to the weekend.

It's supposed to be just for managers, there will be team building, personal development, it'll be exciting, you'll love it. It's at the Cotswold Water Park in South Cerney. There's a centre there for

141

management development. We spend a weekend out in the wilderness, well, not the wilderness exactly, there's chalets and catering, there's even a bar. It'll do wonders for your personal development."

Back at the office it was more or less home time, though Rob felt he'd done bugger all bar sit in the lounge of the Retreat, which was his idea of time well spent. He was packing up his brown leather man-bag to head home: iPod, copy of the Metro from this morning, Thunderbirds sandwich box which made him feel ridiculous but the PUA website assured him it would be a perfect ice-breaker for meeting women. Apparently, they would be unable to contain their curiosity as to its provenance...

All three wise monkeys had gone and Rob's work pod was populated only by himself and the little black cloud in a dress hunched up opposite him.

"Why have you got that fucking silly child's lunchbox?" asked Sue.

It was the first proper sentence she had spoken to him all day.

'It *works!*' thought Rob.

"My nephew," he came up with, off the top of his head.

Sue glanced at him over her inappropriate eye-wear.

"I didn't know you had a nephew."

He didn't but managed to come out with, "Yeah? Well, there's all sorts you don't know about me pet. I'm an international man of mystery."

She pulled an onion-sucking face at him. "An ocean-going knob-head more like. Do you know I waited in all night last night for you to come and help me out like you said you would? Politeness costs fuck all you know."

He nodded and bowed his head a little in a show of contrition, which he did actually feel, one way and another.

"Look," Sue said, with the air of a woman giving a second chance despite her better judgement. "I *was* busy tonight but I can cancel if you promise to come."

He would have made an excuse even so but she brushed her pale hair away from her face and looked at him through her daft wire-framed glasses in such an honest way, he just nodded and said, "I'll be over at around seven."

"I'll pick you up in the car, it'll be easier," she said, as though that was the end of the matter."

"No," he said, heading out of the door. I'll see you at seven," which was a mistake he reflected as soon as he was in the lift.

It meant getting the bus over to Gloucester, then back again into Cheltenham, just to avoid appearing weak, which he was probably doing anyway by turning up at hers because she'd snapped her fingers.

Besides, he'd gone off this one, hadn't he? It was all about Alice now, or maybe Lou? It was five thirty and there was no earthly point in getting the brace of buses, so he made his way up the Promenade past Montpellier with its snowy, plump-breasted Caryatids, staring sternly into the fading sunshine.

He stopped at the Co-op near the roundabout and bought a lads' mag, felt embarrassed as he paid for it because it seemed like porn. As he left the shop he glanced over at the marble statue of George IV in the centre of the road and noticed that, from this angle, it looked exactly as though the old king was showing his penis to the small stone child who held his hand. 'It's all about perception,' he thought, 'It's all about the angle you see things from.'

He headed up through the genteel Victorian streets of the Suffolks and as he did so, he felt suddenly happy and at peace. Life had plenty to offer him, there was pale blue sky, there were high bright clouds, there was the evening sun which percolated among the buildings around him, teasing honey from the Cotswold stone. On top of that there was the modern world, filled with all its music in his hip pocket. He only had to think of a song which would inspire or elate him and it was there. Oh and there was a phone too if he wanted to speak to his father or his sister, though this was an unlikely scenario; perhaps to Alice then, or Sue... or maybe not. If he wanted to speak to Sam, he could do so, right here in Suffolk Parade.

He went back to the Retreat for the third time that day, sat in the corner on his own, ate spaghetti Bolognaise and drank a pint of cider, then downed another; he wanted to be relaxed for his meeting with Sue.

Sue's house was terrifyingly neat. He wondered whether she had tidied it for him coming. Nothing was out of place, nothing much was even there to *be* out of place. There wasn't a speck of dust on the glass-topped sideboard in the hall. It looked like she'd just put the Dyson away and he guessed it was always like this.

"I need a man around here. They're useful for some things." She gave him a lascivious grin and threw her whole featherweight into a cartoon nudge at his ribs.

"DIY for example. My big light's buggered in the front room, the old boy from B&Q sold me a new fitting."

She ushered him through to the lounge which was even more pristine than the hall. Rob had done a few weeks on property during his induction to the paper and this looked like one of the showhomes they have on new estates, the sort they show prospective buyers what delights their new abode has in store for them, when it's no longer a pile of mud and breezeblocks.

"So, I bought it," she went on, "but I don't know what to do with the wiry bastard - you're useful for that." she beamed at Rob, half expecting him to be delighted at his new found utility. Then her eyes flicked across to something she'd spotted over his shoulder and they hardened into a glare.

"What's *that* doing there?" She yelped and picked up a small scrap of crumpled paper from the floor near the electric fire, which wasn't a fire as such but a TV screen with an image of fish swimming on it.

"Did that drop out of your pocket?"

Alarmed he shook his head. He'd only been there five minutes and already stood accused of making the place look untidy.

She bustled off to deposit the offending dab of litter in the kitchen bin and Rob surveyed the white plastic light fitting, most of which was hanging limply from its socket on the ceiling. The twirly metal light shade beneath it was dangling at a precarious angle.

Frankly Rob had no idea how to fix it, whatever the bloke from B&Q had provided for the job. Rob was no use at all at DIY which never held any appeal for him whatsoever. In fact he could do nothing of value with his hands which, when called upon to make or mend something, behaved as though they were encased in rubber mittens.

When he was a kid, his dad had been a one-man makeover show, dexterously able to perform handy tasks large and small. He had rewired their semi from foundations to loft conversion, fitted a new kitchen, plumbed the bathroom and installed double-glazed windows throughout. He also spent Saturdays with his head buried under the bonnet of a series of garishly coloured old Fords and had encouraged Rob to join him there at which point Rob had indeed learned the mystic sacraments of basic car maintenance.

Dissecting a carburettor and learning to use the slender tools that set the timing under the distributor cap. It hadn't interested him to be honest and in the long run he'd learned nothing from it except perhaps the value of patience and introspection. The sad fact was it all counted for nothing in this modern vehicular world where car bonnets hid three black plastic boxes to which you had no key.

Rob's dad had built a sailing boat in the garage at home, starting with a few lengths of wood, some screws and glue. He had plans which absorbed him fully and the rest of the world disappeared into a grey outline on the periphery of his vision while he planed, hammered and sawed until the ship resembled what it had looked like inside his head.

He painted the boat white with a red stripe down the side and sewed the expanse of tough grey fabric for the sail on a geriatric hand-cranked sewing machine borrowed from his mother. He studied a book about boat names for a few days before naming the craft 'Foamcrest'. It amazed Rob to see him do that, because he had never in all his life seen dad read a book before. To Rob's mind, back then as a boy, it seemed like a form of sorcery that his father could create something so big, real and fully formed with his own hands.

Rob believed it must be something all men found they could do when they reached maturity, that magical age when they knew everything and the workings of the world came under their mastery.

Somehow, things never seemed as easy for Rob as they'd looked in his father's hands when he was just a child.

Sue had been busy fetching gear from her shed for him to fix the light. She had a small stepladder, the new light fitting, a Phillips-head screwdriver. She assembled everything in a tidy bundle on the living room carpet, stood up and brushed her hands together, exhaling like she'd exerted herself - it was cute, domestic and he found himself grinning at her.

"Will you hold the ladder for me?"

She thought about it briefly and shook her head.

"Nah, you might fall on me. I'll make you a cup of coffee."

He picked up the aluminium stepladder and positioned it under the light. Three steps up and he was so close to the ceiling he had to crick his head sideways to get a proper look at the fitting.

It didn't look like too much of a job, even for him. The lampshade dangled from a wonky wire, the plastic casing which held it to the Artexed ceiling had cracked, quite probably through age and that's why the rest of it was dangling at such a peculiar angle.

The casing needed to come off first, that was attached by a small screw on one side, then the new one had to go on and he could see the new shade would slot over the bulb.

He'd be a hero come Monday, all manly and capable. Maybe Sue would tell Alice? Maybe Alice would tell Louise?

He fished out the screwdriver and realised the screw was a flathead, still it was tiny and loose and he managed to get some purchase on it. Within seconds it was shifting. The light was shining in his eyes and he squinted through it. Shit... maybe he shouldn't have it *on* while he was fixing it? It seemed obvious now - what an *idiot*. He backed down the ladder and turned it off by the switch at the door, safety first and all that.

He shinned back up the ladder and the little screw was soon out and in his palm. He placed it carefully on the flat bit at the top of the ladder as Sue shouted through from the kitchen.

"I'm glad you've come to help me, you're not a bad lad after all. I don't know why you'd want to hang out with that Alice though, she's a right dopey bitch... dresses like a whore!"

The fitting slid off as far as the lamp shade. He had to take the still warm bulb out, unscrew a plastic widget on it which was holding the shade onto the wire then it all came apart, the old shade came off and the cracked fitting slipped off too.

All good up to this point.

He felt empowered, capable even. This must be how his dad spent much of his life feeling, with the notion he was useful and in demand.

Sue was still talking to him from the kitchen. He soon realised that if he concentrated really hard on what he was doing with the light fitting, he was actually able to phase her out completely.

"He *said* he was my friend," she piped up. "I've met girls like me in support groups and things, they always seem angry and they hide it by hurting themselves with pills and razor blades and hanging around with the wrong sort of men. I don't do that. Well, not very often anyway."

He took a look at the wires underneath the fitting all coiled up on the ceiling in the snug plastic cavity he'd exposed. It resembled an exotic nest of baby snakes. One of the wires seemed to have worked loose, he'd just tighten it up a little before sticking the new cover back on and it was a job done. He reached up and poked his screwdriver into the cavity... and went bang.

The shock threw him off the ladder and halfway across the room. He didn't know too much about it right away, one moment he remembered standing on the ladder, craning up with the screwdriver in his hand, the next he was waking up on the floor rubbing the back of his head which had come into contact with something hard and unyielding. His heart was pounding, he hurt but couldn't quite work out where or why.

He felt like he'd been clubbed on the head from behind and mugged, probably by Sue, though he couldn't see why she would do such a thing. Come to that, he didn't see her at all, she wasn't in the room.

Sue appeared at the doorway looked startled and let out a shriek.

"What the fuck's going on in here?"

She hurried over to him, picking her way past the toppled stepladder.

"Have you fallen? What was that bang? There was the crash of the steps falling but that *other* bang. Sounded like a bomb going off!"

Momentarily, he realised he couldn't answer her. Though he had thoughts in his head (in a vague, scrambled form) there didn't seem to be a way of getting them to come out of his mouth. It was as though his software had crashed and he needed to reboot. He managed a thin sound through his parched lips, an animal sound, like an anxious cat.

"You look like *shit!*" Sue knelt down beside him to scrutinize his face and determine precisely how shit he looked.

"I think you must have cracked your head on the coffee table when you fell," then, suddenly alarmed, "I hope it hasn't got a dink in it?"

She ran her fingers over the antique pine, exhaled, "No... you're alright, it seems fine."

She looked at him again, ruffled his hair in a comforting way. "I think you must have copped an electric shock. You *did* turn the power off at the mains didn't you? Shit. You *didn't?* I couldn't have made the tea if you had! You've had a big shock you dick."

She leapt to her feet and headed for the hall.

"I'd better dial 999 or something. You might be dying for all I know. We need to get you to the hospital."

The thought of being wheeled out on a trolley under a pink blanket for all the neighbours to gawp at didn't appeal to Rob. He found his voice, quavering and diminished.

"I'm okay. Kind of. Give me a run to casualty. I think I can get up now and sit on the couch. Get the car. I'm not too bad, just feel a bit cold, like shivery you know?"

He was dizzy with a side order of damp and queasy. It was as thought

147

he'd been walking home drunk and got chucked in the canal.

He kept saying, "I'm alright, I'm alright," but was aware that there were tears welling in his eyes.

When one finally broke free and trickled down his cheek, Sue shot to her feet, lithe and purposeful and said, "Right that's it, I'm calling the doctor's surgery," and she fished around in her pocket for her mobile phone, hand rifling repeatedly through her short blonde mop as she spoke sharply down the phone.

"He's alright... I mean he's alive, he's lying down. I think maybe he's in shock."

She looked over at him critically. "He looks terrible actually, really awful." She put the phone back in her pocket.

"The nurse says you should go to hospital. She even said phone an ambulance but it will be quicker in my car."

He didn't remember a lot about the journey in her shiny, metallic-blue Beetle, just the big red silk Gerbera in the bud vase on the dash and the strong smell of vanilla car freshener.

As Sue swung the Beetle into the hospital car park, Rob bent over and threw up in the footwell.

"Shit," said Sue annoyed. "I just spent the whole morning cleaning this."

"Sorry," Rob replied abjectly and vomited again, loudly and copiously. He remembered wondering where it had all come from as he couldn't remember eating anything.

Sue screeched to a halt outside the door of casualty and bundled Rob out of the car; more so - he sensed - to protect her upholstery, which was no longer scented with vanilla, than for concern about his medical welfare.

He fell to his knees on the pavement and she helped him up and guided him to the door like a blind man.

He half expected they'd turn him away, perhaps with a lecture about wasting valuable NHS time but instead they found him a bed on a ward which was otherwise filled with querulous, pungent pensioners and told him at length he was being kept in for observation.

He was suddenly tired, the whole thing seemed absurd and wearing and despite the strangeness of the setting, he slept soundly.

He woke once with a full bladder and endured a baffled and protracted foray for the loo, down dimly lit corridors with his arse hanging forlornly out of the back of his hospital gown.

Later, after he had more or less dozed off, he was woken again by the high pitched one-sided chatter of a demented old man in the next bed who argued bitterly with his dead wife over some ancient grudge about a missing bicycle.

This argument continued 'til dawn, despite protests from the other beds and several interventions from the nurse who pleaded with him to, "Settle down, Mr Nutter, there's other people trying to sleep".

"It's a racer, it has twelve gears," he trilled, as the rest of the ward cackled bleakly at his name.

So no more sleep as such but by sticking his head under the pillow Rob was able to doze a little under the cool starchy sheets. When morning came and with it a curiously thin and sterile breakfast of cold toast and bland scrambled egg, he was feeling more himself, though a trifle washed out, not to mention embarrassed by the fuss of being in a strange nightgown surrounded by old men.

There were twelve beds in the ward laid out along the sides of the room which was bare and clinical but for the garish get well cards and arrangements of carnations and dahlias on the bedside tables. He was the only patient on the ward who was not a pensioner and he tried not to look around too much for fear of the whey-faced old man in the bed opposite who stared bleary-eyed at him, keen to engage him in conversation.

The nurses were wondrous though. He'd never been in hospital before and expected it would be like a TV medical drama where they were very stiff and proper, refusing robotically to have any emotional attachment to the patients. On the contrary, they were warm and flirtatious, stopping off for regular visits up and down the ward, as they ministered to the confused old men. They were pretty, dumpy, mouthy girls in their early twenties with a broad sense of humour who would clearly rather be messing with him than dealing with bedpans and pills.

The little blonde one seemed most keen he indulge in a little basic PUA play with the 'Yes Ladder', which was intended to give her a series of questions she could say yes to, right up until the one where he asked her out. People like to please other people, they like to say yes but she had to answer the querulous demands of the old boy opposite, who wanted to know when his wife would be here, so Rob never got chance to see if his skills were working.

At one point, there were three at once around his bed sniggering at the story of his electrocution, though quietly so as not to disrupt the rest of the ward, but the sister appeared, stern, frosty and middle-aged. She stood at the end of the bed and they scattered like starlings with a cat on the lawn.

Rob squinted up at her ID badge which appeared to say, 'Mortality Manager' he swore bleakly under his breath, believing his time had come.

"No," she snapped. "It says 'Modality Manager', it means I'm the ward sister."

"It must be funny when that happens," said Rob, greatly relieved.

"Maybe the first few times", she admitted.

Rob tried wheedling to her about how he didn't need to be in here now and could he just go home but she cut him dead saying he had to wait until the doctor came round at eleven to take a look at him. Once he'd been properly processed and examined, if it was established there was little wrong with him a dose of common sense wouldn't cure, he'd be on his way leaving the bed free for more deserving patients.

In the meantime, she'd be grateful if he stopped bothering the nursing staff while they were busy carrying out their duties on the ward.

Duly chastened, he spent an atrophying hour listening to hospital radio, which was beyond dreadful and seemed to consist entirely of requests for Neil Diamond and Glen Campbell by men called Albert.

The nurses smirked at him and gave him the eye when they could on their way past his bed but he couldn't be bothered to respond beyond winking the odd time, or putting his tongue out at them, which they seemed to appreciate.

'If I was a *real* PUA,' he thought, 'if I knew what I was doing and had properly learned the craft, I'd have the mobile numbers of most of this lot already.'

He recounted the advice: approach with confidence, high energy opening, some patterning maybe, then give them a command, write down your details, they would do it. Don't end the conversation right there though and risk looking predatory - carry it on a little while until a natural break.

Perhaps there was still time?

Visiting started at 10am and Alice was at his bedside by ten past. His heart sank when he saw her, it just seemed like hard work and that wasn't what he needed right now. What he wanted most was to creep off home to his own bed and sleep for a week immersed in silence and darkness, waking maybe on Friday evening to a knock on the door from Sam with a McDonalds chicken nugget Happy Meal and a lemongrass smoothie from that place in the Regent Arcade.

Instead, what he got was a full half hour of Alice being prepared to forgive him under the circumstances. Forgive, yes, but not forget, not yet, maybe not ever.

There were some wounds which went deeper than the word 'sorry' could cure, some hurts which mere electrocution was not enough to cleanse. She gave him to understand that karma had indeed made a good fist of helping him atone for his sins, although she did hint that perhaps the jolt to his system had not been quite fierce enough, as he'd more or less recovered and was comfortably sitting up in bed trying not to stare at her tits. Meanwhile Hamish, *poor* Hamish, was but a bump in the herbaceous border following a simple yet dignified service for a few nearest and dearest chez Crazy Al's the previous evening.

Rob got the impression that if he'd ended up under his own heap in Cheltenham cemetery, Alice would have turned up in a short black frock and wept for him certainly, yet she would have believed deep down that natural justice had been served.

She softened a little later on and asked if he would like her to log into his Facebook account for him. He indicated in the negative, given he didn't make that much use of it.

"But how will you know who's commented on your status?" she wanted to know, concerned. "How will you even update your status? You really need to update."

He told her he was sorry again, of course and asked if she wouldn't mind filling his water jug for him because he was parched. He also needed to give his brain a break, as she was filling it with a big memory dump which could loosely be labelled as, 'Everything I remember about Hamish.'

She'd reached about six months old when he was still a cute ball of fluff given to doing occasional dumps on the drawing room carpet. There was clearly quite a way to go in the narrative, as it appeared the animal had been about a hundred and eighty in dog years when it reached its sudden demise.

Rob was reminded of the way criminals were sometimes made to face their victims, sat down in an interview room somewhere and subjected to an impact statement with all the grief, all the damage and the sour fruits of their heinous crime.

While she was gone, he lay back in his bed and drifted, wondering how long this doctor was going to be and wishing Sam would come and pick him up in the car. The old bloke across the ward had started mumbling plaintively about racing bikes again and Rob found it comforting almost, after all these hours, a torment perhaps but a familiar one.

Suddenly, there was a new noise, the pop and crackle of a distant fracas under way, not here on his ward but not far beyond it, echoing perhaps from the corridor outside where voices were raised.

Then the door swung open fiercely and here was Alice again, followed swiftly by Sue who said nothing but picked up one of the plastic pee bottles from a small metal table and chucked it unceremoniously at Alice whereupon it bounced off her head and hit the ward floor with the hollow rattle of imploding Tupperware.

Alice howled as though she'd been hit with a brick and pulled an expression of pained surprise which made Rob blurt out a nervous laugh, though he was mostly shocked by the whole thing. It wasn't just the appearance of Sue or the notion that the two of them weren't currently the best of pals, but the fact that they were willing to go at it here in the hospital which was a place that reeked of authority, where you were supposed to be on your very best behaviour.

Rob hadn't even been prepared to politely check out before he was allowed to, never mind chuck bottles of piss around like it was a Wild-West saloon. The bottle appeared to have been empty... luckily. Alice span round and told Sue crisply to fuck off. Sue raced over and grabbed her by the hair extensions, pulling her face down to hip height, seemingly ready to give it a good shoeing - Rob knew she would do it too.

"Wait! What are you doing?" he yelled in alarm.

Sue looked up at him, as if surprised to see him there and stood still for a moment, still clamping Alice's head to her waspish waist. Alice was howling and clawing at Sue with her acrylic nails but they didn't seem to leave much of a mark. Sue tugged her hair one more time and let her go with a slap, Alice fell back and started giving out to Sue in the strongest possible terms but she didn't come back within hair-grabbing

152

range that's for sure.

Sue ignored her and turned her attention to Rob in the bed, where he lay nervous now her eye had fallen and rested on him.

"What's this slag doing here?" she wanted to know, as though there was some kind of hard and fast anti-slag rule in operation which he had known about all along but chosen to ignore.

Alice cut in, "What do you think you're doing, you mad bitch? This is a hospital not some crack house for you and your skanky council estate mates."

Sue looked over at her and carried on as though she hadn't spoken.

"I come over here to find out how you are and this overfed posh whore is in the waiting room trying to tell *me* what I can and can't do!"

"I only said he was sleeping and it might be better to leave him until he was feeling stronger. You are a fucking psycho woman and I'm going to make sure everyone at work hears about what you've done."

Alice was crying now, she was shocked and frightened sure but the tears were useful to her too.

Sue turned, poised and ready to have another go at Alice but as she homed in, Alice ducked and came up holding her shoe which she used to rap Sue sharply in the middle of the forehead as soon as she came within range.

It was a court shoe with a one inch heel in patent leather and it made a clock noise as it landed.

Sue yelped and grabbed her head. Alice hadn't hit her hard enough to do any lasting damage but it brought her to a standstill sure enough and at that stage, a couple of Rob's nurse chums came tumbling through the door shrieking for order and pulling the pair of them apart before they could do any more damage with their curiously chosen weaponry.

They were hustled swiftly out of the door, both yelling at each other, then over their shoulders to Rob saying, 'See you hun,' as if they were just popping out to the WRVS bar for a magazine.

Alice used her free hand, (the one that didn't have a plump blonde nurse hanging off it) to make a phone sign for him, holding her little finger and thumb up to her ear as the swing door banged behind her.

The ward fell deathly quiet. The old men peered at Rob with a mixture of fear and awe, he sank down in his bed and pretended to be asleep. Pretty soon maybe he *was* asleep, or very nearly anyway. When the tall, saturnine doctor came and lazily prodded him for a short while and pronounced him fit to go home, Rob was a bit put out at having to give up his warm bed and slide back into his jeans.

Through the door, sat on faux leather furniture, he found Sam waiting for him and gratefully accepted a lift home.

When he got there he headed straight back to bed again, suddenly so profoundly tired it was too much work to peel his jeans off once more and get under the covers. He was feeling pretty sorry for himself too, it was as though the electric shock which had flowed through him had only just hit his system, depressing and debilitating him, closing him down.

He slept through the rest of the day, woke in the early evening for beans on toast and found messages on his Ansaphone from Sue and Alice (inevitably) but also from Lou who wanted to wish him well, Sue having filled her in on the details of his incapacity. She hoped he would be back on top form in time for the away trip to the Going Forward symposium on Thursday and Friday.

"Get some rest and look after yourself," she told him. "We need all the electricity we can get this week!" and she laughed, delighted at her own quip.

Rob had a bleak vision that there would be many more low voltage power-based puns to come later in the week and he wasn't looking forward to it. On the one hand you could say it might be exciting, something different for a couple of days that he would otherwise have spent sat at his desk or out on the ring road pestering advertising budget out of grumpy businessmen but he knew he'd also be out of his comfort zone. A whole two days in a strange place dealing with the senior people from work, the ones he usually avoided or mollified so he wouldn't have to interact with them in any deeper way.

They made him feel uncomfortable because they were more serious than him. They exuded confidence and expertise and he could only pretend he had those qualities for a short while in an attempt to impress women.

He feared that an extended period in their company might leave him vulnerable and exposed as a shallow, useless fraud. He went back to bed with his laptop and comforted himself by going through a few PUA drills.

Ultimate opening lines for groups of girls in bars: "I'm on a blind date and I'm nervous about it. Are there any tips you can give me so I don't make an idiot of myself?" Other responses included: "Are you girls shy?

We've been standing here talking to each other for five minutes and you haven't spoken to us?" Along with, "Do you believe in ESP? Think of drawing a number between one and four on a blackboard, you drew a number three. Now a number between one and ten, you drew a seven."

There was also, "I'm lost! I can't find my friends and I'm scared. Remember when we were kids and you could just be friends with whoever you wanted? D'you want to be my new friend?" and, "Hi, we're picking up chicks!"

Most of these he couldn't imagine using but then again, after a few drinks in a bar, who knew what might work. Simply having *something* to say was a big improvement on his situation a few weeks ago when he'd either been tongue-tied or talked pure gibberish.

"How come you're not into Facebook then?" Sam wanted to know. "It's the totally best way to be boosting that there is, better than all that unfortunate 'meeting people' and 'talking to them' nonsense."

"There are a range of reasons but first among them is that I am a very private person, even secret," said Rob, mock aloof.

"My idea of a good time is not to spread every nuance of who I am all over the interweb like Rob marmalade, telling people what my 'status' is, flashing pictures of me in my pants on the beach. The weird thing for me is that anyone *wants* to do it!"

Sam shrugged, "Well, women like it, you know and showing off is a big part of human nature, we all show-off don't we? That's what you're doing when you strut your PUA stuff, you've just been taught to show-off more effectively."

"Yeah," Rob admitted, "I'm in control of that now. I get to decide what I say, though I know I've been tutored, it's my choice if I say it and who to. On Facebook, anyone could look one way or another, friends of friends, you lose that personal control."

Sam laughed at him. "You're a bit of a young fart in some ways. This is the future mate and I'm all over it. You want to know about what's going on tomorrow, ask Sammy, I'll hook you up with what's happening."

"Hmm, the future's always better, that's what we're meant to believe isn't it?" said Rob, "but I know that's not always true. You asked me on my 15th birthday whether the future would be better. I would have said yes, of course, bring it on. Wonderful world, can only get better. Six months later, my mum dies, everything *isn't* better and it never got better again if I'm honest."

Sam was solemn for a while. Neither of them said anything.
"So you won't use Facebook 'cos your mum died?"
Rob nodded thoughtfully.
"That does appear to be it, yes."

CHAPTER 8

'Johnno!' the blog of Robert Johnson, July 22:
"So, I electrocuted myself and it's not even the most shocking thing that's happened to me this week, or even today. I feel weak and spaced out but I was like that before I plugged myself into the mains. Now I feel much the same, only I have a hangover too. Life is more real to me than it used to be. Before it was like watching telly. Now I know I'm in it.

Whatever happens I think that's a good thing. Even if it can mean you get knocked on your back and end up in casualty. The part where your heart is thumping so hard you think it's broken and you're terrified in case you have done something you can't take back - that's called living and I've never really had that before.

I used to spend my life trying to do what was expected of me, so as not to upset anyone, or do anything they wouldn't approve of. In the end though, the people who love you want you to have a good life, don't they? Maybe not a great one but a good one. It's hard to guess sometimes what a person would have wanted. And you forget what they were like too, what their tolerances were. Plus, times change. In some ways people are the same now as they were ten thousand years ago but still you can shock someone just a generation older than you are, without meaning to. You have to deal with today."

Sonof: The image you project to the world, it's important right, I'm sure we can agree on that?
Rob: Yeah, of course. I mean I think the AA guys in the town centre are real.
Sonof: ??

Rob: In the High Street there are blokes in AA uniforms: hats, badges, high-vis vests, the works and they're out selling car breakdown membership.

Sonof: Mmm, I am aware of the phenomenon.

Rob: And I believe that they can fix my car. I mean, if I had a problem with it I would ask them, about the carburettor or the head gasket or whatever they have on cars because they are AA men.

Sonof: Even though you know that they are salesmen earning commission by signing people up to membership in the street?

Rob: Yep.

Sonof: And that, if they were actually trained mechanics, they would probably be out on the road rescuing single mums with flat batteries.

Rob: Yeah, I know, when you expose it to the harsh spotlight of logic it seems a bit mental but I'm supporting your point here. If I had a car and it was broken I would expect them to fix it.

There was a holiday atmosphere on the bus: laughter, shouting, some singing of lewd songs from the girls at the back and some of the guys played cards and hooted with stag do bonhomie. Rob sat on his own first rather than with either Sue or Alice and later moved over with Jayden to join in with five card stud poker for a little while. He bailed at three quid down and when he went back to his seat Alice was there waiting.

She wanted to talk it seemed but not about dead dogs or lost weekends, not about what a bastard Rob was thankfully. She seemed to want to be friends again and you can never have too many friends thought Rob.

They chatted amiably for a while and it was only when Rob mentioned Sue and asked whether the pair of them had recovered from their spat at the hospital, that the mood turned chilly. Alice wrinkled her nose like she'd inhaled something putrid.

"She's a total bitch and there's never any bog roll left in the ladies loo 'cos she eats it all."

Rob was nonplussed. He wondered whether this was some curious euphemism which was new on him but was all the go if you were a girl.

"What? You mean she actually eats it?" he asked cautiously. "With her mouth?"

Alice looked at him like he was the weird one.

"Yeah. She fills up on Andrex. It makes you feel full and it's free. If you're a noob you have it with pickle to start with but she just gobbles hers down with a swig of water. No bloody thought for any of us with a wet vag."

She hooted with laughter at her own off-colour joke and Rob joined in self-consciously, because he felt he had to. There was something in him which was still squeamish sometimes about the matter-of-fact way girls spoke about their bodies. He couldn't deny it was fair enough, though he wouldn't be tempted to start going on to them about his bits and pieces in quite so much glaring detail.

Girls hadn't been like this at his school, certainly not the ones he'd known anyway. Something had happened to them in the last few years, to them or to the world it seemed. These days, *everything* was open, transparent and clear. Anything could be said by anyone it seemed though nothing had been announced, he hadn't seen anything on Google news about it, there had been no documentary on the box. He laughed again for Alice. She was made for this world, she would do well in it he knew, her honesty would be her charm.

Rob looked down the bus and was alarmed to see Sue craning her neck around to look at them. Her face was cold and angry, though she could not surely have heard what was being said about her. When she saw she had been spotted she smiled at him vaguely and turned back to talk to one of her friends as though it had been nothing and she had better things to do than gawp at them.

Rob was among the last off the bus. He'd never been to the water park before and was amazed when he saw lakes through the windows of the coach. They didn't seem to belong there, they weren't part of the natural landscape yet as he passed one, then another, then a third expansive lake, they all looked quite mature, seemingly natural. He assumed Mother Nature had caught him out and was showing him he knew sod all about the way the world was formed.

In fact the lakes had been made by man, indirectly and were originally dug out as quarries to mine the precious honey-coloured Cotswold stone. Over time they filled with water and were softened by the actions of the wind and rain. Plants grew, birds and animals arrived and liked what they saw and stayed. People liked it too, this strange half man-made, half natural confection. They came to see it as a place for leisure. They introduced fish, brought boats and wind-surfers.

The coach pulled to a halt at the side of one of the smaller lakes. An artificial beach had been manufactured with lorry loads of sand and shale leading to the water's edge. There was a jetty and there were lots of Scotch pines. Up a slight rise surrounded by woodland were a cluster of Swiss-style log cabins. Lamps hung from the eves and soft yellow spotlights in the grass threw a warm glow over the wooden walls. It looked magical, all the members of the coach party were thrilled. This was not like work and some of the girls squealed in delight, then there was laughter again and a race for the cabins.

Stepping down from the coach onto dry grass, Rob glanced over at the chalets, then back towards the shingle shore, the jetty and the open expanse of dark water. He knew he should be racing after the rest of them, scrabbling to secure himself a space in the cabin, close to Lou and a safe distance from Sue and Alice but he found he couldn't drag his eyes away from the water.

The sun was setting over the trees behind the lake, it cast a rich golden shadow over the body of water which was still, calm and waiting.

Rob began to run. He didn't call out or whoop like the others, he was heading up the slope in the other direction. He was silent, smiling and open-mouthed. He accelerated onto the pebbles and the others heard him, then came the urgent crunch of high tops on loose shale. Somehow even through their heightened manufactured excitement they were brought to a halt by that sound which they found irresistible and head-turning. By the time Rob hit the jetty - still speeding up - they were all looking back at him and some were already venturing back down the grassy slope for a closer look.

Rob's feet rattled over the hollow echoing planks, he was not considering what he was going to do - he wasn't thinking anything at all, just feeling the evening air and the cool of the breeze over the water.

Soon enough he reached the end of the jetty and effortlessly launched himself into the air, floating, flying, then plunging down into the water like a brick which was so icy cold it shocked him - just as the electricity had - and made him fight to get his head above the waterline. He gasped and yelped with laughter into the cold, wooden gold all around him.

He was still recovering his senses when he heard the first big splash nearby, then another and a third. Rob had company and looked around him to see Jayden and one or two of the other guys as their heads bobbed up and they made shocked 'so cold it's hard to breathe' faces. More splashes followed and calmly treading water, Rob saw a line of runners heading down the jetty towards him, so he swam off to the side to clear their landing area.

One or two of the women headed in too, Alice the first among them accompanied by a huge throaty yell. Others came up to the bank wanting to join in the fun without getting quite so cold and wet. Lou dabbled her ballet pumps in the shallows, Sue hitched up her jeans and waded in awkwardly.

Rob still hadn't spoken but the others were hollering and laughing, splashing about like starlings in a bird bath. He looked around at them, their young faces full of joy. There was something liberating about the way they all seemed so thrilled to be out here at nightfall, up to their necks in ice cold water.

Rob laughed - at himself, at them, at what they'd done together and he swam back to shore, scrambling up onto the shingle beach, ungainly and already shivering.

Lou was waiting for him, smiling. "You are a nutcase!" she told him, part mortified, part thrilled, the way mothers are when a precocious child does something daring.

As he splashed towards her, water dripping everywhere, she was laughing and somehow her arms seemed to beckon him.

"You are going to catch your death!"

"Put your arm round me then - warm me up."

And she did, though somewhat gingerly and it made barely any difference to the deluge of biting water which consumed him and thrilled his blood. She was hugging him - sort of - rubbing her hands up and down his arms to try to get them warm and leaning in gamely at first, then pulling away in mock horror from the wet and the cold.

"Eeewww, you're like a drowned rat!" But she didn't pull away too far and he moved in again, responding loudly so the others could hear.

"Hey, it's great you staying nice and dry watching us lot suffer. I think it would be good for 'team building' and morale if senior management got into the spirit of things."

She grinned at him vaguely because she didn't really get what he was implying, then it dawned on her and a look of genuine shock and horror spread over her face.

"Oh... no way... you do and I'll..."

But he leaned in and grabbed the top of her legs, just beneath her bum and tipped her into his arms. Lou was absurdly light, like her bones were hollow and it hardly felt like carrying an adult at all. She seemed caught between wanting to maintain appearances and vent her emotions but as he whisked her into the air she came to a decision and just let out a shrill scream.

"Don't you bastard, if you do I'll..." but he had already turned and started trotting back down towards the jetty.

Clump, clump, hollow again but fuller and louder this time with the extra weight. He took it slowly and gave her time to beg.

"Oh *please* don't! I've not brought my straighteners and I wasn't intending to go swimming!"

He slowed to a halt, three quarters of the way down the jetty.

"Oh well then, if you've not brought your straighteners."

There was a groan of disappointment from the swimmers and those on the shore.

"Yes," said Lou stern and relieved, summoning all the dignity she could with her arse in the air and her arms draped round his neck, "and I wasn't intending to swim this weekend. You put me down like a good boy and I'll forgive you."

"You're *so* going in," he told her, ignoring her yells of protest as he sprinted the last thirty feet and propelled them both into the golden darkness.

After they had processed wet and shivering to the chalets and changed, they got together under the stars around a fire in the brick barbecue which Sue and Jayden eventually managed to light with much swearing and use of scrunched up newspaper as kindling.

Rob was the subject of much good natured abuse, he had got them all wet they said, 'they got themselves wet,' he responded with mock indignation. All apart from Lou anyway, who came out to the fire wrapped in a blanket, her wet blonde hair scrapped back. She was giggly and full of fun, tingling, she said with the cold. She came to stand next to Rob, bumping up against him in the dark as they all chatted and laughed over beer and white wine plucked from urban cool bags.

He lent in and said, sounding serious, "Hey, you're not cross with me about your dip are you?"

"Would you care if I was?" she teased.

"Well, you're the boss," he said, unconcerned.

"Hmm, it didn't feel like it when you picked me up and chucked me in the lake. I think *you* were the boss then don't you?"

"Better not get on the wrong side of me then, or you might find

162

yourself getting another cold bath."

She pouted, "You're too rough. I thought we might be friends, I've let you come to our special, very important weekend. You could at least be grateful!"

"Oh, I am, I'm thrilled to be here with you."

Alice came up behind them.

"How are you two?" she said with forced cheeriness bright and brassy. "Dried off yet?"

"Toasty warm," Rob said.

"Good, good," said Alice, her voice brittle.

Rob realised he hated it when she said good twice like that.

"We better be off to bed hadn't we Lou?" Alice asked.

"Big day in the morning... packed programme of team building."

Louise shrugged. "There's no hurry, people are bonding, it's good for team spirit."

"We're all going off to bed anyway. Rob, come on, we're all heading back to the huts. Everyone's decided we're going back up there now."

Rob lifted up his bottle to show it was still half full of lukewarm lager. "I'll be in there later. I'm okay here right now." He tried to sound nonchalant. Truth was he really wanted to stay out here with Lou, close in the gathering darkness, talking about nothing.

Alice shot him a look, hurt maybe, it said, 'wait til I get you on your own,' then she bustled off, bristling with fake sociability. Out of the shadows, Sue followed her, stopped in front of Rob without looking at him, spat on the grass and slunk off into the darkness like a skinny cat.

For a moment, Rob thought that was it for the evening. They would stand there awkwardly for a short while until Lou had finished dragging on her fag then she'd make her excuses about how she needed to get her beauty sleep and he'd follow her, yawning and nodding so as not to get left out there in the darkness on his own.

Instead, she pulled her coat around her shoulders and said, "Let's go for a walk, down by the lake. No throwing me in this time though."

She seemed tipsy, warm to him and was clearly having fun. She took his arm as they walked down the slope into the fading light and when they reached the shoreline she took his face in her hands, pointed it towards her own and made him promise gravely not to throw her in the water. He did so, equally seriously and they stared into each other's eyes for a moment, until her attention wandered.

163

"Look." she said. "A boat!" There was indeed a small, aluminium rowing boat tied to the far side of the pier. She wandered along the wet planks towards it, there was nothing much inside it, oars, sacking on the floor, it was dry though.

"Let's get in," Lou said, decisively. "Let's go for a sail." She clambered in, hanging onto his arm and he jumped in after her. The tiny boat swayed alarmingly so they had to sit down quickly, issuing muffled whoops of alarm but it didn't capsize. Louise lifted off the loop of rope attaching it to the jetty and gave the wooden post a gentle shove and the craft floated serenely along the shore for twenty or thirty metres until it sat becalmed again. It was so close to the pebbles, Rob could have leapt over the side and walked back to dry land without getting wet above his waist. That seemed to be enough sailing for Lou. She didn't bother with the oars, just lay back on the bottom of the boat, looking at the sky. After sitting awkwardly beside her for a while Rob joined her lying down and looking up, she didn't seem to mind.

"Do you Twitter?" she asked him, with the air of someone who was saying something cool.

"Nah. I just bought some stamps - lol!' It's not for me. It's for older people isn't it?" He glanced sideways at her see if he'd scored a hit. "I do a blog though."

She seemed interested. Blogs were one of the magical 'social networking' sacraments, along with Tweets and going-viral, all regularly discussed in hushed, excited tones at marketing meetings.

"Oh, where can I read that?"

He cringed a little there in the twilight when she said that, wondered whether to lie or to try to sort it out later before she could check. He quickly realised that wasn't practical.

"I don't actually put it online," he admitted. Feeling embarrassed, jejune.

"Well," she said in mollifying tones, "I'd like to read it anyway. I'm sure it would be a fascinating place to be, inside your head."

"And in yours," he said. "So how's your love life?"

He chanced his arm with a bit of cheek, not able to remember whether this was a good strategy or not in PUA terms, thinking he has to move things on in some way to prevent this whole conversation, this whole relationship, becoming bogged down in the workaday and mundane.

"I don't know," she seemed sad suddenly. "It's all very complicated.

164

Very, very." She trailed her hand in the chilly water, splashed a little up at him as he stared over the side of the boat at her bare arm, ghostlike in the half-light. He rubbed drops of water from his nose.

"Want me to chuck you in again?" he grumbled.

"No," she admitted, solemnly. "Another two hours with Susan's manky hair straighteners does not appeal."

"Yeah well, mind your manners then," he said, more ruffled than he ought to have been over a few drops of water and percolating over what she might have meant by 'complicated.'

His love life could not be more simple in that he still did not have one worth the name.

After all this work, all these plans and manoeuvres, he still couldn't say to Louise, 'Yes, mine's complicated too,' with any degree of honesty.

"I know where you're coming from with that," he said. "Mine's a bit complicated too at the moment."

She laughed but not so he felt he hadn't been believed.

"I'm sure it is from what I've seen. I never would have had you down as such a Don Juan. You've got the office girls in a total flap, the talk in the cigarette corner is of little else."

The moon was bloated, orange, low and the stars seemed to multiply as you looked at them, just a few at first then more coming out of hiding, further back and forever.

"I don't know you. I don't know enough about you and I want to know everything," he grumbled.

"Well, what do you want to know?" she said patiently, huge sky behind her, shadows around her, sound of the water hollow around the fibreglass boat. "Hey," she added, "do you write about me in your blog?"

She seemed to be hoping he did which was flattering but he didn't want to gush so he took a couple of seconds and said, "Of course. I write about *all* my girls."

She laughed, told him he was getting too big for his boots and needed taking down a peg or two. She was up against him in the bottom of the boat and he could feel her through their clothes.

"Get me my coat," she said. "I'm cold."

"No," he said flatly, "can't be bothered." It was just a compliance routine and he treated it with the contempt it deserved. The difference

165

between him and an Average Frustrated Chump is that he wouldn't over-comply with any demand made of him in a desperate attempt to gain approval. This just seems needy and unattractive. Not very alpha male at all.

"And stop interrupting. I want to know who you are," he told her. "Say if we were on a desert island together..."

"If I was on a desert island I wouldn't be *cold*," she grumbled.

He put his arm further around her and pulled her in a bit. Kino escalation. Touch is the most powerful non-verbal means of communication and he had a feeling now was the time to communicate that he was feeling horny - within reason of course, he didn't want to scare her off.

"We'll have to find some way of staying warm," he told her. "It's for the good of the company."

She made an appreciative purring noise in the back of her throat. "So you're coming on to me for business reasons?"

"Partly work related," he said briskly, "and partly because you are very sexy." He used the word - sexy - no confusing that with anything else - no 'just good friends' about it. That word put him out on a limb, it frightened him but sooner or later he had to face the fear.

Remember, he told himself: bait, hook, reel, release.

"You're sexy and you've got a good job, bet you can't cook though." (Bait.)

"I can!" she pouted, "I can cook curry."

"God I love curry. How's your saag alloo?"

"It's the dog's bollocks," she said proudly, "I'll show you when we get out of here." (Hook.)

"It's a date then. You do the saag and I'll do my takka daal." (Reel.)

"Alright then, it is a date."

"Don't get any saucy ideas when I come over though, it's just the curry that's supposed to be hot, in fact, it might be better over at mine so I'll feel safer." (And release, with a tricky role reversal thrown in; truly he was getting quite good at this stuff.)

She sighed at the moon and pouted in a way that made him want her more than the others.

"I think maybe what I need is a younger man."

'Pick me!' he wanted to stand up in the boat and yell. 'I'll be your younger man,' but he remembered there was nothing worse than appearing too needy and available.

"I'll have to see if I can fit you in."

She laughed again obligingly and moved in closer to him. "It's getting colder here isn't it?"

He repositioned his arm around her shoulder and she looked at him in half surprise so he was no longer sure whether she had been inviting him to do that or not. Had he gone too far? It was only an arm keeping her warm. It could still be friendly rather than sexual.

While he was debating with himself and working out how to back away with dignity, she bent towards him and kissed him on his dry mouth. Her kiss was curiously soft and lacking in substance, like being settled on by a jellyfish or being the toast under a poached egg. It was as if her mind was elsewhere, thinking deep managerial thoughts.

She wasn't quite engaged with him there in the boat, she was up there in the stars: alien, intense, intelligent beyond his comprehension. Nevertheless, he took the opportunity to move his free arm hurriedly up and down the front of her dress, as if he was stroking a dog.

When they disengaged, with a slight popping noise, she asked him, "Did you know that sometimes stars move? They drift through the galaxy in groups. You see the Great Bear up there? In a short while, maybe 50,000 years or so, that will be gone. Nothing lasts forever."

He replied, "Did you know all polar bears are left-handed?"

"Yes," she said. "You told me before."

He moved his hand in instinctively to grope her breast, thought about the word 'grope' in relation to what he was doing and immediately regretted it. She'd find him crude, dirty and would surely loathe him forever but it didn't work out that way and she made appreciative noises and stuck her tongue in his mouth which made his brain burst with rich, intoxicating chemicals. He could feel her nipple hard under his thumb; it was getting chilly.

He had the sort of 'look at me' erection that could not be ignored and she didn't ignore it, running her hand down the front of his jeans to investigate.

She made an, 'Mmm' noise which, while it didn't say, 'I'm impressed', certainly seemed to convey, 'this'll do nicely.'

The arm he had behind her shoulders was going to sleep but he didn't want to move it for fear of ruining the moment. He tried to ignore the pins and needles as he sneaked his other hand down her dress and ran it

167

up the inside of her bare leg.

"Christ," he gave out.

"Sorry?" she asked.

"No, it's just my arm, it's..." He pulled it out from behind her head and it was around that moment that she stuck her hand inside his pants.

'Blimey' he thought. His first impulse was to yell and pull away again but he managed to resist it by lying very still, as if dead, in the bottom of the boat, while she fumbled around.

This was going quite well, except she might as well be interfering with a shop dummy. He managed to move his hand weakly up and down her leg and made strange sounds which he hoped were encouraging. She moved in to kiss him and he closed his eyes. The kiss was good, the hand down the pants was definitely good and getting better. He moved his hand back up under Lou's skirt and pushed her pants aside, where, despite all he had carefully learned from porn, he was still surprised to find an almost total absence of hair.

This was it then, he figured, nothing could stop them now, things had gone too far for that.

There was an echoing thump on the side of their boat. Someone had grabbed a rollock and was nosily peering in.

'God, no,' he was thinking, 'not *Sue!*'

Lou disengaged with remarkable rapidity, brushing him aside. She sat up in the boat, back straight, all hair in place looking cool and aloof there in the almost dark.

Rob lay in the bottom of the rowing boat not knowing quite what to do. Should he sit up too?

"Hi," Louise said flatly. "Can I help you?"

"The others were asking where you were," said a voice. "They thought you'd got lost, they were talking about calling the police."

Voice sounded wounded, small, voice did not belong to Sue, but *Alice*.

He propped himself up on one arm not sitting up fully but enough so it didn't look as though he was carrying on some ridiculous pretence that he was invisible.

"Hi Rob," said Alice. There was something in her tone which made him feel cold and meek and guilty. Sue could not have done this to him he realised. She could have punched him in the mouth and hurt him plenty that way, but she couldn't have made him feel like this inside.

"Look at that moon," said Rob. "Isn't it wonderful?" He gestured up

168

at it, glowing majestically as though he had produced it in some kind of magic trick.

Both women stared over his shoulder at it briefly making appreciative noises, which he felt diffused the situation a little.

He could hear Alice sloshing about in the freezing cold, coal-black water of the lake, she must have been in it almost to her waist. He thought briefly how hard her nipples would be and wondered what the chances were of her getting into the boat with him and Lou, this was the 21st Century after all.

On balance, he decided against suggesting it. There was to be no readers' wives-style saucy outcome to this evening, only chill, damp and another period in the dog house.

Under the cover of the side of the boat, he moved his free hand over and put it on Lou's knee. She immediately shifted her leg out of his reach. Could it be that she was angry with him too? How the hell had that happened given what they had been up to just moments ago? It wasn't his fault Alice had decided she was the sex police.

Lou stood up, wobbling only slightly then slipped over the side of the boat with a little squeak and a splash as she hit the water.

"It's getting late, I suppose I had better get back in. We've got a busy day tomorrow."

She didn't offer Alice any explanation for what she had been up to under the stars with Rob and Alice didn't ask her for one. She was, after all, still the boss.

Later that evening, dry and warm in his bedroom, he rang to keep Sam up to speed with developments. Told the story about Lou and the boat, the soft-boiled kiss, the interruption of what might have become something close to sex. There was a long crackly silence on the line and he thought for a while the signal had been lost out there in the lonesome plastic wilderness of man-made cliffs and fake lakes.

"Hello? Helloo?"

More hissy quiet then, "What's that word, that 'hates women' word?"

"Misanthrope," Rob offered.

"Nah, that's 'hates people' you cock. Misanthropists hate you, philanthropists buy you a museum."

Rob was stung, he had been doing his best to sort out this lexicographical puzzler but his efforts had been greeted with scorn.

Sound of Sam thinking then, "Misogynist - that's you."

"I wasn't that far off then," said Rob wounded and a pace behind the conversation. "Hang on though, that isn't me at all. I'm finding I quite like them if anything. What's a word for men who love women?"

"There isn't one," Sam sounded grumpy now.

"Yeah well, there should be. Philogynist, how's that? That's me that is."

He was conscious that Sam, as a deputy head of department, might feel left out of the loop by not being included in the trip to the lake. Especially as Rob wasn't deputy of anything and was technically the most junior member of a department with several older, wiser heads in it. He was too excited about the whole thing to play it down too much and besides, there wasn't any boring work stuff to report right now, just the bus trip and the impromptu swimming expedition. Rob went through the whole thing in some detail. Dwelling on the moments of Lou's anguish, the jog down the jetty with her nestled close to him and her entertaining yelp as they met the cold water.

There was pensive silence down the line for a moment.

"So you really like Lou then?" Sam asked.

"Yeah," Rob admitted. "Frightened of her of course. Well, that's a common theme with me and women right? But yes. She's fragrant, wise, accomplished. She's only an ounce of low self-esteem away from being the next ex-Mrs Johnson."

Sam laughed an empty, distant crackle down the line.

"So you know what you want then? That's a first. Maybe that's what's been holding you back. If you don't really have an aim you just drift? It's probably quite confusing for these girls too, don't you think? One minute you're all over them, the next you're distant or off flirting with someone else. I know this perhaps isn't PUA orthodoxy and I might get stoned to death as a heretic but girls are people too you know?"

Rob did know but he didn't think they were people like him, not really. When he made small-talk in the office with them, he assumed they were basically the same as him but perhaps had a different set of priorities. Now he knew there was far more to it than that.

It wasn't just their aims and ambitions which differed from his, it was the way they approached them, the way they thought and the manner in which they put those thoughts into action. It was as though men and women were both computers but each of them were running different software – he felt like a geek.

Sam was talking again but he'd missed half of it because he was deep in reverie.

"Sorry?"

"I was saying, why don't you try something with Lou? Ask her out, do whatever. Otherwise you'll be knobbing about like this 'til next Christmas not getting anywhere with *any* of them, just pissing them off by farting around."

"I *know* you're right. You are so right, it's just easier said than done. This is *Lou* we're talking about. Consider the extreme terror of trying to get into her very expensive pants. I mean Sue's scary 'cos she might kill me and Alice is scary 'cos she might eat me for breakfast, but it's like they're both slightly nippy Siamese cats and Lou's a sabre-toothed tiger."

"And *she's* the one you've decided it's a good idea to go after?"

"Well, no," Rob said in piss-take officious. "Us PUAs don't go after anyone in particular, the idea is to maximize your number of potential targets in the hope that one of them will pay off. We recognise not all women will like us, whatever we do. The point is to improve your odds, create a situation where some women *do* like you. The difference between a PUA and an Average Frustrated Chump is that we make a focussed effort, where as they just flail around, sometimes scoring lucky but more often not."

Sam laughed down the line, hollow and far away.

"You make it sound like a fishing trip."

"It is," said Rob, "and now I've been taught how to fish, I know the proper spot on the canal, I've got the right bait and I know that if I cast my line carelessly, I'll catch it in the overhead cables and fry!"

"Did you know," asked Sam, "that fishing is the single most dangerous sport in the world? Responsible for more deaths than mountain climbing, boxing and motorsports? People either electrocute themselves on the wires, or they drown."

"Yes," said Rob. "I did know that but do I seem like the sort of lad who's likely to go mucking around with live wires, or going for drunken swims in open water?"

"Was she not pissed off?"

"Pardon?"

"That you got her wet - her hair, clothes, make-up; it wasn't exactly dignified was it? Can you imagine how wee Willie would have taken it

171

if you'd done that to him? She's got to be a boss to these people tomorrow."

Rob had thought this of course, starting right from the moment the cold water enveloped him and the adrenaline swiftly wore off but it seemed he had nothing much to worry about.

"I think she quite liked being the centre of attention," he said. "I mean she pretended not to but did really, the way girls do. It brought her closer to the rest of people here I think and I reckon she knows that for this weekend, that's a good thing. Anyway, we're all supposed to be 'mucking in together' and all that, y'know? Here, all bets are off."

"Carnival time," said Sam. "The normal social conventions are suspended; the master becomes the servant, the servant the master."

Eloquently put Rob thought and was about to say so when Sam went on.

"If you believe you are a mug, what goes on at the lake, stays at the lake? You just watch your step. It's like getting drunk at the Christmas party and expecting it to be forgotten New Year. It's *never* forgotten mate. Why do you think I'm deputy of my department and sweet dopey Justine is there with you? I'll tell you why, two years ago, staff Christmas party, I had a run in with Willie. Things got said. That's why I wasn't floating around in the lake with you this evening. Just don't do anything you can't take back that's all and remember, Lou will still be your boss on Monday."

CHAPTER 9

'Johnno!' the blog of Robert Johnson, July 23:

"Women are still a bit mysterious - on all sorts of levels. Even in a mechanical way they function differently from men. When you watch the adverts on TV there seems to be a whole wide range of weird ailments just for them.

Why do they need good bacteria in their guts? What happens to them if they don't get it? Is it really serious, can they die from it? Or do they just slow down and feel lethargic with having all that bad bacteria sloshing around in there? And bloating - what's that all about? It's as though they blow up and float around like a little hot air balloon in a frock. Tena Lady - I know that one, it's when they wee themselves when they laugh, but I don't think the ones I'm interested in get that. It happens in their thirties, or older... Bio-oil? What the hell's that used for? Do you rub it on or drink it? Is it supposed to lubricate you, make you slippery? What?

Any advert where there's a bunch of women sitting around together laughing uproariously at nothing in particular, you know there's an evil, yet poorly described, health condition lurking ready to lay them all low unless they neck some drink and strap on a towel.

I used to think it was just having the decorators in that laid them low. Or should that be painters? Decorators sounds a bit too structural - why not knock down a couple of internal walls and erect an RSJ lintel while you're at it? They look as solid and straightforward as men but it seems they're not - they've got more going on inside somehow, they're far more complex and it's like my old dad used to say about electric windows when he bought a second-hand car - it's just more to go wrong."

There was a 'continental business' breakfast at 8am. Continental meant old croissants and lukewarm coffee and business meant having to listen to Jayden give a half-hearted ten minute presentation on the structure of the retail department in adverse trading conditions.

People clearly couldn't be bothered with it because they felt like they were on their holidays and wanted to be goofing around and giggling, not frowning and nodding as Jayden made a telling point about the changing demographic of the newspaper reading public.

At one point, people thought he'd finished because he sat down but it was only to turn on the overhead Powerpoint projector and there was a slideshow with statistics for another five long minutes, by which time even Jayden had lost faith in it and petered out into silence.

People were not sure whether they were supposed to clap or not so one or two did but most just turned their attention to talking amongst themselves. Lou let them do that for thirty seconds or so then stood up rapping the butt of her knife on the table so they all turned to her with a start.

"First of all I'd like to thank Jayden for that presentation. There was certainly a lot of food for thought in it and I'm sure I speak for the room when I say we will be thinking of some of the points he made and acting upon them over the weeks and months going forward."

She paused there and people did clap then because they knew they were supposed to. Jayden looked suitably gratified wearing a 'trying to hide it but can't' smile people have when the boss has told them how special they are. He even bobbed up again from his seat and took a little bow which got a laugh.

Lou cut back in. "I asked Jayden to speak first to remind us that it's not all fun and games here this weekend," she said sternly. "Oh no, not one bit of it."

She had her fair hair scraped back as though she hadn't had time to do much with it. She was wearing a white T-shirt, blue jeans and very little make-up. She looked fresh, alive and hot.

"Of course, there *will be* fun and games," she said with a twinkle, "and I of course shall join in - whether I want to or not - just ask Rob."

There was polite laughter and Lou seemed pleased with herself demonstrating she was one of the gang. As they filed outside the huts, she ruffled his hair.

The morning was bright, airy and fresh with possibilities. It felt like the start of a day when things happen and all the junior and middle managers on the company away day were tickled by it somehow, giddy and misbehaving in a gaggle outside the huts.

Jayden slapped Sue on her bony arse and ran away giggling and Sue pretended to be annoyed and chased him with Lou cooing the odd, 'now, now and 'settle down' like she was their mum and they were naughty children.

Two tall, gangly men approached wearing red T-shirts with 'Staff' printed on them and preposterously tight lycra shorts. Immediately the girls began cooing and cackling over them.

"They look like boy scouts" giggled Sue, "I can see that one's woggle," hooted Alice.

The two young men seemed ill at ease in the face of this ribbing. Their suntanned faces went red and they shuffled around from one hiking boot to the other until something like silence fell. Then the taller of the two broke into a wooden and obviously rehearsed welcome message / safety announcement about the importance of not larking about too much near open water and proper safety procedures when using tools.

It appeared they were about to be split into teams to make rafts which they then had to sail out to a buoy in the lake, negotiate their way round this and paddle back to the shore with ivory, apes and peacocks to the first team to complete said feat.

Naturally, Rob wanted to be on Lou's team but several of the brown-noses amongst them raced over to her side as soon as the word team was mentioned and so he ended up with Alice and a couple of the older guys from property who were being solemn-faced about the whole affair.

Down by the shore they found their raft-making equipment: wooden pallets, bamboo poles, nylon cord and bright orange plastic oil drums for buoyancy.

Sue's team (with Sue as captain) were situated at the next pile along from Rob and she soon had them whipped into shape, lashing together poles and pallets.

Rob's team didn't have a captain, so he and Alice set to work sorting out some poles into a pile while the two blokes from property just stood around scratching their behinds, smoking and grumbling about not being at home with their families.

It appeared Alice wasn't really talking to Rob which made the whole raft building thing more difficult, though not impossible, given that there wasn't a whole lot of philosophical discourse to be undertaken about the design of the craft, given that the parts only fitted together in one obvious way; two pallets, poles at the side and an oil drum at each corner.

For the first half hour or so the only sentence Alice spoke to Rob was, "Give me the rope".

She looked great this morning he thought, tight T-shirt, small shorts and dark hair tied back in a pony tail. He liked it when she bent over the oil drums and wondered whether the decision to focus his attentions on Lou had been premature.

What was wrong with Alice? It wasn't her fault he'd trod on her dog and seduced her mum. Alice was an innocent party in this, pure and without stain. He grinned at her and she half smiled back. She also seemed prepared to forgive him for his indiscretions with Lou. The worse he behaved it seemed, the easier he was forgiven.

They still didn't speak much but began messing around, nudging each other and sniggering. Alice's hair was in her face and Rob delighted in brushing it away. Later, Alice picked up one of the bamboo poles and suggestively put it up to her mouth. When Rob laughed, she went further and pretended to fellate it.

There was an angry yelp from a few feet away. Sue had been looking over from her raft. She dropped her oil drum with a hollow clatter and marched over to them.

"I'm not being funny," she announced, unnecessarily since she wasn't wearing a comedy face but the pasty death-mask of fight or flight. "But she's just a cheap little whore and you're a stupid little boy who leads her on 'cos he doesn't know what he wants."

Alice smirked and barked out, "Oh, he knows what he wants alright."

Sue said nothing else but bent down and picked up the bamboo pole Alice had dropped. She opened her mouth then, as if she might have something else to say but all that came out was a whiny hiss of rage.

She lifted the pole high above her head and made as if to bring it down on Alice's back. Alice ran shrieking for the chalets and Sue pursued her for thirty yards or so, swinging the pole, then brought herself up sharp and turned to face Rob. He had been watching, blankly, intently and detached from the action but he realised suddenly he was in danger.

"Crap," he said, redundantly, running for the half-finished raft by the water's edge as she bore down on him, waving the pole round her head like a Samurai warrior issuing an ululating cry of pain and anger.

Their raft, such as it was, currently consisted of two oil drums, one lashed to either side of a palette. Rob bundled it into the water and shoved away from the beach not minding the soaking he was getting. He pushed until his feet left the floor and started kicking. He was saved only because Sue gave up the chase at the water's edge, though she did fling the bamboo pole after him like a javelin.

It glanced off his shoulder and hit one of the big orange oil drums with a resounding boing. Out on the water now he looked back to see Sue and the two property guys watching him from the shore. She still looked furious, they were baffled, fags in hand.

The teams from the other rafts had halted their manufacturing process and downed tools to watch. There was laughter, it seemed they believed that the whole business with Sue and the chase had been high jinks rather than attempted murder.

Out on the water, consumed by the cold, Rob was curiously calm. In the distance, the middle management team whooped and hollered in good natured encouragement at his pre-emptive attempt to reach the buoy. When he looked back over his shoulder he saw Lou's team trying to launch their raft in belated pursuit but it only amounted to three planks and a drum so it wasn't going anywhere even though it only had Lou perched on it who didn't weigh much at all. It dragged on the pebbles in the shallows and she sat upright at the prow like a prim Boudicca as her underlings tried to haul her into deeper water.

Rob kicked lazily through the cold water. When he looked up into the mid-morning sunshine, the pines glistened around the edges of the man-made lake and the sky was a slaked blue, the colour of old jeans.

When a man argues with a woman it's like a ship in a storm. When two women argue it's like two storms which bellow into each other until they blow themselves out. Must be hard having an argument with another woman he pondered, neither one wanting to be the sensible, logical one, both wanting to rely on emotional arguments. He realised his bollocks were getting numb. Better kick on.

Floating around with his half-finished raft beneath him, Rob realised he might as well keep on trucking towards the buoy. He circumnavigated it within five minutes and headed back to the shore. When he cast up on the pebbles, Sue had calmed down a little it seemed and anyway, there were authority figures around. Lou had come over from her raft and the two boy scouts with the staff T-shirts were there to pronounce Rob's team the winner. It was unorthodox they said, but there was nothing in the rules about the raft being finished, only that it had to float and that a team member had to get around the buoy.

Rob was presented with a gold coloured medal on a red, white and blue ribbon. The medal said 'Winner' on it and Rob could not have been more proud.

Lou didn't seem particularly pleased that he'd won the raft race. His team all got a medal and they were still wearing them at lunch. He wondered whether to go and sit by Sue to try to make up with her. He didn't think it would be all that tough, after all she was often in a towering rage and it soon passed, especially if someone was prepared to grovel.

As he approached her table she shot to her feet without looking at him and stalked quickly over to talk to Jayden by the breakfast bar, laughing and bumping hips with him, ruffling his razor-cut hair. He loved it but was careful not to show it too much. At one point, he even ignored her for a bit and pretended he was more interested in reading the weekly rag which was on the bar. Sue was clearly put out and made more effort to win his attention. Was he a PUA too? Rob wondered. Maybe some people were just naturally good at this stuff.

Rob decided to go find Lou and showed her his medal with faux pride, like a caveman bringing meat home to his woman. She tolerated him sitting down next to her but he could tell she was still irked that he had won a contest in which she had been a competitor.

Rob looked over to where Sue was flirting with Jayden, arm round his waist, wriggling and giggling as he tickled her and felt an absurd bolt of jealousy. He had feelings he did not know what to do with and they crowded in on him in dark and quiet moments of the day. They made him feel prey to their whims. It was as though someone was injecting him with chemicals to make him bend to their will.

He turned back to Lou who was telling him that he only won by dumb luck and that if he had followed the rules properly and built the raft correctly before trying to launch it, he would probably have come last and she, Louise, would instead have the gaudy plastic medal dangling between her petite bosoms.

"It was a physical challenge," he told her, voice rich with ennui. "You need man strength for that stuff. Perhaps they should have given you girls a head start and I'd have let you win if you'd told me it was so important to you."

She shrieked in mocking horror and gave him a slap on the chest, "You're a bad lad," she told him, looking deep into his eyes.

Rob wanted to glance over to see if Sue was looking but managed to resist. It didn't seem so bad somehow that a woman he was kind of involved with was flirting with someone else, so long as he was doing the same. It was like a competition. 'You're making me feel bad but I bet I can make you feel even worse'. It was a contest in which women always had a built in advantage, since they only had to walk into a room to get flirted with *if* they wanted to. After lunch it was abseiling. Rob wasn't the best with heights but he wasn't particularly worried because he didn't know what abseiling was. He assumed from the sound of the word it had something in common with sailing, perhaps it was a fancy name for windsurfing - he resigned himself to getting wet again.

Even when he trooped onto the minibus with the rest and it shot off towards the hills, he still assumed they were heading for some other pond set back in the Cotswolds. As they rattled through B-roads with one of the boy scouts at the wheel, Alice explained to him that he was going to fall backwards off a cliff top with a rope round his waist.

"Crap," Rob said, crisply, as the bus pulled to a halt in a dusty quarry at the foot of a wall of honey-coloured Cotswold stone.

"You scared pet?" cooed Alice, not without malice, she was enjoying his discomfort it seemed.

They stepped down from the bus into a powdery compound which was surrounded by tall pines, trees which - like everything else about the environment here - seemed to be placed there by man rather than nature. There was a slight artificiality about the place, it was stilted, prettified and improved.

The other boy scout came bounding up in a florescent orange hard hat, there was a trailer full of similar luminescent headgear behind him attached to a battered Land Rover that had been painted up to look like a leopard and had 'Cotswold Safari' emblazoned on the side with a face of a big cat roaring.

There were three candy-coloured ropes dangling down from the rockface. The scout was wearing a leopard print T-shirt, a pair of football shorts, bright red socks, climbing boots and a harness which seemed to be way too tight around the crotch.

"You can tell he's excited to be here," beamed Alice.

Once he'd got going with his safety lecture it became clear he was thrilled to be in charge of something which would give most of them the willies. 'They had to have respect for the rock,' he said, slapping it with a chunky red hand and pacing back and forth. Apparently, there was nothing to fear so long as you obeyed the rules. There were lots of rules but the main one was always obey the instructor.

"What's the main rule?" he barked, pointing at Lou.

"Never wear socks with shorts," she shot back and everybody laughed.

He blushed but carried on. "Get in threes. Adrian will get you suited and booted and take you to the peak."

He counted off down the line as the groups peeled away. "You, you and you." Lou, Susan, Rob.

They put on their helmets and boots, Adrian tightened a harness around each of their waists, flirting with the girls as he fitted theirs and making them giggle. Rob wished a rock would fall on his head.

At the top of the cliff they waited their turn. The vegetation told a tale of a different climate, a Mediterranean one, spacious and sandy, with outbreaks of rock through the weeds and thin soil. For a short while Rob was frightened, then he tried to suck up to Sue who ignored him completely, then he was bored.

He lay in the sun and stared at an ant's nest. The black dots scuttled about industriously, each seeming sure of its destination, as if acting on orders. People were a lot like ants, Rob thought to himself, blowing at the insects so they braced themselves as if caught in a gale.

Maybe ants were like people. Maybe they believed they had their own lives when *really* they were just part of a bigger machine, an economic and social organism for which they worked, from birth to death. All the little triumphs and woes and chasing after the opposite sex in the context of their ants' nest. It wasn't all that important really and if one ant went missing there were always more to take its place.

High up on the ridge the air moved warm and lazy. Rob stared out over a handful of quarry pigeons that hung beneath him over the escarpment, glittering all purple, green and confident.

"They used to be rare birds," Lou said breathily. "They were called rock doves and it was hard to even find them, then they realised a building was as good as a cliff face. Now they're everywhere and people think of them as vermin."

"Very clever," Sue chipped in. "You are so *very* clever Louise."

The abseilers were let down in groups of three. A row of them stood on the edge of the abyss, laughing nervously at first as their harnesses were attached to the lines and they were given a recap on the instructions they'd already received at the foot of the cliff. Then whey-faced and quiet, they leaned backwards over the drop, suspended in mid-air like cartoon characters who never fall until they realise they have run out of road.

Their gloved-hands clung grimly to the nylon rope which appeared to be all that kept them from plummeting to a messy death, ending their lives as a blob of raspberry jam and man-made fibres on the floor of the quarry.

Rob intently watched three groups make the descent before it was his turn. He observed the tops of their orange hard hats disappear over the lip, then heard a period of grunting and straining accompanied by the tap-dance of boots on the cliff face, and (eventually) some low-key applause complete with shrieks of personal victory welling up from below.

When it was his turn, he allowed the boy scout to lead him forward like a meek old Labrador and attach him to his lead. He got the middle rope with Sue to his left and Louise on his right. He felt fine really, vague and faintly numb like he was somewhere else watching events unfold on the sports channel. It was all fine right up to the bit when the boy scout told him it was time to turn his back to the drop and take the slack up on the rope.

Suddenly, his head was light, his mouth was dry and his stomach dropped as though he was in a fast lift. Desperately, he tried to remember what he had been told to do with his feet and his hands. One section of the rope acted as a brake, the other he was supposed to feed upwards as he fell, in a controlled manner, towards the second tier management gathered beneath. Unfortunately, he couldn't remember which bit of rope did what, even though he had *just* had it explained to him. If he cocked it up, would he crash to the ground? He had been told he would be fine but that's what people always believe just before an unexpected disaster - that's why it was 'unexpected'.

That's also why, when a devil-dog attacks a little old lady, the chav supposed to be looking after it always says, "He's never done that before. He's soft as shite is Fang."

Rob wondered whether it was too late to pull out of the whole thing. Feign an injury maybe and limp back down the path to join the others at the bottom but he could imagine Jayden and the lads laughing at him for bottling out. He thought of Lou's face once she had abseiled serenely to the ground, her puzzled expression as she mulled over his cowardice. He knew he had to go over, whatever the consequences.

With his arse hanging over edge of the cliff, Rob had no faith at all in the whole endeavour. What *was* he trying to prove after all? He didn't want to be a mountain climber, he *certainly* didn't want to be a middle manager. The only question that remained was, would leaping backwards off a mountain impress women? The answer he arrived at, with his toes clinging to the cliff edge, his tense butt cheeks constricted by the DayGlo harness and the boy scout more or less shoving him off the edge, was probably *no!*

Well, no more than it would if he showed his sensitive side by backing out. Did PUAs show their sensitive sides? He strove to remember, couldn't and was still trying to work it out, when he slipped off the side of the cliff.

"Fucking shite," he exclaimed involuntarily as he fell backwards, the words wheezed out of him in a high wild girlish scream. He could hear Sue, to his left, further down the cliff laughing in sarcastic triumph.

The rope stopped his descent sharply, his head snapped back and his feet skittered on the rockface like a cartoon cat running on marbles. The boy scout was yelling at him to keep his body taught and to remember to feed the rope through, like he'd been shown.

Sue's laugh flooded his ears again and Rob, floundering and panicking, suddenly thought, 'Do you know what? She's right, this *is* funny,' and he laughed which calmed him down.

His trainers gained a little traction and the rope he was holding didn't seem likely to fail him. He stood there on the rockface for a short while, just breathing heavily.

"You alright Robbie?"

It was Lou, down to his right. What to say? To be honest, any words he spoke would be weak and quavering. Sweat was pouring from his brow stinging his eyes. Instead of saying anything he shuffled down the

182

cliff a few steps, moving his left arm away from his body gingerly to release the brake on his rope enough to allow him down.

"Yeah!" he managed to croak. "Having a right laugh."

He descended gently, then a tad more realising that the more he fell in this controlled, non-dying kind of way, the nearer he would be to getting his feet back on the ground. He hated it though and knew when he reached the foot of the cliff he'd be telling everybody it was 'nowt really' and that he fancied doing it again some other time. In truth, it was a cruel kind of torture combining his fear of heights with an even greater fear of making an ass of himself in front of everybody and particularly in front of Lou.

He let himself down some more and glancing to his left could see the sun glinting off the top of Sue's plastic orange helmet. She appeared to have stopped, perhaps waiting to give him a hand?

"I think I'm alright," he called down to her in a trembling voice. "Don't worry, I'm getting the hang of it now."

There was a derisive snort and he let the rope out a bit further until he was more or less level with her. He looked across with a watery smile and she sneered back at him, face full of aggression.

"Suffering?" she snapped. "Now you know what it's like then." and she dug her heels against the side of the pale cliff and swung over to him.

"Hey don't... you'll have us both off," he yelped in panic.

He thought she was going to grab him with her legs but she changed course at the last minute and caught him a bony knee in the chest.

"Woof?" he said, his hands slipping from the rope and his feet dangling.

The pendulum swing of the rope took her away from him again and she dropped out of sight, slipping the line though her fingers, leaving him lost and helpless like a marionette with cut strings. He felt his head tipping backwards again and his feet lifting into the air. Queasy with fear, he grabbed at the rope and clung to it, although he had lost the line he was supposed to use to lower himself to the ground.

He heard the calming voice of the boy scout who was peering over the edge of the cliff. "Steady – steady - don't panic - you won't fall but you have to calm down enough to right yourself".

Rob couldn't utter a word and instead made a meek wailing noise, the sort he'd last made when dragged onto amusement park rides as a child.

He was going to die, he felt sure of it, whether it was quickly with a sickening fall and a snapped neck, or slowly through dehydration as the emergency services fought to rescue him.

He was dead meat, hanging like a side of beef on an abattoir rail. His feet were above his head now, he hung uselessly, the fight draining out of him.

He felt a hand on his shoulder, another human being. Had the boy scout come down to rescue him? He turned his head as much as he dared and saw Lou, her blonde mane sticking out from under her hard hat, big grey eyes full of proper concern.

"Rob. It's okay hun honest. Let me get you upright and we'll get down nice and easy."

She was pushing at his feet and he let her guide them gently down so his head swung back up with a sick-making swirl of colour and light. He felt dizzy and frightened, mainly relieved and part-grateful that his feet were back on the rockface. He planted them there firmly and felt Lou slipping the rope back into his hand.

"You're okay - just feed this through like you were before - you're halfway down - do it with me."

He did and they started to descend together, her keeping pace with him as he scrambled in an ungainly skitter down the rock.

"That's it," she repeated in a soothing way. "Nearly there, not far to go now."

He realised she was able to look down and see the ground approach, something he couldn't bring himself to do.

"Thirty feet," she said. "Twenty," then, "your almost on the ground."

She managed to calm him to such an extent that, when the other boy scout grabbed him round the waist and lifted him off the rock, uttering gruff words of reassurance, he had the presence of mind to be embarrassed about the whole thing. He even thought about struggling and protesting so that he could, 'get down on my own thank you'.

There was an ironic cheer and some laughter from the others as his feet finally found terra firma but there were murmurs of sympathy too, particularly from the girls, which was gratifying.

Maybe this wouldn't be as bad for his credibility as he had feared.

Once he'd steadied himself, he felt so relieved he wanted to cry. Equally though, if he was honest with himself, he was quite exhilarated with the decent and the fuss which had accompanied it.

There had been something intense and life-affirming in it. That was what was so addictive about Sue, she was less sexy than either Lou or Alice but strangely attractive nonetheless.

Mind you, she had just tried to kill him, so maybe not.

He felt dizzy suddenly, his feet gave way underneath him and he fell heavily on his backside. Darkness came, like he'd taken a short nap, then there was light and the heat of the sun on his face. Sitting down there in the dust, his head swam and he felt sick but mostly he felt foolish and unmanned.

Louise and Sue were both untangling themselves from their harnesses and seemed not to have registered his collapse. Alice, thankfully, was still at the cliff top awaiting her descent. Jayden moved in, laughing and offered him a friendly hand.

"Made a meal of that mate," he commented cheerfully. "Think you *actually* fainted! Thought we might have to call the paramedics for a minute."

"Yeah... I don't know what happened," Rob replied hesitantly.

He didn't know how to play this at all, whether he was supposed to be howling with rage at Sue or pretending nothing had happened. Avoiding the issue was his default setting certainly, it felt comfortable and sustainable. Denial was a very underrated skill and he couldn't work out why it always seemed to get such a bad rap; it had served his mother well, he remembered, in her final days.

"I think I slipped and Sue came to help me?"

"Funny fucking help," Jayden remarked thoughtfully, as he led Rob over to the bus.

"Then Lou helped me out too. She got me back on track. It's okay once you get the hang of it, isn't it?"

"Yeah," Jayden said, not unkindly, "but I don't really think you've got the hang of it yet - do you buddy?"

When they got back to the lodge Rob was hoping to let bygones be bygones but Louise snapped at Sue pretty much as soon as they both got their skinny arses through the door. Lou wanted to see her for a private chat.

Neither had said anything as they sat at the opposite ends of the bus on the trip back, neither to each other nor to Rob, who'd sat with his head down worried that people might take the piss out of his inelegant descent. Now they were back, it seemed Louise had things to say.

She led Sue to her bedroom, as these were the only rooms in the place which afforded a degree of privacy, although they still had matchwood-thin walls which issued booming echoes.

The pair of them stomped off and Rob could hear raised voices resounding back and forth indistinctly as he sat in the kitchen diner with a calming cup of tea, studiously avoiding Alice's gaze. The altercation was accompanied by the occasional bass beat of foot thumping and now and then, the high shrill treble of a forced laugh.

Rob knew the acoustics of the place made any conversation in the rooms sound like a wild night out at the Vodka Revolution but still it was clear there was a forthright exchange of ideas taking place. After perhaps ten minutes, Sue returned to the dining area dabbing her eyes with a piece of toilet roll, in a very un-Sue-like show of her soft feminine side.

"She wants to see you now," she said with a catch in her voice, barely glancing at Rob, then sat down next to Alice who seemed inclined to offer her clucking and comfort despite the fact that they had been wrenching each other's hair extensions out at Rob's sickbed a couple of days earlier.

'You know what I've got?' Rob thought to himself, silently. 'I've got the future. However things are now, this is just the start, they will change, they will get better. There's no reason the future can't be great, even greater than this and this is pretty good sometimes, though not right now admittedly with the sky falling in and furious women plotting my downfall.'

He wondered precisely what his future would hold but only caught glimpses of his fate vaguely through a clouded glass, nothing distinct, only an impression.

There was an overwhelming feeling of happiness and an end to his loneliness. Right now, he'd settle for that, whatever the details turned out to be.

He rapped on Lou's door and her voice said, "Come," all cold and official. When he stepped into her room he was alarmed to see she'd it set up as an office. The dressing table had been dragged into the middle of the room and her chair was placed behind it. He was supposed to sit on the bed, which he did awkwardly, perched on the edge.

Who had dragged the dressing table out of whack? Sue *and* Lou? It must have been a struggle, the pair of them together probably didn't weigh as much as those sticks of laminated marble look MDF. Even with all Sue's pent up aggression it must have been tough but they'd done it and on the night table was a jug of water and a glass, presumably for him as Lou had her own.

"It's a delicate situation," she said gravely. "There has been a charge made against you - of sexual harassment."

It was early stages, Lou told him, the full details would have to be raked over in a formal hearing, probably a series of hearings but in the meantime he was advised to seek legal guidance. He was to be assured that the company took allegations of this nature very seriously but also that he would receive a fair trial.

What was he supposed to have done? He wanted to know. Lou could not tell him, all she was in a position to divulge at this stage, was that his colleague, Susan Preston, had made a serious and formal allegation that he had behaved inappropriately towards her both in and outside of the workplace and that, as a result, her work had been affected.

As a result of this allegation, a formal investigation was to take place with a view to possible disciplinary procedures. He was to go away now and she would see him again briefly tomorrow when she'd have more information about the way forward for the case.

Blank and vague Rob left her in the room and wandered down the corridor. He let himself out the back door of the echoing wooden house and drifted down to the shore of the lake, his feet popping and cracking on the gravel-like breakfast cereal.

What was it he wondered that had made Sue hate him so much? Was he as evil as she seemed to believe? There must be something in it, something which had turned her so deeply and powerfully against him that she was willing to destroy him.

He thought back to just a few days before when they had been entwined on his armchair, then back further to when they walked arm in arm on the hill. They felt like scenes from a chick flick - how had they gone from that to the Bride of Frankenstein in less than a week?

He picked up a pebble about the size of a hen's egg and weighed it in his hand and flung it into the darkness of the lake. There was silence followed by a hollow clanking sound.

"Hey, *fuck off!*" came an aggrieved voice out of the blackness, behind it was a squeal, then a girlie-giggle.

"Sorry," Rob shouted, raising his arm, though he realised when it was up there that nobody could see it. "Sorry Jayden - sorry whoever."

"Yeah?" a female voice came back over the water. "Well pack it in you dick head." He recognised the voice he thought, or maybe he didn't.

There was nothing doing out here except to play gooseberry so he went to his room which felt small and oppressive, cold and bare. He wished he was home in his own bed, even if he still had this hanging over him. At least there it would feel less alien and intense, more like something which was part of his real life.

He had to talk to Sam but the call just went to ansaphone. Sam's voice, blunt and unapologetic said, "I'm out - leave a message dude."

So instead he logged onto the PUA site and went to the chat area. There he saw a few of his regular guys were online. Chilled was there, so was Pies and lonesome Bob who all sympathised with his plight, in the bowdlerised way he felt able to explain it to them.

There was no sign of Sonof, the one chat member he thought might really be able to help him, so he left a private message for him, spelling out the situation slightly more frankly than he did for the others, then he logged off, let his laptop drop to the side of the bed and tried to get some sleep.

He woke startled to hear the door of his room bang open. Squinted into the lit corridor to see Jayden, quite apologetic at having woken him.

"Hey - visitor for you outside."

"What time is it?" Rob wanted to know, still muzzy with sleep.

"Not late - 'bout half one, there's people still up, so put your kegs on."

'People' turned out to be Sue, perched on a stool with the remains of a bottle of red wine on the breakfast bar in front of her. Maybe she'd been drinking with Jayden. Sue ignored him with an energy of passion, like the inner workings of a half-empty wine bottle, was what she was doing her dissertation on.

There was no sign of any visitor though.

He wondered whether he should ask Sue but to be honest, she wasn't looking very approachable, besides, he wasn't sure whether he was allowed to talk to her, whether it was sub judice or whatever. He didn't want to prejudice his trial... crap, this was terrible.

Right about then the front door, which had been left ajar, banged open in the wind and there was a figure backlit by the patio spotlight. Someone with a shock of red hair lit up like a Belisha beacon.

Sue slipped off her stool and stalked over towards the door to investigate. The figure spoke.

"Here we are - stupid o'clock - it's dark and it's raining - what the *fuck* am I doing here?"

Sue stopped dead still, a few steps from the door, her back stiffened like an angry cat.

"What are *you* doing here?"

"I was summoned," Sam spoke softly in the night air, "Sue - come out here for a moment, I want a word with you."

Sue didn't move. She stood frozen, ready to leap. She was attempting nonchalance but appeared baffled and diminished.

"What you doing way out here?" she said at length. "This is just management this weekend. Senior and second tier."

The figure in the doorway shook its head, hair flaming orange, accompanying their mood well.

"I'm here to see you. It's a personal matter, it's important. I wouldn't have dragged myself out of bed for it otherwise."

Sue made as if to move towards the door but then she changed her mind and turned her back on it, setting off with purpose across the lounge diner, shoes clacking on the laminate flooring in the direction of the bedrooms.

"I don't have time for any of your shit," Sue shot back dismissively over her shoulder. "I have a long day tomorrow and there's work to do. I'm going to bed and I suggest you get back to your rust heap of a car and head home to yours."

Sam didn't move but replied in a raised voice, strong and level which allowed for no misinterpretation.

"If you don't step out on this porch with me now, I'll drag you out by your hair. You *know* I can do it and that I will."

That stopped her. She half turned back to the doorway and didn't seem so sure of herself any more.

"I know you," Sam told her. "You're a bully but you're weak. What do you think you're going to get from destroying this young lad?" Sam waved a dismissive arm in Rob's direction. "He's an idiot."

Rob was put out, if this was help then maybe he'd been doing okay on his own.

"But he's harmless and he's certainly done nothing at all to you."

Sue reared up, prickly with indignation.

"He *has* done, you don't know, he's to blame!" she insisted shrilly.

She pushed towards the open door as if to slam it shut on Sam, to close down the challenge to her point of view but Sam refused to budge, when Sue's hand came up to grab the door frame, it was slapped back down again.

"You're not angry with Robbie, you don't give a *shit* about the daft little sod either way. He's just someone for you to take your rage out on, just another man. I know about you Sue, let's not forget that. There's been enough drunken evenings. I know what goes on inside your head. All that pain in there but I won't let you take it out on him."

"Just because you got interfered with by one man, doesn't mean they're all the same you know. The world's not made up of guys like your *brother!*"

There was a terrible emptiness in the room, it was like the silence after the dropping of a small, lounge-sized atom bomb. No birds sang, no flies buzzed. The air had been sucked out of Sue too, she stood silent as a child who hopes standing still will make her disappear.

Sam played statues too, alert and expectant.

Rob stood quietly in the corner, unheeded, feeling surplus.

Then Sue began to cry. Her body started shaking, softly at first then decidedly violently. She made a sniffing noise.

"Is she okay?" asked Rob.

"Oh, *what?* " Sam exploded. "Look, I wouldn't worry about it. She's what the 'It's Complicated' relationship status was invented for."

Rob moved over to Sue where she stood, frail and shaking and took her up in his arms and hugged her but not too tight. She felt like a fledgling he might inadvertently crush. And she was crying, or maybe he was now, stood there in the dark and quiet. It took Rob some minutes to register that Sam had gone, the sound of a car engine a lonely rattle in the distance.

He was left feeling terribly self-conscious. Where was this 'cuddling Sue' thing heading? He snuggled in closer to be polite but she pulled away, dealing him a bony arm in the ribs and backed off, hissing.

"You tell anyone..." and she was off to bed, leaving Rob feeling sad that she would ever think he would, he could...

There was nothing doing anywhere in the darkened house so he went to bed too.

The next morning, waking from uneasy dreams, he breakfasted on cardboard and water and bathed in the cold, damp fear of the condemned man. As he sat drinking coffee, Jayden came up, stood next to his table and awkwardly addressed Rob.

"Hey - the boss sent me over to tell you to go speak to her," they both looked over to where Lou was sitting with her back to them.

"I mean - I dunno why she couldn't just come over herself," Jayden shrugged apologetically and then couldn't get away fast enough.

When Rob went over, Lou addressed him without even looking up from her document folder.

"I need to speak to you in my office about that matter I outlined yesterday. Take ten minutes to pre-prepare and then we'll conversate about it."

He took ten minutes to go to the loo then knocked on her bedroom door. The room was still set out like an office and he assumed she must have slept in her bed but it didn't look like it, all straightened out for him to sit on again.

When he entered, she was roosting behind her dressing table with her mobile clamped to her ear.

"It's the flagship proposal in our new raft of measures, we hope to deliver to benchmarked targets going forward..."

The call ended and she looked up as if noticing him for the first time and waved him to sit down.

"Sorry, just interfacing with regional - now."

Rob's words came out with a big rush of air. Things he hadn't even known he was thinking spilled out of him in a stream of consciousness rush.

"I mean, I didn't think I was but you know, when you put yourself in the other person's shoes and I wouldn't, I mean I never, not in a million years but perhaps I was. Guilty I mean of doing what she said."

He focussed on Lou to find she was frowning and waving at him to shut up.

"No," she said firmly. "You did not. You did nothing."

He stared at her all sweaty and dumb.

"Sue has dropped the allegations," she told him calmly. "She says she has been under a lot of strain... personal issues... now she's had chance to sleep on it, she realises her earlier statement was precipitative."

They stood in silence for a while. Rob didn't feel particularly relieved, just a bit depressed about the whole thing, that it had happened at all, that everyone had got so upset. It was alright now though he supposed, everything was okay, for *him* anyway - he felt sorry for Sue.

Standing there in the bedroom, Rob became aware for the first time that he and Lou were alone together. Lou seemed to realise it too and as she perched her birdlike bottom on the end of the bed, she stiffened a little. They had been together during the 'business' part of the proceedings sure enough but in the room with them had been a weight of work and bureaucratic language, procedure and formal process. Now it was just him and her for the first time since they'd groped and wrestled together in the bottom of the boat. A place where he might have hoped things would be easy and relaxed and perhaps they could slip back into the mood which had led to such shenanigans.

Instead, they both found the atmosphere awkward.

"I wouldn't worry," Lou said vaguely, "about anything."

She seemed to be interested in the window, what was going on out there in the car park, rather more than she was engaged with Rob. He found himself looking out there too but there was nothing to see except swirls of dust and a magpie worrying a crisp packet.

"Oh and," she looked back at him, "you know that when we get back to the office, I'm the boss again and you work for me. As a fairly junior employee."

Rob bridled at junior a little but didn't say anything. He understood she had to put the fence back up again somehow but knew there was a gap in it now and maybe he could squeeze through again if he wanted.

He smirked and she didn't like that. She frowned and seemed to be preparing to give him a bollocking but apparently there *was* action out in the car park.

The magpie had tired of eating crisps and rose into the air with a squawk as if being pursued. There was the sound of a car behind the hedge and Lou leapt up as it turned into the car park but lost interest when she saw it was only the boy scouts in their cloudy red Citroen arriving to organise the morning's fun and games.

She sat back down again and Rob was wondering if he could back out of the room without her noticing but she patted the duvet beside her for him to sit next to her which he did, though still feeling stilted and out of sorts.

"You know what I'm going to say to you now, don't you?" Lou said with a forced smile. He didn't. Not really.

"About last night!" she said with a mirthless giggle. "About last night."

But she didn't seem to have anything to say about last night of any consequence and just sat there looking at him with panic in her eyes waiting for him to rescue her.

Which he did in the end, by saying, "It's okay, I get it, what goes at camp, stays at camp, right?"

She nodded, obviously embarrassed and surprisingly poor at covering it up given her usual poise. The nodding went on rather too long, she made an, 'Mmm', sound to go with it, then said, "It's not... it's just..."

"Oh you don't..." said Rob but she had more.

"No I mean, I shouldn't have you see, I'm in a relationship - kind of."

He didn't like the sound of that. He'd thought since the divorce she was married to the office and didn't have time for anything more. He hadn't heard about a man from the back door fag smokers and that nugget would certainly have been gossip worthy.

He found he was nodding, then she started up again too. They sat nodding at each other for a while, who knows how long that might have gone on for but out of the window there was the sound of another car approaching. There was the drone of an engine and the prickle of the wheels on gravel which broke their uncomfortable trance.

They both jumped to their feet again but he got the impression that, if she could have held him back down on the bed, prevented him from seeing who had arrived, then she would have done.

He looked out of the window to see a big black BMW 7 series pulling up, dust swirling around it. In the driver's seat looking rather out of sorts was their permanently under-whelmed MD, Wee Willie McBean.

"Aw bollocks, what's he doing here?" Rob vented. "He must have heard we were having a laugh and come along to suck the blood out of it." He looked over at Lou to make sure he had not overstepped the mark and was astonished to see how excited she seemed. She glowed, she was thrilled with the whole concept of Wee Willie's surprise arrival. In fact, it transpired it was not much of a surprise at all.

"It's okay," she said. "He's not stopping," and she bent and slid her suitcase out from under her bed, pink leather, pricey looking.

"I have to go now, I have another commitment. Jayden is aware he's now acting up into my role for the rest of today so," she took a look at him and realised he was smashed by this turn of events.

She paused, brushed his hair from where it had fallen over his eye said, "Hey - we had fun though, right?"

"Yeah," he said flatly, "...fun!"

Then with a swift, "See you Monday," she was gone, skittering excitedly out of the room and down the hall.

The door slammed and there she was again out of the window, heading over to the big black Beamer with her bag trailing behind her. She waved at the car and Wee Willie looked back at her, clearly pissed off. She let herself in the driver's side, dumped the case on the back seat and after she had slammed the door behind her, she did something which would stay in Rob's mind a long while to come; she lent over and kissed Willie on the cheek. He scowled as though it had been an imposition, slammed the car into reverse and was gone from the place in a cloud of pale pink dust.

Rob stood and stared out of the window for a while, even though there was nothing to see apart from the magpie that had come back. Presently, he found he was talking to himself, out loud, pondering what he'd witnessed.

"He's married. What about his family, his kids, his wife? It's not right," he said primly, though there was a cold wind blowing up on the moral high ground.

He wondered bleakly about what they got up to, the two of them. Where they met, what they talked about? Was Wee Willie *still* the boss in their private time? Did they talk endlessly about work? Did they whisper to each other in management speak when they met secretly in bars and restaurants late in the after-work evenings? When would they have time to be together given that he had to attend to his kids and keep his wife sweet? There were conferences of course, always plenty of those, team building exercises, awards evenings. Lots of overnights in hotel bedrooms.

Rob thought about the pair of them having sex and it plunged him into a dull flat spin of depression. He thumped his head forward so it banged on the window pane and scared off the magpie which disappeared over the boundary hedge with a clatter of wings.

"Bollocks," he said. Then, for some reason, which wasn't entirely clear to him, he flattened his face on the glass, shut his eyes and filled his mouth with air so it blew his cheeks out. It felt cathartic and took him back to a simpler time in his childhood when nothing really mattered much and there wasn't a problem in creation his mum couldn't sort out.

When he opened his eyes again, Alice and Jayden were standing among the low bushes on the other side of the window staring at him.

"Jesus Christ," he yelled, leaping back. It wasn't just that he'd got caught making a blowfish face, it was the whole issue of where had they had appeared from so quickly. They must have just stood up out of the undergrowth but what the hell would they have been doing in there in the first place?

They seemed surprised to see him too, they weren't laughing for a start, instead they looked startled, clearly caught out doing something they ought not to have been doing.

While he stared at them, they stared back without moving away, they fidgeted a little, at a loss for what to do. Rob decided to go to the loo but before turning away he lifted his arm and brushed the imprint of his face from the window with his hand, like a window cleaner waving goodbye, goodbye.

CHAPTER 10

'Johnno!' the blog of Robert Johnson, July 24:
"What's the point of this sodding thing anyway? Who the hell cares what I think? I promise to keep my naïve, stupid thoughts to myself from now on."

The three wise monkeys could see Rob Johnson was in turmoil and were considerate of his pain.

"Tough weekend then my lovely?" Jude enquired, after he had stared at his coffee mug for half an hour.

Rob shrugged and gave her a little grin, grateful for the concern but too weary to go into everything. Instead of an explanation, he came up with a question.

"So how do you get them to fancy you?" he wanted to know, "and how do you know if they are likely to, or when it's worked?"

"Ah, Colin replied sadly. "As the great poet and philosopher Betty Boo once wrote,'I've used up all my tissues on this most serious of issues'."

"Perhaps you're just heading off in the wrong direction?" Alan interjected from the far side of the desk, his glasses glinting with sincerity as he peered around his flat screen.

Jude got excited. This is what she'd been saying for ages, she put in breathlessly, Alan was just being an energy thief.

"What you want..." she said triumphantly, "is a nice girl who likes you for who you are. Now I know there aren't going to be many of those around but what about that Sam?"

Colin nodded solemnly. "Nowt wrong with her son, she's a bit of alright... for a ginner."

"Nothing the matter with a ginner," Alan contended, "they're very passionate people."

"Ginger pubes are a real turn off though," Colin said thoughtfully.

Jude tutted and broke in crossly, like she was the only adult there.

"She's a lovely young lass and she obviously cares for you. You care for each other. I don't see what the problem is or why you've had to go all round the houses with these other sorts, some of whom are no better than they ought to be."

"Oh, they're okay," Rob said, absently. "They're all kind of being themselves but I mean, Sam? We're just friends."

He picked up a paper clip and peered at it as though he'd never seen one before.

"There's nothing wrong with shagging your friends," Jude said firmly. "I would highly recommend it. Me and my Dave were friends before we got together, we still are friends, that's what keeps you together when you get bored of having sex with each other."

Colin and Alan made supportive noises.

"Mind you," Jude added. "It won't last. She's way too good for you but if you're lucky, it'll take her a few months to realise that."

Rob studied his paper clip. It wasn't as though he'd never thought of Sam in that way, it's just that he had put it out of his mind as impractical and toweringly unlikely. They were mates, buddies, like lads together down the pub or, if he was going to acknowledge Sam's sex at all, like brother and sister. He felt sure that's how she would see it but then, that was a big assumption.

Why was he making it?

Perhaps because he was afraid. To make a sexual approach to Sue say, or Alice, meant risking nothing very much apart from a loss of dignity and he had never been very big on dignity anyway. To make such an approach to Sam and be rebuffed would be the death of their friendship, something which he cared about deeply because he realised she was one of the very few people he would truly call a friend.

He was still thinking about it half an hour later in the tea room.

"What are you doing?" said Sam, her copper hair shone in stripes where the sun caught it through the blinds.

"I'm trying to get the top off this jar," Rob admitted, the low-sugar black cherry jam Lou had with her breakfast wholemeal which, as a special treat, he was permitted to prepare.

"Give it here," Sam commanded.

"No." Rob hugged it to his chest with the soiled Weston Super Mare tea-towel he was using to try and shift the stubborn lid.

"Give." Samantha held out a slender hand.

He looked at the hand for a moment, then at her face. She had a snubbed nosed, serious freckles from the summer sun and the start of a tan. She laughed at his deliberations and took the jar from him, gripping it to her chest and wrestling it with a grimace.

There was a sucking pop as the lid came free.

"You must have loosened it," she said soothingly as she handed it back to him.

He stared at the jar contemplatively, stirred the purple syrup with his knife and said, "I mean Vagicil. What the hell's that? I don't know but I can guess from the name that it's something I wouldn't want to order a pint of."

"Just stop about the woman's complaints will you, it's getting older than Lou."

"I can't help it, you're all just so badly designed, too complex, bits breaking down."

"I never thought I'd say this but this is why men don't have babies."

He glanced over at her as she stared at the toaster. "Want to go somewhere?" he said.

"What, now?"

"No, later. After work, you and me?"

She thought about it. "Mmm, okay, but I pick. If you choose it will be somewhere crap. Meet me at my car when you can get away. I'll think of somewhere good to go. Somewhere fun."

Swindon dog track was a short way off the ring road tucked away in the midst of an industrial estate which must have grown up around its sixties concrete architecture. It reminded Rob of a non-league football ground, low rise and slightly crumbling but not seedy. Dilapidated but decent.

They paid a paltry amount at the turnstile and wandered through the twilight past men in tweed coats with patches on the sleeves. They mounted dimly lit stairs to the bar which overlooked the track. Its décor was early '80s transport café, there were pale Formica tables and orange and brown carpet tiles on the floor. Behind the bar was a guy with greasy shoulder-length hair and a prodigious beer gut which made him look like he was about seven months pregnant. He took Rob's order for a pint of cider and a blueberry J2O.

The dogs were both ugly and beautiful at the same time Rob thought, he made a joke about greyhounds being the Sarah Jessica Parker of the dog world.

Sam laughed politely. "You're supposed to bet on the ones that take a dump on the track before the start of the race," she told him knowledgeably. "It's a well-known fact, makes them lighter."

He bet instead on the greyhounds which were the prettiest colours. Men in white coats marched the dogs on their leads up and down the sandy track before they shut them in the white metal traps and set the teddy bear hare loose.

They bet a pound each a race. Rob was embarrassed that he didn't know the procedure, never having been to a race meeting before, not even the Gold Cup which filled Cheltenham with rowdy Irishmen each spring but was too expensive to tempt him through the gates. Still, he felt betting was a man thing and he should know how to do it.

Sam seemed to know, what's more, some of her dogs won while none of his pretty ones did. The dog shit method clearly worked and after a few races he abandoned his plan and followed her tips instead; they both won a little money.

"Do you miss your mum?" she asked him, as they stared out over the track. He nodded without looking at her. "I think that if I do the right thing, then maybe she'll come back."

It was only as she drove him home again through the darkness, that he realised that not once during the evening had he thought about being a PUA, or about what to say, or how to say it. He felt embarrassed mentioning it, like it was a phase he'd grown out of. Instead he asked her how she'd known to come to the chalet on the evening of his row with Sue? He was grateful of course but her turning up like that...

"You told me," she said. "Well, you told Sonof and that's me."

He let that sink in for a while then said, "Maybe I should grow a beard?

"All the cool kids have them right now. The kids in cool bands, they all have beards and shaggy hair."

He stroked his chin, imagining the luxuriant growth.

Sam didn't look up from the road ahead.

"You'd look a right cock with a beard."

Rob pouted in the dark.

"Okay - it was just an idea."

"Yeah well, you're best off not having ideas. I don't know what you ever saw in any of those girls, they're all various kinds of mental. You only have to take a look at the resting bitch face on Sue to know she's a psycho."

"I thought she looked enigmatic," said Rob, knowing it would wind her up."

"Yeah, like a rattlesnake looks before it bites the head off your chicken."

"I feel sorry for her now," Rob said. "She must have had the world's worst childhood. You think you've had bad things happen, then you hear what other people have to deal with."

"Yeah," admitted Sam. "I don't know any more than she told me when she was drunk a few times. She had a hard time growing up. It's a real shame but she's mad with the world so best not get in her way. And how could you *not* know about Louise and the Chief Exec? Do you ever listen to what anyone says?"

"People *knew?*"

"There's practically posters up in the tea room. I figure the only reason you wouldn't know, is if you didn't want to."

"Well, maybe I didn't, it's not the best thing for her, is it?"

"No, probably not but she's writing her own script just like the rest of us, it's up to her."

"What about Alice? Alice is nice."

"She'd have you for breakfast, mind you, they all would. It's like you are too good for them really."

"Or not good enough," he said, looking out of the window. "So, if you were interested in me, why didn't you just say?"

"Because you weren't interested in me," she said. "What would have been the point? As far as you were concerned, I was one of the guys."

He knew this was maybe right, in as much as anything ever was when it came to people, they were too complicated it seemed to him. Whatever you could reasonably say about women, the exact opposite was also true.

"I always liked you," he said after a while. "We've always clicked, been friends. I suppose I just wasn't looking at you right."

"So *that's* why," she said, "I wanted you to look at me differently but I wanted *you* to do it! I wasn't going to come running after you. I wanted you to want me."

"Is that what women want?"

"That's what *this* woman wants."

They drove in silence for a while, then she said, "Tell me a joke."

He shook his head, still mourning his imaginary beard. "I don't know any jokes. I can tell you a thing."

"Okay, tell me a thing."

"When I last stayed at yours, you know, when we got pissed at that leaving do? I had a bath in the morning and used that bar I thought was soap and it turned out to be a something."

"A Lush massage bar."

"Yeah and it had all gold glitter in it. I spent the rest of the weekend looking like Ziggy Stardust. I managed to scrub it off my face and behind my ears - but Monday, when I went to the loo, my little soldier was all glittery. I got a hell of a shock. It was like Harry Potter's magic wand!"

Sam snorted in mirth.

"That is a thing, as you say. Don't make me laugh when I'm driving."

They were silent again for a spell, until a lamp-eyed fox flashed across the road in front of them, making them gasp at the uniqueness of it.

"Did you see that?" asked Sam. "Maybe that must be lucky, or unlucky, or something."

Thrilled as Rob was with the nocturnal wildlife, something was bothering him.

"So how much did you know about the PUA thing then?"

"A fair bit – it was me who told you about the site remember? I used to go on there for a laugh to see what the boys were up to – the bunch of numb-nuts. I was a member which meant when you showed up I could chat to you and be your little buddy. Did you not *ever* have a clue I was Sonof?" She sniggered.

"Erm, no... but why Sonof?" Rob wanted to know.

Sam looked pleased with herself. "Haven't you heard of Son of Sam? It's a thing, it was kind of a clue to see if you were paying attention. Which you clearly weren't."

"The American serial killer Son of Sam? Eww – you named yourself after a serial killer? Is that the vibe you were going for?"

Sam pouted. "It was the only Sam related thing I could think of. I admit I didn't really think it through."

"Yeah well, they'll probably put that phrase on my gravestone but what about Sam I Am from Dr Zeus? You could have been I-am."

"Well, now you say it, okay yeah, that would probably have been better. Next time I have to adopt a fake online identity with a sly nod to my real name, I will consult you first."

"Unless it's me you're trying to fool."

"It's unlikely to be you I'd be trying to fool."

They were approaching the outskirts of Cheltenham, suburban street-lights bathed the road in an amber glow.

"What's happening now?" Rob asked her. "With us I mean. What comes next?"

"That's the beautiful thing," Sam told him. "We don't know."

He had another question. "How many people have you had sex with? How many men?"

She shook her head still looking at the road.

"None. None that matter. It's... nothing you know, unless you care."

When they got back to town they stopped outside Sam's place and without any discussion, both got out of the car. It appeared he was staying the night and that night became the first of many nights, which seemed natural somehow. Normal. Right.

So it transpired that they were wrong for once, those long gone three wise monkeys, when they suggested (all those years ago) that Sam and Rob, Samantha and I, would not last.

Because we did last, for the longest time.

Longer than anyone else, even Sam, might reasonably have predicted.

We were together as a couple for ten full years. Rob and Sam, Sam and Rob, until life eventually took us off in different directions.

And what years they were! Times, when I look back upon them now, which were happy, fulfilled and brimming with life.

If I close my eyes, I can picture her now, my Samantha, in all her raging beauty, because though it all ended a long time ago, I will always have her with me.

It was Sam who taught me the truth about women - their truth.

She gave me the confidence to see them as friends and as partners and that's a gift, right there, that all men should be given.

ABOUT THE AUTHOR

Chris Hill's first novel Song of the Sea God was short listed for the Daily Telegraph Novel in a Year prize and won the eFestival of Words award for Best Literary Fiction. As a short story, it also won The Bridport Prize.

Chris works as a PR officer for UK children's charity WellChild and spent more than 20 years as a journalist on regional newspapers. First as a crime reporter and later as news editor of Gloucester's evening newspaper The Citizen and editor of the weekly Gloucestershire News Series.

He was born on Walney Island off the coast of Cumbria in the North of England but now lives in Gloucester with his wife, their two teenage sons and Murphy, a Cockerpoo. Chris is a social media addict with over 21,000 followers on Twitter and a popular blog where he talks about reading, writing and more.

See ChrisHillAuthor.co.uk for details.

Children from the Kundeni School planting trees

Be PART OF THe MAGIC OXYGen WORD FOReST

As well as delivering great content to our readers, we are also the home of the Magic Oxygen Literary Prize.

It is a global writing competition like no other, as we plant a tree for every entry in our tropical Word Forest. We publish the shortlist and winners in an anthology and plant an additional tree for every copy sold.

The forest is situated beside the Kundeni School in Bore, Kenya, a remote community that has suffered greatly from deforestation. Trees planted near the equator are the most efficient at capturing carbon from the atmosphere - 250kg per tree - and keeping our planet cool. The forest will also reintroduce biodiversity and provide food and income for the community.

Visit MagicOxygen.co.uk to buy the anthology and find out about the next MOLP, then spread news of it far and wide on your blogs and social media and be part of a pioneering literary legacy.

Visit CarbonLink.org for updates on our project.

Lightning Source UK Ltd.
Milton Keynes UK
UKOW06f1336230315

248343UK00009B/243/P